Rig Penlip and
THE DEATH of MAGIC

First independently published in Great Britain
Text copyright © Myles Howard 2025

All rights reserved.

No part of this publication may be reproduced, distributed, or transmitted in any form by any means, including photocopying, recording, or other electronic or mechanical methods without prior permission from the author.

Names, places and incidents are either entirely fictional, or used to enhance the story only. This work is in no way religious, is not intended to offend any faith, and is for entertainment only. Any resemblance to actual persons, living or dead, is entirely coincidental.

Acknowledgments

I cannot allow this to be published without raising a glass half empty to my family, in particular my brother Julian for his undying support and enthusiasm. His brotherly encouragement of dangerous sports now that my Last Will and Testament has been written is duly noted. For his and Sue's children C & J who are no longer little, but grown up as marvellous human beings. They are travellers, always far away and free as birds and the best of us.

My deep love for Anya who is in many senses a fictional widow, having allowed me to focus on my writing when needed, but who is always supportive – even if she hasn't read any of my novels. To cousin Katherine who always has my back. Can you return it because what I have is awful, and thank you for being who you are so expertly, and for being such a great friend. To cousin Carol who seems so far away and yet she always offers such warmth and enthusiasm. To my dear pal Anthony who has passed on. I can't find the words to express what a loss you are. Thank you for your long friendship over many years.

To Steve, Sam, Lisa and Chris and Tawnya, F & F. I can't tell you how much love and admiration I have for you all. Seriously, I can't tell you. We've enjoyed so many good times together that we always slot into our little family dynamics as soon as we meet, as if it were so many years ago. To Steve who knew me as an odd red headed boy with a funny accent. Your friendship has meant everything.

For mum and dad. Everything I do is to honour and respect our memories, my memories of you, and the unconditional love and joy I feel for all that you did for me and Julian. I thank you every day and know you are never far from my side.

Finally for Kiersha, my constant companion. Yes, you can have special biscuits and yes you are much loved. No, you can't go out at night as you're bound to meet Mr Fox.

With thanks to my editor, Lauren Dooley.

For a clever and enthralling detective story set in the heart of Sydney have a look on Amazon for Love Lies Bleeding, by J. S. Howard.

For Anthony

Worlds in the Immediate Galaxy

Gamma 7 (Neva One)
Magic has been used for a long time, and a lot of monsters have come with it. Wizards and those with magic ability much respected. This is where Aurielle is from and most Protectors.

Gamma 8 (Earth)
Rig lives here. Magic not been available long, lots of people are upset by it. Those with magical potential get lots of attention, some are obsessed but others full of envy and curiousity, but not in a good way.

Gamma 9 (New World)
Entirely magic free world and likely to continue like this. Magic can't be used here.

Magical *Potential* and Magical *Confluence*

The gods decided magic could be used on Gamma 7 and Gamma 8. Biologically speaking, there are sleeping cells in the body which wake when needed, they then clash with magic particles in the air. This is how magic happens. Everyone has different amounts of these cells in their body, and the amount of cells is generally referred to as *magical potential*.

When the magic particles in the body are activated and smash into magical elements in the air, *magical confluence* occurs – it is in this precise moment that magic can occur.

Chapters

Prologue – The Host

Chapter 1 – Rig Penlip Wakes Up Before Going to Sleep

Chapter 2 – The Dinosaur and the Monster

Chapter 3 – The Trouble with Meeting a God

Chapter 4 – The Room with No View

Chapter 5 – The Hunt for Blackjack

Chapter 6 – Still Hunting Blackjack

Chapter 7 – Blackjack asks Prod Visceral for Help

Chapter 8 – Turning the Screw with Red

Chapter 9 – Awkward Travel Arrangements

Chapter 10 – Blaam Rises Again

Chapter 11 – The Ghost, The Drunk and the Powerless Wizard

Chapter 12 – Gamma Nine with None

Chapter 13 – All Powerful Magic

Chapter 14 – The Creature Hung Up

Chapter 15 – Dimwit in a Cellar

Chapter 16 – Fun for the Tourists

Chapter 17 – The Decision

Chapter 18 – Home and Away

Chapter 19 – Prod Considers

Chapter 20 – Godmaker

Chapter 21 – Jeep

Chapter 22 – Frank Merlot

Chapter 23 – Humphrey the Ghostly Traveller

Chapter 24 – King of Monsters

Chapter 25 – Crash

Chapter 26 – Well

Chapter 27 – The Reunion

Chapter 28 – The Voices

Chapter 29 – Left-handed Magic

Chapter 30 – Strange Battle

Chapter 31 – Aurielle Merlot: Angry Killer And Hero

Chapter 32 – Blue Awakens

Chapter 33 – The Facility

Chapter 34 – Jordi Longstaff

Chapter 35 – Scarlett Crook

Chapter 36 – Mr Melvyn Penlip

Chapter 37 – Henrietta the Horrible

Chapter 38 – Meeting Dad Again

Chapter 39 – The Death of Magic

Chapter 40 – Other

Chapter 41 – Dangerous Interview

Chapter 42 – Remember Me?

Chapter 43 – Half an Ear

Chapter 44 – Lab Chat

Chapter 45 – Detective Love

Chapter 46 – DNA

Chapter 47 – Garden

Chapter 48 – Message

Prologue
The Host

Prod Visceral climbed the hill with ease, although he was uncomfortable. His soaking shirt clung to his skin, while his thigh muscles ached as he pounded up the slope. The warmth of the air was suffocating with its moisture coating his throat like a blanket. Jungle scents hung in the air like mist, as if hesitant to leave. Often, they would overlap and mingle with new smells, but they would also change suddenly when a different more dominant odour cut through the others. His senses were continually alerted to the aliveness of the world in which he trekked through.

He paused for a moment at the hill's peak. The sight of the thick jungle that stretched far into the distance was both exciting and tiring to see. Prod rubbed his eyes. Somewhere in that green bush was another Source, and once they found it, his real work would begin. Finding it was the issue. He had led this kind of trip many times before and had never struggled for fitness – it was the insects and stifling heat that bothered him most, and then there was his accomplice.

Prod gulped water from his flask and waited for his group to catch up. The local tribesman made no complaints as they heaved equipment, and for all Prod knew, they had no complaints at all. They worked incredibly hard, but once they rested, it was difficult to get them moving again, much like a stroppy donkey, and there were a few of those in the group. No, it was his young Protector, Jordi Longstaff, that tested the nerves at times. He was intense but reliable. He was good at killing things too, and that was a definite plus on these missions. If you were willingly searching for a Source of negative magic, why wouldn't you take a killer with you? It was a must; you just had to accept your Protector's oddness and do your best to stay alive.

The team of Asian helpers reached the hilltop, gathered together, and chattered, pointing ahead as they did so. It was never clear whether they were bickering or talking agreeably together. Embarrassingly, Prod couldn't tell the difference, but then he didn't need to.

The young lad lumbered along at his own pace, not concerned with catching up. Prod sat down. And after a few minutes, Jordi neared, mumbling gloomily.

'You alright?' asked Prod.

'Course I am. No problem,' said the teen Protector trying to catch his breath.

Prod took another swig of water and offered it to his accomplice, 'Just sounded like you were doing a lot of complaining and muttering.'

Jordi took the bottle and drank greedily. 'What? Me? No, I don't complain, I like it, like the challenge. I could complain though … I mean, why do I have to carry my own kit when we've got these Sherpas and donkeys to do it?'

'I told you, they're not Sherpas. Sherpas live in Nepal and the Himalayas, not Southern Malaysia. Anyway, if you're unhappy give them your stuff.'

'Yeah alright, could do, but do you trust them though? Look at them. They don't look after themselves much so it's not like they're going to look after my stuff, are they?' Jordi's gaze took in the abandoned luggage behind the men. 'Throwing bags around.'

'They look after us, no point disrespecting them is there?'

'No. I like them, I do, just don't get them, that's all.'

'Well, hand over your staff and knives and they can carry them.'

'What? No way, I'm not giving up my gear. What if something were to, like, jump out of them bushes and attack us. We'd be done for; nah I'm keeping my kit. If you want me to do my job.'

'Good, glad we sorted that out. Let's get going.'

They didn't. Not for a while. Jordi, who again pointed out their safety depended entirely on him when it came to nasty monsters, needed to rest. He didn't appreciate that he wouldn't find his way out even with a satnav and road signs, not that there were any roads; that was one glorious fact about the jungle. Jordi was full of confidence about himself, but anything that made life uncomfortable was an inconvenience worth groaning about, endlessly. Prod agreed the jungle was dangerous, of course it was. At each turn it contained creatures that would happily sting you, eat you, or bury you given the chance, and that was not including the monsters that were borne out of these pools of waste magic.

Three roasting hours later, they stopped again. This time they were in a small clearing the size of a tennis court, a perfect site to rest a while. The sun poked through the tall trees, lighting up the dry brown earth in its centre, whereas the edges provided shadows of cover.

The helpers sat in a huddle away from Jordi and Prod and nattered in their own language, they could be a jolly bunch and before long were laughing hysterically, loud enough to wake the dead. They could do without that.

Jordi perched on a rucksack under a huge leaf shaped like an elephant's ear. He shook his head. He hated sitting on the leafy floor, which was understandable because underfoot the rainforest often seemed alive, whether with ants, spiders, or bugs of some type. The possibilities were endless.

'My feet are red raw again,' the Protector announced, rubbing them.

Prod began unlacing his boots. 'Yeah, think mine are too. We won't go much further, we'll set up camp for the night soon.'

'If I could just get one good night's sleep, I think I'd feel normal again. I just don't think marching through miles and miles of jungle is a quick way of getting what you want. I mean, why not use satellite images and helicopters to find these places? Oh no, instead we have to hike around mountains, through valleys full of spiders' webs, risk falling and breaking necks in dips and gullies we can't see, and practically starve ourselves to death in the process. I mean, c'mon, this is nuts. You need to get high tech. *Then* we can go in.'

'Does it beat school?'

'Oh yeah, definitely.'

'We'll keep doing it my way then. Anyway, satellite images won't help us with forests this dense, and you need some local knowledge when it comes to actually identifying where the pools are likely to be.'

'Keep telling yourself that. So long as you're paying, I ain't gonna moan about it.'

Prod frowned. Thank gods for the Consortium investors. He wasn't going to pay a penny for all this, or the teen's wages.

Jordi reached into his shorts, then urgently rifled through the contents of his rucksack, pouches in his belt, and shirt pockets. 'Where's my penknife? Had it on me earlier, it's gone!'

'Where did you last see it?' asked Prod.

'How's that gonna help? Oh, for the gods!'

'It's under your boot.'

'What?' Jordi lifted his socks and boots and grabbed his tiny knife from the twigs. 'Brilliant, thanks.'

The men were shouting and gesturing.

Prod scanned the clearing.

All looked in order.

No … the donkeys. Two were roped to a tree, should be three. The men scurried in different directions, yelling as they went. Jordi scrambled to get his boots back on.

'Typical … just when I was starting to chill,' he said, tying his laces speedily.

The men searched the area, scattering like thieves and rummaging through natural pathways, cutting through undergrowth with heavy machetes as they rushed.

The call came fast enough, 'Please, here, come, please, here,' said one of the men in perfectly broken English.

Jordi sprinted, with his oak-staff at his side.

They gathered by the stray donkey.

It had cleverly sought water and found a tropical spring protected by a boundary of large rocks, tall trees, and the usual dense layers of forest beyond. At a glance, the spring was maybe twenty metres by ten, certainly large and long, and a few metres deep as far as Prod could tell. It could be a Source.

Jordi went into action.

He gestured that everyone hush.

The Protector thrust a pointed finger at the donkey, then the way out, like he was leading a special-forces mission in enemy territory. The men understood, one pulled the donkey clear and hustled from the site. Jordi took a moment to listen for anything unusual, he spied the pool warily, as though something vicious were lurking beneath. Prod didn't twitch a muscle; he'd been through this routine before. Let the boy check the area, anything suspicious and he'll alert Prod, or kill it. But he had to do a security sweep of the pool's edge and behind the immediate undergrowth. An entirely reasonable thing to do, necessary. That was his purpose here.

Twenty minutes later, seemed an hour, the kid returned with his boots cracking dry branches as he trudged back.

He shouted to Prod as he clambered past some enormous stones. 'Damn the heat here, I swear it's getting worse, shouldn't it be getting cooler? I mean the day is nearly done. For the sake of the gods! This place seriously sucks. Why have they got such big rocks here? I mean, how did they get here anyway?'

Prod wiped the sweat from his forehead. 'Hungry?'

'Starving.'

'Thought so.'

'I'd kill for a kebab right now ... wonder where the nearest takeaway is.'

The boy had an ability to switch from grumbling teen to talented fighter, and back within minutes, the change was remarkable and didn't require any wizard's magic at all.

'Nearer than you'd think,' Prod blinked and rubbed his eyes. 'The place is clear of undesirables then?'

'Yep. No monsters here, boss.'

As a security report it really wasn't very good, but there was no point going on about it. The boy was casual about nearly everything, but when it came to it, if you were about to have your limbs torn from your body, he was the best at what he did, for the price – although that was not his concern. Prod appreciated that running down nasties and dispatching them was a great skill, and a much-needed resource for daring adventurers like himself. Dispatching monsters successfully every time was important business for Jordi, but for Prod the attraction was the mystery, the puzzle. Problems like negative magic had to be explored, examined, and studied. They had to be understood if the killing by monsters, and of monsters, was to stop and their world improved, otherwise they would have to stop magic itself, and that would be seriously unpopular, impossible perhaps. Banning all television and internet access would be simpler.

The men returned gradually while Prod took his time unpacking. Jordi was still in irritable teen mode. The clicking of insects and the chirping of birds gave a pleasant background tune to the scene. Dragonflies perched on the water's edge, flies buzzed back and forth, and a single bright, red-coloured butterfly flew the length of the pool, disappearing beyond and into the forest.

The water was colourless and so inviting. It was tempting to drink, but they all knew to avoid this until it had been tested for negative magic particles. The water could be toxic and even lethal to humans. Initial testing was simple; but the analysis of the chemical structures was possible only to a fraction of the degree required. Samples had to be transported back to the laboratory in London for the full range of tests.

'So, how is it that all our monsters can come from nice looking water like this? How does it happen?' asked Jordi swinging in his hammock across the pond.

Prod stood back and considered the positioning of his equipment. The testing apparatus was ready. The test-tubes stood in a line on the flimsy trestle table. The syringes, funnel, and gauze for sifting samples were ready to the side. His diary and recording manual poked through the lip of his bag.

'We've gone through this before, Jordi …'

If only he would listen.

'…We all have a different amount of magical potential inside us. Magic molecules in the air collide with our basic magical potential, this collision allows magical acts to happen. It's called magical confluence. Remember?'

'Ugh?'

'Look, when wizards or sorcerers conjure magic, negatively charged magic particles are produced. They're like a by-product, a side-effect. These tiny elements drift in the air until they can gather in pools of water like this, referred to as a Source – meaning a source from which monsters are grown. These pools, they're always hidden and out of the way. But we don't know why, and we don't know how monsters are cultivated out of these waste particles. We don't know how they're born, if you like. That's what we're studying. Got it?'

'Umm, yeah mostly.'

Prod adjusted the tubes and their rubber connectors, making sure they were firmly fastened. He didn't want toxic water leaking everywhere. 'And then there's the idea that magic can now be made from nothing, just normal oxygenated air, without these invisible magical molecules all around us, but there's no evidence of that. Just gossip. Utter nonsense.'

Prod stood back and admired his temporary laboratory setup. 'So, that's how magic works, Jordi.'

'Cool.'

'Yes, it is.'

Prod wished he was cool; he was sweating rivers and they were all running out of energy.

'Sounds like them waste particles are a sort of pollution, don't it? It's everywhere I reckon.' Jordi shook his head miserably. 'Anyway,' he continued, 'if there are lots of monsters on this island 'cause of these negative pools, how come they end up all over the place? I mean, how do they get off the island, y'know?'

As he took his boots off, Prod replied, 'Well, they don't organise boat trips if that's what you mean, but they're not bound to the island either. In fact, there is an old legend about this island. Did you know that? Have you read about it?'

'Nah. I don't read very much. Too busy practicing, or hunting, or sleeping. Y'know?'

'Quite. Anyway, legend says a princess was bound here, stopped from seeing her sister by a jealous god, but that's about it. It's just an old story, that's all. The fact is there's a lot we don't know. That's why science and exploration are so important.'

'Gotcha. Yeah, nice one.'

Prod sighed. He chucked his boots to the side and wriggled his toes, happy for the relief of it.

Jordi seemed deep in thought, relatively speaking.

'Don't worry about it, there are no kings, queens, or princesses here, and no-one will be forced to stay … unless you annoy me. It's just a myth, Jordi. Okay?'

'I hate myths and legends, I do,' said the Protector. 'Just stories with no truth.'

'Quite right, forget about it.'

He should ask the men to start building camp while he collected samples and started the first stage of testing. Jordi wriggled into his hammock and shut his eyes. Another butterfly appeared, fluttering from one side of the pond to the other. It paused by a lily.

Prod decided twelve test-tubes were not sufficient, he took a syringe by the bulging "C" logo to get a better grip and squatted in reach of the pond. He could see to the shale at the bottom. It looked like a big bath. He longed for home, a small glass of white Chardonnay wine in his jacuzzi, and good quality sleep in his own comfortable bed. He poked the syringe into the water and pulled on the plunger. He peered at his unmoving accomplice and found the vibrantly red butterfly zigzagging towards him. Oddly, it hovered in front of him before accepting the invitation and resting on Prod's open palm. Its wings slowed to a stop. The wingspan of this beauty covered his entire hand, such a delicate creature with rich crimson tones.

'Ouch! Hell!' Prod yelped.

The butterfly fluttered away as Prod recoiled, stumbling, tripping over a spare case. The men stood; one ran off.

'What?' shouted Jordi, wrestling his way out of the hammock.

Prod got to his feet. 'Watch out!'

A black cloud loomed at the end of the pool, dipping low then rising. Within the shape was a writhing mass of insects. No, it wasn't black, but red, blood red. Butterflies?

Prod turned to the men. 'Run!' he shouted with all his might.

They understood, and didn't need asking twice.

Jordi skirted the pool, his gangly legs following its perimeter. Prod grabbed his diary, but before he could turn, they were on him, his head in the centre of a hoard of insects nipping and biting. Blindly, he struck out, but the bites increased, his skin already burning from his wounds. In the corner of his eye, he saw Jordi cutting and slicing, then he rushed to the shadows of the forest.

Swatting uselessly, Prod took the last option.

He dived into the water.

It was a dumb idea. Submerging himself in acid would have been less harmful. The butterflies were clearly deranged, affected somehow. Most likely the water was mixture of waste energy, the bad stuff – highly concentrated negative magic. He drifted under water, observing above him.

The swarm waited.

His breath running out.

Done for.

What a way to go.

His body's instinct for survival took him to the surface. He gasped, struggling to heave in air fast enough, body retching, complaining. He pushed to the pond's edge, waiting for the attack. He glanced above, one single far-away tuft of cloud in an otherwise totally clear sky. He swivelled, check around him, protecting his eyes from the unforgiving sun. Nothing. The seething mass had gone. An intense ache in his head had replaced them. Coming and going, waves of it. His burning skin had cooled at least. So much for his expedition, the team had disappeared entirely. Surely, they would be return, useless lot. How was he going to get all his stuff back? Maybe he shouldn't bother. He gripped his head. Someone was pushing razor-wire through his brain. It was almost as if … as if someone was in his brain.

An invader.

What poison was in his blood?

Wrong question. Who, not what.

Not thinking straight, new thoughts pushing away old thoughts.

Someone was in his head. How?

Not important.

Was this dying? But why?

What if it is?

Hold on. Why did he travel here? Magic particles?

They don't need studying.

Negative energy … a bad side effect … of abnormal behaviour.

So?

Must be studied, understood.
No. A disease state – a state of magic, one in the same.
Why couldn't he see that before?
There is no before.
There is only now.
This is me.

Chapter 1. Rig Penlip Wakes up Before Going to Sleep

The night had a cool edge to it, which wouldn't leave Rig alone. He turned and lolled in his bed for what seemed like hours as he struggled to sleep in the frosty air. Grumbling fiercely, he got up and closed the window. Keeping the atmosphere cold was a good idea if it was going to help him sleep, but it didn't. He'd taken the advice a bit far. He did sleep before long, and the dreams came again, one after another. Some he feared. Many were difficult to understand while others were full of darkness, dread, and worry.

The images took him back to tunnels underground, gave him visions of hateful demonic beings, others simply hinted at shapes which cornered him and yet could not be clearly seen. He knew they were there. The dreams hounded him with problems, but their detail always escaped him. The emotion of it was draining. His dark past shadowed every quiet moment and tonight there were even images of murder. The gruesome pictures came and went, but between the dreams there was some relief and quiet, and also some fascination.

At the midpoint of the night and from the comfort of his star patterned duvet he would watch them come and go – the unseen. They would appear and disappear without a single complaint wandering from one side of his bedroom to the other. Rig wondered why his carpet had been chosen as a footpath for the departed. His wonderings didn't stay long, and sleep did find him again, and then later, but not much later … there was a sharp poke from the finger of a dead man.

Rig woke with a start. 'What?!' he blurted in a daze sitting up.

'I couldn't get you to wake up,' said the visitor.

'You should've come earlier; I couldn't get to sleep no matter how hard I tried. Anyway, who are you? And what do you want with me at …' Rig looked to his alarm clock, but it had broken again, 'well, it's the middle of the night.'

'Oh, sorry. Is it? Oh dear, I do get a bit muddled with time. Well, what with being, y'know …' The apparition looked down at his form as if it were new to him, because it was see-through and ghostly.

'Well?'

'What?'

'What do you want?' Rig had experienced many unnecessarily long discussions with ghosts before, just not at this hour or in his bedroom.

'You're asking, what do I want?'

'Yes!'

'Oh … oh my! I'm feeling a bit lost now, it's the emotion of it you see. Oh, goodness … can I sit down?'

'What?'

The ghost was middle aged and had an ample middle too. His hair was messed up like he had just fallen out of the shower, which was ridiculous because he was a ghost and as far as Rig knew, ghosts didn't shower. In fact, in his experience they didn't do much at all but complain and moan.

'No, I'm sorry, Rig. I really must sit down, it's all too much,' said the spectre with an unusual amount of theatrical hand movements.

'What is?'

'All this … y'know,' the ghost bunched his eyebrows suggestively.

A thought ignited in Rig's head. 'You can't say it, can you?'

'Say what?'

'You know you're a ghost, just can't say it, can you?'

'Yes, I can.'

'Go on then.'

'No.'

'Why not?'

'There's no need.'

'You said, "*it's all too much*". What is? Why can't you say it?'

'It's unseemly. It's obvious too, I mean look at me. I don't really need to announce it. Do I?'

'Oh, for the gods! What do you want anyway?'

The ghost wafted a hand in the air. 'Me? Oh … yes, now hold on, don't rush me. I know what it was … it'll come back.'

'Hurry up!'

'Ooh you are pushy, aren't you? Has anyone ever told you that?'

'I've been told plenty by all sorts.'

'Bet you have. I like what you've done to your room. It's a bit gloomy though.'

'I told you its night-time, when normal people sleep?'

'Ah … yes, I think you did say something about that.'

The ghost crossed his legs and flicked his hair from his eyes. He produced a small notebook from nowhere and thumbed through the pages. 'It's not in here. Why isn't it in here?'

'Are you asking me?'

'Oh, goodness … I put anything important in here,' he examined some pages close up, 'I think I do, used to. Must have changed my mind.'

Rig pulled the duvet up close. 'Look, I don't know why you're here, and the chances of you telling me seem to be fading. Are you going to tell me or not?'

The ghost's expression hit the floor.

'Sorry,' said Rig. 'When I said "fading" I wasn't talking about your, um, your state.'

'My *state*? Well … you really are a brute, aren't you, Rig Penlip? You don't care what you say.'

'I've been called worse than that. A lot worse, but I'm sorry, I didn't mean to hurt your feelings or anything, just tell me why you're here. What can I help you with?' He really wanted to end this soon, there was a large amount of sleeping to be done.

The ghost turned his head from Rig. 'I'm sure it'll come back, maybe if you're nice to me, it might help.' He fumbled his notepad into his back pocket.

'I really don't have time for this. Do you want to come back tomorrow? Preferably when I'm not sleeping, or eating, or chatting to friends. Anytime really, when I'm alone.'

The visitor spun round.

Rig continued, 'I mean we could agree a time even, like some normal people. How about that?'

He ruffled his hair deep in thought, 'Eating? Friends? Breakfast, lunch, dinner, sleep … um, there's something I have to tell you.'

'Yes?'

'The chicken that you eat, dead chicken, there's something wrong with it.'

'Eh?'

'The chicken is dead. No, the meat is dead. Um … that's not quite right.' The ghost looked about the room as if looking for a clue or inspiration.

'What are you talking about? Have you got a message for me or not?'

The visitor's eyes bulged. 'Ah, got it!'

'Yeah … go on.'

'Your friend Aurielle Merlot has been taken, and unless you find her before four moons pass, she's dead meat.'

Rig gasped; his senses froze. *Oh, no. Not her.*

'Yes, I've got it right.' The ghost looked pleased as punch he'd remembered the message.

'And?' said Rig.

'Oh, sorry … um … that's it.'

'That's it?'

'Yes.'

'Are you sure?' Rig's fingers scrunched his hair. *Not again, not her. I can't do it.*

'Yes. No. Err … yes.'

Rig looked up in a fever. 'Who gave you the message? Where's my friend? What happened?'

'Sorry, to who?'

'To my friend: Aurielle Merlot! Also answers to Flash, likes killing monsters, most things actually, got an attitude, hates almost everything. Short-ish. What's happened to my friend, you numbskull?'

'You know I really don't care for your tone, I really don't, but then … I suppose you've had some bad news. I really don't know anything else; I don't think so anyway.'

Rig clasped his legs and started rocking.

The visitor jumped up and straightened his clothes, so they were perfect. 'Right then, I'll be off.' Examining his profile he said, 'Do I look big in this outfit?'

'What are you going to do? Change what you're wearing?

'Well, I—'

'No, you're stuck with it. You're a ghost … remember.'

You really are an unpleasant boy, no wonder you've no friends to talk to.' 'Bugger off!'

'You are rude and childish,' the being turned his translucent form away from Rig.

Rig sighed, 'I'm sorry.'

'Accepted,' the apparition twirled merrily.

It was clear who was behind the abduction. He had heard the phrase before, *dead meat*. It was a calling card, a message within a message.

'You said you didn't know who gave you the message?'

'Did I? Yes, that's right, it just appeared in my head, they often do, and I asked myself … *Humphrey, is this important*?'

'And you thought "yes, it is", well thanks for bringing it to me. I know who gave it to you anyway.'

'You do?'

'Yep.'

'Oh, good.'

'Not really.'

'Why's that?'

'Because the message came from a sorcerer called Blackjack, and he's got form. Lots of it.'

'Oh, how ugly.'

'Yes, he is.'

Text to Uncle James

Hey Unc. My friend's missing. Got to go.
It's bad. Look after Dad + cover for me.
Will be ok. Yeh, will call if have to.
Have a good day lol. Rig x

Chapter 2. The Dinosaur and the Monster

The air was dead cold, and there was no life apparent in the makeshift prison. Although, there was slime, lots of it. The stuff seemed to grow in abundance here, probably because the walls of rock and boulders were damp and hadn't been moved for a long time. It was hard to see anything much by the small candle Aurielle Merlot had been allowed. The atmosphere was definitely heavy, and that wasn't just because she'd been here for longer than was polite, nor was it due to her not being able to kill or maim her captor yet, although it was just a matter of time. There was not much point in having a prisoner unless you could torture them through some means, and so far, Henrietta the Horrible had been pathetic. But to be fair to her, torture may not be her thing, because *horrible* appeared to be a simple reference to her personal hygiene.

Aurielle rubbed her hands and found some warmth, this was going to be fun, if a tad inconvenient.

It wasn't long before the lazy footsteps and slap of tail from her dastardly captor were echoing in the cave system. A beaker of water appeared soon after. The emerald scales of a hand and the talons that sprung from them struggled to place the large cup on the slab of rock. The snout of something reptilian appeared. Bright eyes shone through the gap, gawping at the prisoner.

'Good to see you're alive young un', I don't wants you dying too quickly, do I? There's a lot to be done yet, isn't there? It'll be slow, most likely, and I want to see it, see. But you, you don't know what we're up to do you, and you never will I reckon, will you?'

Aurielle straightened her back. 'Are you asking me actual questions? Or are you going to bore me to death? I can't decide which it is Henni.'

'Well, I—'

'Thought so. You're going to bore me to death. We'll see if you manage that before I cut off your long pointy nose and vile arms.'

'Look, Miss, all this that you do, clever words and like, won't help you, see. Not at all, not once we do the deed we'll do.'

'All I need to decide is whether to cut your green hands off and make you eat them or lop your scaly tail off and feed you that instead.'

'Got nine lives so you can't kill me, see. Oh … shouldn't have told you that. You is some monster. All your trickery. They warned me about all this, these words that spill out.' Her gargantuan tongue made talking difficult, and apparently thinking.

'Look at yourself. Calling me a monster? And no, these words won't be familiar to you, I realise that. Collectively it's known as wit. You seem incredibly short of it. And yes, I will kill you, repeatedly, however long it takes.'

The dinosaur was moderately interesting now, Aurielle had never met a creature who could regenerate at all, let alone nine times.

'I'm not short, no way!' Her nuzzle struck the rocks, loosening them a fraction as it pulled away in a fluster. 'I'm a good five feet tall, aren't I? And that's not counting my ears, is it?'

Aurielle peeped through the gap. 'Again with the questions, Henni. Did your family abandon you? Hmm … yes, I'll definitely take your legs first, get rid of those stumpy things.'

'I don't like you. Got a real nasty side to you.'

The prisoner took the beaker of water and studied Henni, her jaws were snapping as she nattered on. She was strong and muscular in this form, but her heavy tail made her slow. An easy kill. Aurielle gave the rubble in her window a prod and found them loose enough. She'd be out later, or if she could cope with the chill, she could stay another night and get some rest. The world was full of possibilities. Getting caught by a bunch of thugs while taking a quick nap had been a stupid mistake, although it would work out quite well in the end, always did. She just needed one last bit of information before she retrieved her trusty swords and attended to her hopeless guard.

The dinosaur continued, relentless in her efforts at boring Aurielle to death. The sweep of her tail sounded out on the wet rocks underfoot. 'And I said, I did, we shouldn't keep the likes of you here long. It's not the best, is it? But you behave like that, don't you? No gratitude. If I was really cross, you'd regret it all but I get no thanks, do I?'

'I get it now, they're rhetorical questions. I mean, you don't want a reply, do you? You must get so lonely here. Is that why they let you keep people hidden away?'

'Suppose so … I mean no, 'course not. I'm a fierce warrior I don't need no company.'

'Hard to be fierce without company to see it, and a bit of advice, people that are really fierce don't need to explain it. Should be obvious. See what I mean?'

'Oh.'

'Yeah. And who is this ruthless boss you work for?'

'What, Blackjack?'

'Yeah.'

'Not allowed to tell you, see.'

'Okay. And what terrible deeds are you all planning?'

'I'm not allowed to tell prisoners any of that, am I?'

'No, I suppose not. How about a clue? We could make a game of it?'

'I should really be getting back, shouldn't I?'

'You can't be mean and wicked unless you actually tell me how bad it's going to be.'

'True. All I'm going to tell you is, it's going to change lives.'

'In a good way?'

'Don't think so.'

'Thought not. Let me guess … your boss is going to do something wicked that ends up with him taking over the world, something like that.'

'How did you know all them details?'

'A wild stab in the dark. And there'll be a few more of those quite soon.'

'Oh. Look, please don't tell anyone I told you all that, see. I'll be in big troubles. Pinky promise?'

The scaly creature held out a hooked red talon. Aurielle obliged and linked it with her little finger.

With the oily blackness starting to engulf her dwindling candle, Aurielle listened to the merry humming of her captor lumbering downwards into the depths of the cave, apparently oblivious to the monster that was about to track her and end her days with a few well aimed cuts.

Chapter 3. The Trouble with Meeting a God

You would naturally believe that meeting a god was impossible, risky, or strange, but for Rig it was none of these things. He had met gods before, got on quite well with them when they weren't plotting to get him murdered. The problem was in meeting this particular god. For Rig it was neither the power she held, nor the respect a god demanded.

It was her womanly shape.

Lycka had chosen the form she preferred and had never changed it, which was understandable but made life difficult, sort of. Rig was at an age when anything with a soft female curve was attractive, and in being attractive, it was usually distracting from the task at hand. It wasn't that he met gods every day. When he did meet them, it didn't include a casual chat in a café but usually something important, like tracking down a Sorcerer in another world, or trying to save someone's life – that kind of meeting. So, to meet a god in a closely fitting red dress complete with impossibly bright jewels and hints of alluring fragrances, made concentrating tricky.

So it was that Rig found himself walking down an exclusive street in West London in the middle of the day. He followed his online map to Lacey's Wine Bar. It would be a simple enough meeting: find out the exact location in which Flash was being held captive, say thank you, and leave.

Easy.

He approached the glass front and clocked Lacey's glittering name across the top of the entrance. He could see inside a long bar, high topped tables with stools; mirrors which stretched across each wall, enormous crystal chandeliers, and a few people yakking. The god was nowhere in sight. Rig pulled on the door. It was heavy so he pulled harder and stepped inside. It was an unfamiliar world to him, not interstellar, it wasn't Gamma Seven or even Gamma Nine, just a bar of sorts. A posh one most likely.

A waiter with an expensive smile intercepted Rig.

'Welcome young man,' he said with a thick foreign accent, possibly Spanish, maybe Italian, or Greek, definitely not back-street English.

'Um … yeah. Hi,' said Rig peeking round the man, scanning the room for a glamorous god.

'Are you looking for someone, my friend?' he said above the mellow music filtering through the room.

Rig's trainers squeaked as he stepped forward. 'Yes, I—'

The waiter held a hand up. 'My friend, I cannot let you in here, you are … what, thirteen?'

'Nearly fifteen actually.'

'Still, my friend, I can't let you in. I'm sorry.'

'Oh.' Rig's shoulders slumped.

He turned to leave. As he spun round his trainers gave a piercing squeak on the tile floor. All heads turned to him, and his hoody snagged the long stems of the adjacent plant. The container tipped and crashed to the polished floor. Dirt sprayed across the tiles in a neat fan shape.

'No worry, no worry, my friend,' the doorman started clearing up.

Rig didn't know where to look. There were some giggles in the room and a clicking noise to his right. Lycka appeared, grinning. She placed a manicured hand on his arm and gave him a peck on the cheek.

'So good to see you, Rig. Let's go somewhere else,' her tone was lined with smooth velvet like her dress.

Rig followed her out the door, still not sure where to look.

She ushered him to the small park across the street where black iron railings and a line of trees brought some posh greenery to suburbia.

'Sit down,' she said.

'Thanks,' his heavy flanks caused the bench to judder as he plonked next to her. They certainly looked odd together, a graceful model in her middle years with a boy who had some weight issues.

'You wanted to see me, darling?'

'How'd you know that?'

'Please Rig, I am still a god, allow me a little credit. I could see you were feeling troubled and that's why I suggested we meet here. There's no point in me being a god without being able to see great suffering and not be able to do something about it.'

'Oh, in that case why haven't you stopped all the suffering and poverty in ... um, Africa, and helped the poor here, there's so much suffering going on and I don't see any of it being, well, sort of fixed. And, as you say, you're meant to be a god.'

'It's not as simple as that, Rig, people have free will, they do as they please ... that's life, but often people don't appreciate the consequences of their actions, see what's ahead. Come on ... let's not get into politics now, okay?'

'I still don't see why you can't do something about it, no matter how small.'

'Rig ... please?'

'Alright, I'm sorry.'

'So, what's on your mind?'

'It's Flash, she's been taken. Do y'know what happened? Where she is? She's in danger. I've got to find her.'

The god sighed, 'No, I don't.'

'But you're a god.'

'Yes, but I don't know *everything*.'

'Great.' Rig buried his head in his hands.

'Rig, darling, I don't get to hear what's going on now. Not even about things like this. I have to find out myself. You remember the Archiver, the higher god that records every thought and action? We have no connection now, after what happened to you ... when you made a link with a higher god, it changed everything.'

'My fault then.'

'No, it was just ... circumstances. You inherited an enormous amount of magic, and the magical potential in you was already strong, but because you hadn't been using it, the energy ... well, it broke through in unusual ways. You heard the thoughts of the Archiver. No one predicted that. It changed everything. So, no, it wasn't your fault, and I don't know everything that's going on. I'm not warned about anything now either, that link to the higher gods has gone.'

Her neckline was long and flowing, almost perfection as if made of the finest crystal. 'Right. Um ... yeah, and what about the other gods? Do they know anything?'

Lycka's flawless beauty suddenly sagged. 'There's just a few of us now. Blaam was discharged from his duties, sacked basically, because his actions led to the suffering that Erat and Santino must endure, their spirits locked in a state of death. There are no replacements for the Gods of War and Love, not yet anyway, and Blaam's position of God of Odium may not be renewed at all.

'Leaving you, and?'

'The new Archiver, and the God of Death.'

'Oh.'

'Quite.'

'Well ... there's always death. It's big business.'

'He's reliable and got a lot of assistants, put it that way.'

Rig glanced at her. 'What you're saying is, you know nothing and can't help.'

'I'm sorry. There's no way round it, you'll have to find her yourself, probably means doing some travelling again?'

'Yeah, again. And I know what you mean by *travelling*.'

'I'll open a Slide for you, but I can't come this time, there's too much to do. There always is for lower gods. You'd know that if you had accepted our offer.'

'Thanks, but I'm not dead yet.'

Lycka's painted lips purred into a smile. 'I can see that. And there's no point rushing into these things, especially things that require such a grave sacrifice.'

Rig's face didn't respond to the humour.

The god looked at him in that way, when someone wants to reassure you but knows nothing is likely to work. 'I remember last time you had Aurielle, Flash as you call her, to help beat off those monsters but there isn't anyone this time. There's no-one to help you. But you have your magic abilities back now don't you, so it's all good?'

'Yeah, it's great.' Rig stood to go.

'Sorry, darling.'

'Yeah.'

Chapter 4. The Room with No View

Aurielle Merlot, trained killer and bodyguard to rubbish wizards, yawned, took a long stretch in the small outcrop of sealed rock that was her prison, and took a step backwards. The rest had done her some good, but it was time to get out and find the light, pay a few debts.

She eyed the loose rock by the hatchway and struck it hard with a sideways karate kick. A large stone shifted without dropping, pebbles dribbled to the cave floor, loosening the structure. She kicked it again with all the force coming from her hip driving down through her heel. The carefully assembled wall crumbled. Apparently, there were rubbish bad guys as well as rubbish wizards, each of the worlds were full of them. On the upside, there was lots of work for the experts. She just needed to get a bit more training with a few more weapons, and that meant going back to school.

She collected the candle and pushed her way through the remaining rocks, exiting her relaxation room. The light from the flame barely lit the cave two feet in front of her. She collected her swords that had been cast aside and examined them with affection. The cool grip of the patterned handle and the pleasantly smooth leather surface of their scabbards was reassuringly familiar. She strung them across her back, feeling whole again. Time to fix the dinosaur; they were meant to be extinct anyway. She'd have a chat with Henni about that and headed down the slope where the temperature dropped even lower.

And there was a distinct smell, she paused to consider it. Her keeper had whiffed but not of this, and the underground cavern had little else to offer. It was a threat. She reached for her sword with a spare hand in the dim light.

A bearded face appeared.

She gasped. The light snuffed out.

She snatched her sword and shuffled to put space between them.

'Can't see us. Can you, girl?'

'When you say "us" you mean you, don't you? Idiot. No, I can't see you and I'm glad for it, but you smell like a corpse, which is funny because that's how you'll end up if this goes on much longer. Anyway, love to stop and chat. Got to move on, people to see, dinosaurs to kill.'

'Have you figured out who I am yet?'

'Like I said, busy, got some killing to do. Move out of my way or I'll introduce you to two of my best friends.' Aurielle chucked the candle and reached for her second sword.

'I don't suppose you can see this flame then, my dear?'

She sensed some warmth, but no matter how hard she looked about her, there was nothing her eyes could lock onto, not even a shadow. 'What of it?'

'We've taken your sight I'm afraid, and soon you'll be as good as done.'

'Oh, yeah? How's that?'

A shift in the air, she spun, blocked to her right, but a terrible force struck her skull from behind. *Cowards*. The ache grew as the blackness raced through her and all thoughts stopped.

***

The surface was flat and firm. It wasn't rock. The throb in her brain had softened but her back hurt. Aurielle opened her eyes to a fog, a bright one but it was a fog. She snatched at the air. There were no clouds of mist dampening her fingers, her vision was stuffed. That was going to make life tricky. But it began to clear, ever so slowly, too slowly. Little by little she could see the room, her new cell. It was stark. A box with plain walls and dull furniture. She sat up. Her swords were where they ought to be. Fools hadn't disarmed her. The room had a CCTV camera high in the top corner, a large ceiling mounted speaker, one cheap table, two chairs, and one seething girl, who was very keen on getting the right information and dispatching some limbs from bodies.

'Hullo Aurielle,' said a soft, creepy voice.

'Why am I here?' She looked at the speaker. It could be unscrewed, dismantled.

'Why, dear Aurielle Merlot, do *you* think you're here with us?'

'Where am I?'

'Where in this world of ours do you want to be?'

'Yeah, you see, now you're just giving me questions, no answers. I had this problem earlier today. Have you got a scaly face, long red talons, and a long spotty chin? I reckon I've already met a member of your clan. Dumb as well as painful on the eye. Or are you the one with the terrible beard?'

'You're not answering *our* questions, are you? And what a shame that is for us all.'

Aurielle started to examine the room. 'What is it with all this "our" and "we" stuff? Never mind, don't answer that, thinking aloud. Anyway, we'll try again … how did I get here?'

'Sweet girl, don't you remember?'

'No, I don't. What happened to me?' She tapped the walls, solid, most likely concrete. Door locked, of course. But she could reach the speaker if she stacked the chair on the table.

'Tell us child, are you frightened?'

'Only by the amount of anger I'm gonna bring on your head with my blades. I get very cross, you see. You going to answer anything?'

'What do you think, my angry little killer?'

'I'm not your anything, you make me sick. Have you got someone else there that can talk without making me want to puke?'

'Need a bucket, my dear?'

'Tell you what … let me out of here now, or I'll come find you and give you some new body piercings.'

'I'm afraid not, you won't be doing anything at all. Not until we say so.'

'You're over-confident. I could get out of here in a few minutes, then we could have a proper chat, one to one.'

'You won't be going anywhere. And I'm going to be the one you're desperate to talk to from now on, do you know why?'

'Because teasing idiots is great sport. And when we meet, you're going to show me how much fun it is squeezing those enormous spots on your face?'

'Because I've got your mother and sister with me right here.'

Aurielle gasped.

'That's right. And if you don't do what I ask, life is going to get pretty hot for them. Do you hear me? Find any fun in that tragic news, Miss Merlot? Or are you going to give me some threats you'll never carry out?'

She clenched her fists and gritted her teeth, that dunce was going to pay heavily for this.

'Silence is your new friend, eh? Very good, this is a *very* good start.'

Chapter 5. The Hunt for Blackjack

Rig embraced his dad. The grip was fierce, the never-letting-go type. After the horrific death of his mother and brothers, they agreed on a strict rule as part of their recovery in grief, something magic couldn't help with. Every day, they would hug. It was always warm, meaningful, and both saw it as reassuring, to help their healing. To change this was not an option, so both knew how important Rig's trip to stay with his uncle really was. It was going to be the first time he had been away since it happened. But his dad didn't really know how important it was going to be for Flash. Rig couldn't tell him, couldn't put his dad through it again. Uncle James would understand.

The waft of butter and brown toast surrounded them. His dad gave him a last squeeze. They separated, but his dad's firm hands gripped Rig's shoulders.

He peered into Rig. 'You will call me every day, repeat after me, "I will call you every day".'

'I will call you every day, I will, Dad. I'll be okay.' The last bit was hardest to say because he wasn't sure about that. He wished he hadn't said it, but to tell his dad the truth would amount to putting either his dad or Flash, or both, in danger. And Rig wasn't going to have that. Dad, Uncle James, and Great Aunt Ida were his only family now, and he'd protect them all no matter what.

'And you'll be back on Thursday?'

Rig poured some orange juice and took a sip. 'Yes, Dad, I'll be back Thursday and I'll call you every day. Everything is fine.'

His dad took a bite of toast and munched on it. 'Good,' he said, 'then you won't mind telling me who that is standing in the hallway, as if he doesn't exist.'

Rig spun on is heels to find his new friend blubbering.

'Sorry! I am, didn't mean to disturb. Oh dear,' said the visitor as if he were about to burst.

'Humphrey! What are you doing here?'

The visitor's expression tightened. 'Well! I can tell I'm not wanted!' he twirled and waltzed towards the door.

'Wait a minute, you might as well meet my dad.'

Dad sat and continued to scoff his morning toast with gulps of coffee, clearly untroubled about meeting a ghost. 'So, who's Humphrey and where's he from?'

'Oh, don't know exactly. I'm not sure even he knows. I hardly ever see him during the day, always at night when I'm not quite with it.'

'I am here you know … honestly, as if I can't speak for myself!'

Rig sat by his dad and glanced at his mobile phone; the taxi would be here soon. 'Alright, tell us … where are you from? Who are you?' asked Rig.

Humphrey crossed his arms in a huff. 'I'm not going to stand here and be questioned. I'm worth more than that.' Humphrey looked away, and there was a pause.

'Can't remember, can you?'

His dad was scanning his newspaper. 'Don't be harsh with him,' he said without looking up.

'See, someone cares,' the ghost complained. 'The details are a bit hazy now, truth be known, still … what's important is right now, best to be in the moment, enjoy life as it is, sort of. You know what I mean. Anyway, nice to meet you Mr … err … Mister … Anyway, we'll be off then.'

'Where are "we" off to then?'

Dad smirked.

Humphrey was already down the hallway, hands aloft like they were being controlled by an invisible puppeteer. 'Your taxi has arrived, sir.'

His dad smothered him with arms and another squeezed hug and saw him to the front door.

Rig climbed into the back of the car with his bag and wound down the window. It was hard to take his eyes off his father. Rig just wanted him safe, he wanted everyone to be safe so he could read again and play out his adventures on the computer screen. Instead, he was going to rescue his favourite assassin from a sorcerer in another world.

He gave a last wave to his dad. Humphrey materialised next to him.

'Straight to the station then, Guv?' asked the hoarse voice of the driver.

Rig shut his eyes, 'Change of plan, take me to Finksbury University, Gladstone Street, please.'

'But Rig, your dad thinks you're going to Uncle James's. What you doing? Where are we going? I really don't know what's happening. What's going on?'

'I don't think you remember, do you?'

'Remember what?'

'Nothing. Don't worry about it. And you're not going anywhere. You need to stay here, it's safer that way, trust me.'

'Oh, something bad has happened, hasn't it?'

'You could say that.'

'Eh?' The taxi man looked at Rig in his mirror.

'Talking to myself.'

The man nodded his understanding.

'Charming,' complained Humphrey, 'I just don't exist at all, do I?'

***

They stood outside the city's only university. People of all shapes, sizes, and colour filed inside the giant building, the tallest in the city.

'I'll say goodbye here,' said Rig.

'Where you going exactly? I mean, I don't see why I can't come, I've got the spare time. But if you really want to be on your own, I understand. I mean if you don't want me there, wherever *there* is.'

'It'll be safer if you're here, that's all.'

'Well, what's the worst that can happen? I mean I can't be killed Rig, can I?'

'I don't know, just don't want you in danger that's all.'

'Oh! You do care Rig Penlip!' Humphrey rubbed his hands in glee, not really knowing where to put them by the look of it.

'I need to go. We can always say goodbye up there if you want,' he said pointing skywards.

Humphrey arced his ghostly head up, as he did so his hollow jaw lowered in awe at the sight of the goliath. Rig walked to the building, pushed on the revolving door, and headed to the lift. The ghost followed behind, chuntering nonsense.

The lift doors pinged open, and they were soon on their way to the 24th floor.

'I don't like heights.' Humphrey confessed.

Rig looked at the apparition, 'I said to stay, didn't I?'

'I'm not your pet dog, y'know. Anyway, why come here? So many nice places we could've gone. What you up to?'

There was a piercing noise from the straining lift.

'What was that? Why would it do that?'

'I expect it's the cables creaking a bit that's all,' offered Rig, but it was too late the apparition had vanished. Now he was truly on his own. The lift jarred to a halt, Rig got out and climbed the stairs to the roof. The stiff breeze buffeted him as he strode purposefully to the centre. The city's skyline was a sight, a blend of sloping Victorian rooves butting against modern apartment buildings and the interestingly shaped new theatre. It looked like the hull of a boat standing on one end. Rig's belly churned. He wasn't the best with heights himself.

The new theatre became blurry, harder to see. The reason why reformed in front of him. Humphrey.

'So, where we going then?' he asked.

'Look, I need to go, I don't have much time. I don't want you getting mixed up in this, okay?'

'Mixed up in what?'

'I need to find Flash, remember? Otherwise, she'll be "dead meat".'

'Ah yes, well I'm going to … what's that?' Humphrey's attention was drawn to something behind Rig.

A large circular shape fizzed and trembled four feet from the University's cement roof. Its middle hummed with static as though it were out of tune.

'It's a Slide,' said Rig.

'Oh, yes … course it is. I can see that now. And it does what?'

'It'll take me to Gamma Seven, where Flash ought to be. I need to see if her family know what happened and find Blackjack, fast.'

'It's a portal then. Why not call it what it is?'

Hands on hips, Rig replied, 'This is what the gods call it, nothing to do with me. Only gods can open them, so they get to name them, I suppose. Anyway, got to go.'

Humphrey gestured to him to wait. 'Hold on a second. How are you going to get back?'

'The same way.'

'What if you get hurt? Who is this Mr Blackjack?'

'Look, I can't be having pointless conversations like this, I'm in a rush. Don't you get it?'

Humphrey swivelled on his heels in a sulk.

Rig went to the Slide and held its zinging edges. The crackling sensation filled his arms, he glanced back at Humphrey, who sneaked a look at Rig.

'Alright, come on then.'

'I'm not going down that thing. See you there, that's if I don't change my mind. You really are a difficult person to be around, Rig Penlip. My mother said to me once—'

Rig didn't hear the rest of it. He was already spinning through a tunnel of twisting colours and fierce sounds.

Woah! The tube pushed, pulled, and squeezed his stomach as he zipped, *just like last time*. A clanging sounded out so loudly he feared his ears would burst. The Slide seemed alive, as though its cramps were driving him downwards. It went on and on, his whole body squished, he fought not to throw up, couldn't even hold onto his thoughts in the torrent. The worst roller-coaster, like an underground tube-train at rush hour but with rolling hills and valleys as extras. A sudden shove to his head, stinging neck.

He flew from the Slide, arms flailing, legs akimbo as he dropped helplessly. He plummeted in the dark, lights in the distance. Signs of life. Still falling, fast.

WHACK! A blow to the ribs.

The ground had smashed into him. It was wet, long grass. Cold as snow. He ached. All over. It reminded him of the second worst day of his young years.

He sat up. Took a moment to clear his head.

His aches calmed. Yep. He was in the middle of a rugby pitch at the back of what looked like a spread of school buildings. He had been dumped and punched to the muddy floor in that game, hated every second of it. 'With that stomach you can go in the scrum Penlip,' he could remember the horror he felt at hearing that from the sports teacher. It was nothing compared to the pain that was to come. That kind of scrap suited his brother. He loved rugby, all sports. Poor Zac. *Not now*. Dwelling on it would lead to a darker place than this, Rig knew it. He feared that place, somewhere magic couldn't reach, no amount of clever or ancient spells could resolve the truth of that loss, the loss of all of them. It disabled him. He lumbered to his feet, rubbing his sore head.

'Hmm …'

Rig jolted, surprised at the sight of Humphrey already scanning the area. 'Don't do that, you made me jump out of my skin.'

Humphrey gave a sly look, 'Doubt that, there's quite a lot of it.'

'Fine,' Rig stomped towards the school.

'Where now?'

'Told you, to see Flash's family, then Blackjack.'

'Who's he?'

Rig cursed. 'Forget it. Let me deal with it.'

'Moody so and so.'

Rig took his mobile out as he squelched from the rugby pitch.

Humphrey piped up, 'You won't get a signal here. You're in another world, aren't you?'

'Yes, I know, just checking.'

'So, where does the girl's family live then?'

Rig approached a door, 'That's what I'm going to find out.'

'Oh, well ... wait for me.'

Rig pulled on the handle. Locked. He peered at the keyhole, his hand warmed. It was automatic now. He and the magic particles around him bonded whenever they were needed, without instruction. It was so automatic he didn't need to demand magic anymore. If he concentrated, it just happened. The energy around his hand bristled as a tinkling sound rang out. It signalled the opening of magic pathways. In his mind he could see what movement the lock had to perform. Rig's hand flicked to the right; the mechanism clunked. Rig opened the door and stepped inside.

Rig wandered through the corridors of the school, some partially lit by night-lights, some possessed shadows cast by lamps from the side road. The light snuck through high windows reaching like long spindly fingers into the school, but some walkways were utterly dark. None of this was concerning. Rig was focussed on finding Flash's family and rescuing his good friend.

'I didn't like school much,' announced Humphrey who had taken to waddling alongside Rig even if it meant walking through obstacles. 'Maybe it just didn't like me,' he said thoughtfully. 'I mean the teachers were okay. I hated games. Some of those boys were really rough, know what I mean, Rig? Girls were nicer, not as nasty, mind you they could be twice as bitchy when they wanted.'

Rig took a left turn and headed for the sign that said "Headmaster's Office".

Humphrey walked through a wall and came out of a notice board, 'If I ever did it again, gods forbid me, I would stand up for myself a bit more, wouldn't you? I mean the teachers are well meaning, but honestly, they don't—'

'Stop it!' Rig blurted. 'Just for a minute, please.' He gave Humphrey a tired look. This time Rig paused with his palm wrapped around the door handle, sensed the warmth enveloping it, waited for the metallic click, and entered. It was a small office with lots of framed certificates on the walls, a large map, and a modest desk and filing cabinet in the corner. Rig approached the larger desk which was swelling with a pile of coloured folders, skewed stacks of paper and random pens.

'Just like that,' said Humphrey stepping inside. 'Your magic comes to you so easily, doesn't it? You must be very powerful. I've never seen anyone control magic as easily as you do. Is that because of what you inherited when your family were murdered?'

Rig froze. His eyes rose from the cluttered desk to find Humphrey. The reminder burned him. Just for a moment he considered throwing a spell, to bind the ghost's mouth shut. That would be harsh, and probably wouldn't work. As it happened, his expression was sufficient.

'I'm sorry, I am.'

Rig used the torch on his mobile to sift through papers. The documents were headed Nightingale Secondary School. 'I wonder if this is Flash's school, we need her address. In fact, I don't even know where we are,' Rig mumbled as he searched.

'The map on the wall behind you might help, so might that computer.'

Rig frowned. 'Yes, I was about to check them, actually.' He turned the computer on, and while it bleeped and whirred on start-up, he examined the chart. 'Now, I'm sure Flash said she lived in a southern state.' Rig found the pencilled circle around the school.

'Rig?'

He traced his finger along the map southwards, hoping to find something recognisable. 'I can't see where she lives, but then I don't actually know the town. I bet it's on file in that computer if it's anywhere. What are you like at passwords?'

'Rig?'

'So, we're here,' his finger pointing on the map, 'just don't know where her town is. Just need an address, something.'

'Rig!'

'What?' He looked up.

Humphrey was cowering. 'Something's creeping along the corridor.'

Rig peered back the way they'd come. 'I can't see anything, it can't hurt you anyway,' he lowered his voice in reply. Humphrey gave a short wave and faded to nothing.

So, that was how it was going to be. He skirted along the wall, hands already warm, his early warning system. Rig stared into the hallway, at the reception desk, posters, doors to other rooms, toilets – noted for later, but saw nothing out of place. And yet, something felt wrong. His senses knew it and so did his frightened ghost. He was about to turn back to the map when the floor moved, or shone, under the limited light. He studied every part of the tiled floor, dull in some places, apparently shiny in others where the light brushed it.

The floor moved.

Rig gasped, stepped backwards.

Grime from the floor gathered into a mass. The gooey blob grew to the size of a large dog. It slid closer. Rig scanned the room for anything that could act as a weapon. A glass paperweight to his left, cricket bat to his right. The thing rose higher, wider, its shape filled the doorframe. Rig stepped nearer the window as the form sculpted into a huge figure with six arms. Its head featureless, as though it didn't need eyes or a mouth. Worrying.

Rig hurled the glass ball at the creature, the weight splodged into its chest making a dent before sliding to the floor, the gap in its body repaired itself. Rig had no choice. He raised his tingling hands.

'I call on the gods and protectors of magic, the ancients' and the collective wisdom of those that have gone before us.' Rig pictured what he needed to happen.

The timber doorframe split and collapsed as though bombed from above.

'What?' The creature can't be shielded from magic, nothing is.

There was a terrible roar as the thing jumped at Rig. A wodge of gunk slipped around Rig's neck and shoved him against the curtained window. Rig grabbed at the creature's arms, pulled chunks of it away, but the gaps swelled and simply replaced themselves. The head had no apparent purpose. How did it see and think?

Rig struggled for air, realising it smelled like a mixture of oil and petrol.

'Why ... don't we ... sit ... tea ... have a ... chat?' gurgled Rig.

Rig sensed extra arms wrap around his middle, trapping him, squeezing him like a fat python snake. Running out of air. It had him pinned.

From the corner of his eye, Rig spotted Humphrey, who gave a little wave.

Rig's eyes implored the ghost because he couldn't speak.

'Oh, yes,' he said. Humphrey produced his notebook and picked through it. The pad's front cover had "HP stamped on it, which was without doubt entirely irrelevant right now.

The monster gave a high -pitched shriek, perhaps it knew Humphrey had arrived, an unknown threat, at least unknown to it anyway.

'Somewhere in here it'll tell us what to do. Now, what was I looking up again?'

Humphrey glanced at Rig just as a lump of stodge poured into Rig's mouth.

'Ooops, that's right,' he said, 'filed under S - school monster, made of sludge.'

Rig gagged.

His eyes watered.

Can't breathe.

About to go.

Never wake up.

'Nearly there.' Humphrey looked again at Rig, busily dying, the creature had almost cocooned him entirely, just his eyes peeked from his head.

'It's made of grease and muck; it's looking for fat and food waste so it can grow stronger and more powerful. I can see why it went for you. Only joking!'

Choking, going to pass out, can't move hands, but they warmed.

Best chance, last chance.

Fingers won't click. Greasy. Short-cut, his hands grabbed at the goo by his throat, it melted and fell away. He pictured what would happen and coughed the fatty goo from his mouth. Rig mumbled the word through the gunk. Didn't work. He spat the last of the goo.

'Ignis,' he said.

There was a very brief but dramatic stillness to the room.

The creature squealed. It was so sharp and surprising that Rig banged his head against the window.

'Oh, that's bad,' said the ghost. 'Fire!'

The creature shrank away as the school's alarm rang out.

Flames raced up the curtains. Rig's legs launched him from the wall just as the entire curtain became a fireball. He wiped the remaining gunk on his sleeve, grabbed the fire extinguisher in the hallway.

'Oh, very good idea,' said Humphrey cheerfully above the bell-ringing din.

Rig rushed to the burning flames that were now scorching the ceiling and blasted them with the extinguisher, foam covered the wall, desk, and half of the floor. Rig battled to save the office from complete destruction.

'Rig? Rig? You missed a bit down there. Oh, no … and look it's gone all the way over there too. Oh dear, you might want to hurry up.' Humphrey was being very supportive.

The walls were looking charcoaled now. He had drowned most of the flames, the edges had a habit of re-lighting once they'd been dowsed.

Rig focussed his mind, recanted the phrases from the old scrolls and released a flood of magic through his fizzing, shaking hands.

'Rig, why don't you—'

The fire ceased. Smoke puffed from the blackened walls; the fumes heavy on the throat.

'You should've done that earlier,' said the spirit above the clanging alarm.

Rig turned to his ghostly friend, and sighed.

Chapter 6. Still Hunting Blackjack

The ghost and the wizard plodded down the school drive. The gap between them had chilled.

'Where did you go when I was fighting the grease-ball?'

'Well, there's no need to be like that, I mean who came up with the answer to that little problem anyway?'

Humphrey crossed his arms and half turned from Rig, drifting now instead of walking. He did that when he was properly annoyed.

'I'd already figured that before you said anything, and anyway, why did you leave it until I couldn't breathe? I've seen that book before. What's in it?'

'Oh sure, you looked fully in control with that blob of fat covering you,' Humphrey looked him up and down. 'It's nothing anyway, I just write a few notes on occasion that's all.'

'Thanks for that. Great help you are.'

'Oh good!' Humphrey said, not recognising the sarcasm. He wafted to Rig's side, walking with a new bounce in his step. 'So, where we going?'

'The records showed Flash isn't studying at Nightingale Secondary anymore … she was expelled, got her address though.' Thankfully the computer system had survived the bonfire, and the grease-ball monster had disappeared. Meeting monsters had become a bit of a hobby after his family had died. Whilst always impressive in their own way, their form and nature no longer surprised him.

'Why we going there then?'

'I told you, to see if we can trace Blackjack.'

'Who's he?'

'Never mind. What was your memory like before becoming … well, dead?'

'There's nothing wrong with my memory, never has been. It's not easy being like this. I can barely touch anything; no-one notices you at all. I could go on, you know.'

'Don't. It's okay. I understand.' Rig marched towards the bus stop.

'I mean, can you imagine not talking to anyone all day, not knowing what you need to do next? It's so frustrating at times. I just can't tell you how awful it can be, no-one cares, I don't even get hugs anymore, a basic human need, don't you think?'

'Well, you're not human, are you?'

'Sometimes I'm not even sure what I ought to do next, what's best. I used to like reading, can't do that anymore, it's not like I can apply to the local library, is it? I mean, where would my local be? I don't have a place to call my own or even where I can simply be me.'

'Sorry, Humps, must be awful, really bad. You manage great, you really do. There's always a positive though, it must be fun going wherever you want to at any time.'

Humphrey looked at Rig as though he were about to stab his pet cat.

'Sorry, Humps.'

They waited about half an hour for the bus, the sky was a patchwork of cloud that dribbled on Rig every few minutes, forcing him to use his hoody which dampened his already soggy mood. At least he didn't have to pay for his invisible companion.

Rig sat at the back of the bus, hoping to avoid people. Generally, he liked people, he just liked to dodge them sometimes, quite frequently actually. The rain stopped. The bus chuntered onwards, and Rig slumped into his plastic seat.

The ghost stood opposite, not needing a seat or stability.

'Why didn't your magic work against the slime ball?' he asked.

'Don't know, don't really want to think about it now,' Rig shut his eyes.

'Well, seems quite important, I mean if you're magic doesn't work sometimes, shouldn't you work it out? Might save your life? I don't know, you're such a lazy wizard, Rig.'

'What?'

Humphrey was glaring at him.

Rig shuffled in his seat, 'Logic says he either had a protective shield of some sort, I used the wrong spell, or … I don't know.'

'It was a hallucination,' said the ghost.

'What? Like seeing things that aren't there? No way.' Rig looked out of a smeary window to find green fields, cows eating grass. Normal stuff.

'Well, you see me. Don't you, Riggy?'

'Don't call me Riggy. Well, if it was a hallucination, you wouldn't see it would you, numbskull?'

Humphrey sat on the seat in front, the back of his translucent head facing Rig.

'Sorry, just making a point, aren't I?'

Humphrey didn't budge.

Rig continued, 'I suppose it could be a group hallucination, more likely it had some sort of protective shield. I don't know.'

The ghost turned one hundred and eighty degrees and looked Rig coolly in the eye.

'What?' asked Rig.

The apparition dissolved.

Typical. Unreliable and massively touchy.

About an hour later, he arrived at the bus stop nearest the Merlot's house. The driver directed him down a winding lane away from the main road, which skirted the edge of a large housing estate surrounded by farmer's fields and sheep. They seemed a little larger than they should be, not that Rig was an expert on these things. He found the house. The garden was neatly pruned. It was used to getting a lot of attention, small orange and yellow flowers topped the shrubs lining the path to the door. Rig knocked, then saw a bell so he pressed it. A high-pitched jingle sounded from inside. It was lifeless behind the net curtains, no response. Rig banged a fist on the door.

'Hullo?' an older man's voice came from above.

The white-haired neighbour stared at Rig from the bedroom window next door. Surprisingly, he was still in his striped pyjamas.

'Hallo,' said Rig.

'Yes? What do you want? If you're selling something, we're not interested.'

'No, I'm—'

'We get enough of your sort round here, selling this, selling that. Well, we watch out for each other here see, we don't need to be buying your wares at our front door, thank you.'

'I'm not selling anything; I'm just trying to find the Merlot's. They're friends of mine. Are they out?'

'Not seen you round here before. I'd never forget a fat stomach like that. How old are you? I don't know, today's generation have it too easy.'

A voice with a Scottish lilt came from somewhere inside, an arm yanked the man away from the window, and a purple perm appeared in an equally purple dressing gown.

'Sorry laddy, never mind him, he's always grumpy in morning. Aurielle, Denyse, and Molly have been missing a few days now, police might tell you more, sorry laddy.'

Rig shuffled on his tired feet, 'Oh, I … that's bad. Thank you for the information.'

With a sigh, Rig turned to go.

'Another thing,' the woman called out, 'that Frank, down the pub or nearby. Where he always is. Try the Cat and Custard Pot, off Grime Street in town.'

The neighbour pointed a crooked finger in a southerly direction, grinned, and slammed the window shut.

Happy days. Rig marched as quickly as his big legs would go, following the bend of the road, past double-glazed windows and double-parked cars, they all looked much the same although he wasn't really looking. His head was soaking up the news: Molly Merlot and Denyse were also missing, presumably taken by Blackjack. Denyse must be the sister Flash had mentioned who was good with the violin and looking pretty but not much else, although she could be a cruel judge. Hell, now there was more on his plate, and not a scrap of food in sight. Rig plodded on, until he saw an unnatural shadow standing by a tree.

'Back again then, is this how it's going to be. Disappearing whenever you feel like it?'

'Yes. Especially when you're being a nasty individual.'

'Sorry.'

The ghost drifted at his side taking in the view. They nattered amiably for a while, Humphrey forgetting what they were doing, Rig reminding him with a sharp tone. The ghost scolded Rig for his lack of patience, yet again. It was now a circular arrangement which Rig struggled to avoid.

There was a large field ahead on their left. In front, iron benches lined the way to what could be Grime Street. A pub on the corner had a white cat on a yellow sign. They passed two old ladies in rain macks on the nearest bench talking about their respective dogs, neither much larger than Rig's left shoe. A vagrant slept on the next, gripping his bottle of plonk as he slept.

'Must be that one I reckon. See the sign? White cat. Must be the Cat and the Custard Pot.'

'What a ridiculous name,' Humphrey stopped and gawped, hands on hips. 'Why not call it something cute and memorable?'

'Look, we need to get a shift on. Flash and her family's lives are at stake and you're complaining about pub names? In any case, it's fine, and it's easy to remember.'

'Who ... you talking to ... young fella?' asked a new husky voice.

Behind Rig the vagrant was standing as though he was on the deck of a boat in rough seas. He was clutching his bottle of drink like his life depended on it, and for all Rig knew, it might well do. His light brown corduroy trousers had dark splotches, the yellow top under a crumpled suit jacket had seen better times as well. The man hadn't shaved for a few days.

'I was thinking aloud, that's all. Is that the Cat and the Mustard Pot up there?'

'Yeah. Wouldn't go there though.'

'Why not?'

'Beer's foul,' he burped loudly, and the old ladies cast a vicious glare. 'Wine's cheap though, tourists like it.'

Rig glanced each way, looking for possible tourists, unlikely.

Humphrey whispered in his ear, 'I bet there's more to it than that.'

Rig faced the man, who couldn't seem to hold still.

The drunk staggered forward, hand outstretched, the other protecting his wine. 'The name's Frank, Frank Merlot. Nice to … to meet you, lad.'

Stunned, Rig shook the man's hand.

Frank stepped backwards, tripped, and fell to a heap on his rear.

'Haven't got a spare tenner have you … boy?' he burped,

Rig looked at the smirking ghost, then the drunk struggling to stand.

'Oh no,' he mumbled, 'what now?'

Chapter 7. Blackjack asks Prod Visceral for help

Prod sank further into his armchair. His apartment was just right, light, and airy with sleek white furniture. The atmosphere quiet, how he liked it. A spider's steps would be an interference. The view was stunning through the two glass walls bordering his home. The city's landscape of buildings and roads had looked more and more like Prod's hunting ground, his city, and from this height, he could see most of it. That's how it should be. As for home comforts, he didn't need much. There was no clutter, but an order to it which seemed just right. To anyone else the rooms might feel cold, empty without personal items, but had any been included they would have been out of place.

And that is exactly how Blackjack looked.

'Why are you here? We discussed this weeks ago, I didn't agree to social visits,' said Prod.

Blackjack was sitting on the edge of the leather sofa, picking at his fingers. Prod eyed fingernail fragments splinter to his wood-slatted flooring. The sorcerer's expression was calm, but his hands betrayed him. A faint creak rang out, Prod's attention switched to his right side. Most likely the ceiling's internal metal framework reacting to the changing temperature, except Prod didn't believe in 'most likely'.

'No, no, of course not. We have the Merlot girl and some of her family, won't be long now.'

'You haven't come here to tell me what I already know, so spit it out, Jack.'

'Thought you'd be happy. It's what we agreed, isn't it?'

Prod stood up. 'Don't question me, Jack. I know it's in your nature, but you don't do it here.'

Blackjack didn't reply, it was difficult to alter what comes naturally. The sorcerer was full of questions, always had been. Prod moved to the window. The skyline was particularly stunning today, the morning sun peppered the streets below, the blue sky was hazy in places, but the sun's rays had managed to warm the twenty-fourth-floor apartment. There was not a single cloud to be seen.

Usually, he could see at least one. Maybe they were hiding. Nonsense. He brushed the thought away.

'Problems?'

Blackjack shifted in his seat. 'None. Just a question, that's all. Just one. It's the transportation, the route more than anything. It's what we agreed, the best way forward.'

'And?'

'We need to get her to Gamma Nine. It's the best place to do it, only we don't have any transport. How can we get her there?'

Prod turned on his heels. Blackjack's beard twitched on its own. He was an unusual looking fellow, black straggly beard, shoulder length hair, and his jeans and shirt a little too modern for Prod's taste. Despite reasonable talents with traditional and dark magic, he was a fool, although on his day a dangerous one, but that's why Prod employed him.

'I asked you to solve this problem, now you come to me with it. Very disappointing.'

'I've never travelled to another world, it's not an everyday thing, even for a sorcerer. Give me the tools for the job and I'll do it.'

Prod sprung over the sofa in one leap, grabbed Blackjack by the throat and raised him up in the air. He wriggled like a salmon on the end of a fishing line. 'Speak to me like that again and I'll rip your arms from your shoulders and kick your head so hard it'll roll free from your weak neck. Got it?'

Blackjack spluttered a lot, but he nodded too. Prod threw him to the floor. Blackjack trembled as he peered back at his master, waiting for the next assault. Prod thought the slovenly man might even cry. He didn't wait to find out. Instead, he returned to the window.

Prod examined the scene below: the cars queuing, the office blocks and apartment buildings standing tall amongst medieval church steeples and occasional lines of slate roof topped houses. Within those streets was the answer. Only the gods can open a Slide to another world. Gamma Nine: that's where they had to go. He didn't have access to the gods, not since Rig Penlip had changed everything, not since he had made history and changed the world –

a simple boy with barely any skills unseated a higher god to save his dying father. And he defeated the Oglith clan in the process. He made what seemed impossible, possible. Rig had travelled across worlds to make that happen, now it was Prod's turn. It was all about having the right knowledge and using your head. If that didn't work, there was always the best, fail-safe plan ever known. If approached in the right way it never failed, through trickery, bluff and applying knowledge Prod would get what he needed. The plan was quite simple really.

To cheat.

He would do it to get what he wanted, and if it allowed him to win, he would do it every time. Rig Penlip had a lot of magical ability, had inherited a lot from his dead family. As they died, their potential transferred to him, as the gods intended. But Prod no longer wanted to study magic; it was for harnessing, controlling, and whoever did that the best would hold all the cards. And yet, it was traditional for those seeking the authority that was naturally theirs to do whatever was required. Removing powerful people who could be a threat was a sensible way forward, any leader needed to have control over, or eliminate, the opposition. Leadership was like vanilla ice-cream, not for sharing. In this new age, ordinary people needed to believe in something, or someone – order and safety were important aspects of modern life. His city, and beyond, was about to get very modern.

The air-conditioning whirred into action, and there was a faint scrape of metal on metal. Prod's hearing was unusually perfect, boosted significantly since his dip in the pool of waste magic. Except for his self-improvement, their scientific expedition to the islands of Malaysia for the group calling themselves "The Consortium" had been pointless. They were idiots. But he was a finely tuned being now, the best he had ever been. He had to admit, he was so strong and certain of purpose that he felt utterly invincible. In a way, he was a god without actually being a god. Yes, he was always meant to go to that island, contract or not.

The shrill bell of the apartment phone rang again. Prod ignored it again. The ringing went on and on, persistent, getting more and more irritable.

Blackjack was tense, 'Do you want me—'

'No, I don't.'

The caller rang off.

Prod scratched his temple. They weren't giving up; someone was very keen to chat. A clump of hair came away. He looked at it with a distant kind of interest, twisting the strands through his fingers. A new symptom, something to be worried about? A side-effect of gloriously real change. Of improvement. Refinement. The cost was irrelevant, he put it in his pocket.

Yes, you're changing. Losing control.

'Who's that?' The tone, the words, they were familiar. Words of doubt. From the person he used to be. How? He was gone, no longer.

No. Still here. You're not well.

'No, no, I'm better than I've ever been.'

'What?' Blackjack gawped at him.

'Shut it.'

Silence is not the answer, you need the answer. Before it's too late.

'Answer? What answer? Of course, I don't.' Prod paced up and down, from one end of the apartment's window to the other. The movement shook his mind. He was in control. No-one else.

Reflected in the large triple-glazed window was a cowering Blackjack. He needed work, direction, and a hard kick.

'You need to find a Seer. There will be one around somewhere.'

'A Seer?'

'That's right.'

'I thought you hated spirit-seekers.'

'I'll do the thinking.'

'There's one that visits the corner shop cafe on West Street, called Scarlett Crook. A small-time Seer but got some decent skills. Does demos there and stuff, card reading, tells peoples futures, all that.'

'Good. Make sure she understands her future depends on her immediate co-operation.'

'What should I get her to do?'

'Tell her you need to get to Gamma Nine with four passengers.'

'Four?'

'Just tell her. Be persuasive. "No" is not an answer.'

Blackjack stood and headed to the door, his large boots squeaked on the shiny wood flooring, which lessened his dangerous sorcerer image somewhat.

'Have you seen him?'

Blackjack paused by the door. 'The boy?'

'You know who.'

'Nothing, no. He'll turn up, curiosity always kills the cat.'

Prod's rigid glare caught Blackjack, 'I'll be the one doing the killing.'

Chapter 8. Turning the Screw with Red

They were called Red and Midnight. Her favoured sword of the two had fine swirls of gold inlay on the handle that contrasted well with the midnight black which surrounded it, hence its name: Midnight. It had style and a vicious serrated edge, and it was cool in her palm, whereas the other was pattern-free in violent red. Red had ridges making it simpler to grip, giving the artist confidence it would never slip away.

She changed her mind.

Red was her favourite today. The steel tip slotted nicely into one of the screws holding the round speaker. The chair wobbled, or was it her knees? She looked down. Mistake. Her head clouded, she looked away, gripping the chair. She never was good with heights. Standing on a chair on top of a rickety desk wouldn't have been her first choice. But needs must. She steadied herself, focused on gripping the blade, feeling the screw's resistance, and forcing the blade to turn, and with it the screw. Her hand strained and turned white, the fixture wouldn't budge. Reluctantly, she let go of the chair, with both hands she squeezed the hilt of the sword anticlockwise. The screw gave way, relief came with it, just a matter of time now before she got going. Annoyingly, the screw was long. Why? Obviously fitted by an amateur. She twisted and turned Red until the long screw finally dropped, clipped the table, bounced to the floor. Only another eleven screws to sort out. She would be ready for a good scrap after all this. She started on the second screw and began thinking about her best options for killing her nutty captor: slow, quick, nasty, or unforgettable? It wasn't a difficult decision to make, but the method, that would take some working out.

It took a while, but the tenth screw tumbled to the floor. She placed Red's pointed tip in the end of the next screw, gripped the handle, squeezed then turned.

Vibrations ran up the chair through the sword, loud rumbling, shouty voices. Problem.

The wall exploded.

She jumped from her perch.

A storm of dust and noise burst the air. A farmyard tractor had smashed through the door sending bricks and rubble everywhere. Through the haze she saw a tall boy jump from the tractor with a long staff, teeth gritted like he was in pain.

'I'm Jordi, come to rescue you.'

'Ha!' the idea tickled Aurielle.

Men were trying to squeeze between bricks and tractor to get at them.

Aurielle pointed to the ceiling with Midnight, 'See up there?'

The teenager frowned at her response and duly looked up.

'You,' she said now aiming Red at him, 'have ruined my escape plan. I was about to tear that speaker off and get out through the ceiling, now look what you've done.'

A man in a facemask and khaki uniform stole through the gap and charged at Jordi-boy from behind. The boy followed her glance and jabbed his staff into the man's face, who promptly slumped to the floor. Jordi had barely turned to face him as he struck. He was a protector, it was obvious.

'You're welcome, I mean I've got better things to do, miss.' He seemed a little annoyed.

She clocked another guard approaching from her side. She unsheathed Midnight and with a quick flick of her wrists, sparks flew as she clashed her blades together, a warning she rarely gave. He stopped, turned, and fled at the sight.

'Yeah, need a good scrub, don't you. Get all that blue off your skin,' she said holstering her swords.

The boy's shoulders drooped a little. 'If you think I've come all the way here to take a load of abuse off the likes of you, well …'

Her hands rested on her hips, 'Well, what?'

A mechanical rat-tat-tat of a high-powered machine gun sounded out. Very old fashioned. She flipped the table and crashed behind it. Jordi scrambled to get all his limbs behind it too as bullets ripped through the room. He was panting heavily. He might be of some use if he didn't get in the way.

'You've really annoyed the locals haven't you, Flash?' he said. The room seemed alive as it burst from the assault of hundreds of bullets tearing across its walls. The din was intense.

'It's Aurielle,' she shouted back, 'and how do you know my name?'

'Stories ... everyone knows what happened to Rig Penlip and his Protector.'

'Killer ... hired by the gods.'

Wood splintered between their heads as a bullet ripped into the back wall. They stared at the hole it had come through.

'Whatever,' said Jordi.

The machine-gunning ceased abruptly, but the ringing in her ears continued. She massaged them, shook her head trying to clear the racket. The boy wiped dust and debris from his arms and stood up.

'They've stopped,' he said.

'Gods! You're gonna be helpful, aren't you?'

He rolled his eyes and turned from her.

She stood, examined their options. Best thing to do would be to reverse the tractor, get drippy boy to distract the attackers, while she searched for her mum and sister and got busy with some payback.

She looked up at his skinny, blue-tinged face. 'So—'

'Look,' he said.

Behind them were tubes jammed through the holes made by the bullets, gas was being pumped into the room. Why? There were too many air-holes and a big one where the tractor had smashed the wall.

She switched back to him, 'Quickly, do you know magic?'

All the evidence so far suggested not.

'I'm a Protector, not a—' Jordi dropped, unconscious.

'I'll take that as a 'no' then.'

Oh.

Her own knees gave way as if slashed from behind. The floor hurt when she hit it, and her remaining thoughts melted.

Chapter 9. Awkward Travel Arrangements

The one -hour journey in the back of the van had not been full of comfort, but that didn't trouble Aurielle, it was that beardy Blackjack finally had the good sense to take her swords. If anything got her miffed, it was someone taking Midnight and Red, her best friends. No-one takes away her best friends.

No-one.

He paraded with them across his back proudly, not realising his days would end with one savage cut by Midnight.

When she really thought about it, getting caught once was embarrassing but getting caught twice was utterly careless and, in normal circumstances, unforgivable. Except this time, she had a decent explanation, or to put it another way, it was entirely Jordi's fault. She had had a perfectly good plan she was about to execute before he'd came along, and now it was him she wanted to execute – if she could just get hold of him.

The day was bright and the sky calm, with a smattering of thinly stretched cloud which looked like an after-thought by the great designer of skies. The trek along the deserted dirt track to the hill's summit was very pleasant, the fresh air energising and the sight of the sprawling town in the distance interesting. A view she rarely saw.

The monster's thighs rubbed furiously as she moved, the chains making her steps shorter. She could easily tumble, except her cumbersome tail anchored her nicely. Aurielle had grown fond of the dimwit dinosaur, even though Henni had wanted to murder her. She couldn't understand why Henni hadn't broken free of her shackles using her powerful haunches and those enormous shoulders. The creature had accepted her fate somehow, whatever that was.

Having only her hands bound was insulting, they would be simple to overcome when ready. The lack of attention to detail was amateurish and laughable, although it might be fun to see what occurred so she wouldn't act just yet. Blackjack led the way like a pantomime pirate with his long-braided hair and scruffy Hollywood beard. He kept Henni in front and prodded her up the hill, whilst Aurielle, her sister Denyse, and mum followed on behind. They had fear in their eyes. They weren't used to these situations, the only trouble that ever found Denyse was domestic, like the time when her hair straighteners blew a fuse, or her finger nails chipped.

Her mum had her scary face on, ready to act. She was itching to get her nails into Blackjack. Jordi Longstaff was quietly seething with his own anger at getting caught. He had threatened and moaned so much that Blackjack had gagged him, not with a spell but a dirty rag. There was fire in the eyes of that blue-boy.

There was someone Aurielle had not seen before. An older woman, decked with jewellery and tattoos wherever there was space to show them. She climbed the winding path alongside Blackjack, mumbling, had been for a while.

The woman gripped her hands tightly. 'Gods are our saviour, forgive us for this trespassing. We are here to obey, we are not worthy.'

'Speak for yourself, witch,' barked Blackjack, 'you can stop that rubbish.'

She had the look about her, the chants and prayers only confirmed what Aurielle had known all along, she was no witch but a spirit guide, enchanter, or visionary perhaps.

Aurielle's mum spoke in an urgent whisper, 'I need a weapon. How can I get a gun? Anything. Any ideas?'

'Leave it mum, it'll be fine. I'm gonna sort it, leave it to me. I'm used to dealing with his sort. When the time is right, I'll do it, don't worry.'

This didn't seem to calm Denyse, who still looked petrified. Aurielle gave her a wink and cheeky smirk. There was no way in hell Aurielle was going to let anything happen to her family.

'Nice this is,' Henreitta's chains clanked as she moved, 'are we going to have a picnic at the top? I love a picnic, don't I?'

The motley bunch of six captives reached the pinnacle of the hill. Blackjack forced them to stand in a line opposite him, prisoners on parade. The town, its sprawling suburbs and the farms beyond, formed a picturesque landscape below, with the few shadows of clouds present giving an even greater patchwork effect.

A view the gods must see every day. It was a curiously twisted moment, such scenic beauty in the company of five fellow hostages and a mad sorcerer.

Henriette the Horrible couldn't help but chat to anyone bored enough to listen.

'Fun, isn't it? All those houses and fields down there. Always like a good view, can't be the only one, can I?'

'Come here,' Blackjack ushered the dinosaur forward. Henni obliged.

Her chains rattled as she stepped, she seemed unaware of them now.

'What we doing now? Like a good surprise, I do.'

Aurielle's mother poked her. 'What's going on?'

'Wait mum,' she whispered.

Blackjack unfolded his crossed arms, 'Lie down and shut up.'

'Alright, no need to be like that, is there?' Henni did what she was told.

Blackjack kneeled and began unlocking the dinosaur's chains.

'Come here, Crook. Get ready,' ordered Blackjack.

Crook jangled forward, her necklaces nudging across her large chest. There was something about the way she moved, with grace, poise. Aurielle reckoned she had had martial arts training, unusual for a spirit guide. They're usually against all violence. For defence most likely.

Blackjack unclipped a scabbard from his hip and pulled a six-inch knife. A spot of sunlight flashed along its edge.

'What you gonna do with that?' asked poor Henni.

'This is going through your fat heart,' said Blackjack. He plunged it, without further warning, through Henni's ribcage skewering her organs.

Henni screamed.

The terrible, monstrous noise ripped through Aurielle.

Denyse gasped and her mum gripped her arm.

Aurielle saw Jordi-boy working furiously on his cuffs.

'Be ready,' Blackjack said to Crook. Something about their body language, combined with his tone didn't seem right to Aurielle. Did they know each other? Were they in cahoots somehow? Her attention switched back to Henni. Her muttering was fading, and then snout locked still. Purple bile oozed, then spurted in dollops from her wound. Her legs wriggled as if shaken by an invisible force but even they quietened, moving just a fraction until they were entirely calm.

The audience was stunned. Aurielle angered, but she remained alert watching Crook and Blackjack closely. The air was hazy, as though a cloud had lowered but when Aurielle looked about her it was just the spot by Henni which had grown dim. Now the air was changing, turning, and a fog had gathered. She turned to her mother and sister.

'Can either of you see a fog gathering by Henni's body?'

Her mum huddled closer. 'What fog? Where?'

Denyse indicated she couldn't see it. In which case Aurielle knew what was to happen.

A figure emerged, slowly, impossibly, through the veil. It was cloaked in brown with an extra-long staff. Ignoring them, the soul in the robe gave a deep sigh and tottered uneasily to the death-ridden body of the dinosaur. The faceless form stood over Henni and peered at her, paused, then stooped to have a closer look. The shrouded spirit rose, hands on hips, head shaking.

'Now!' blurted Blackjack.

Crook's hands were entwined like tree roots, 'Gods, have mercy on us.'

'Now! Do it!' the sorcerer demanded.

Crook didn't know what to do.

'What?' she asked. 'Do what?'

Blackjack bunched a fist. And to Aurielle's surprise, Henni's arm moved.

Her hand swept the blood from her chest. She sat up with her eyes wide, glaring at Blackjack.

'Rude, that is. Killing me like that. I'm not yours to do with what you like, am I?' Her scaly jaw snapped as she spoke, and sludge slipped from her long flicking tongue.

'Yeah, you are Dino and yes, I can! Nine lives or none, I'll do with you what I want,' said Blackjack with a grizzle.

'Eight now,' sulked Henni.

The cloak half-turned to the sorcerer.

'You tricked me, Blackjack, you're a fool for playing the gods like this,' said Death in a surprisingly high-pitched tone.

'Do something, Crook!'

Death shook his head yet again and lumbered into the mist with what appeared to be a painful limp.

The bearded sorcerer rushed at Crook with the blood-stained blade. The woman shrieked as she stumbled backwards.

'Leave her!' Aurielle demanded.

Blackjack snarled in her direction and dragged Crook by the shirt to where the fog had been and whispered into hear ear.

She nodded.

He stood clear of her, 'Do something now, or I'll make you regret it,' he said.

Why whisper to her and then shout? Something isn't right about these two.

Untroubled by the fuss or her recent first death, Henni stood up, looked at the scenery and wandered from the group. Her jaws flexed open at the sweeping view beyond.

'Don't touch her,' warned Aurielle.

Jordi continued to work on the ties fixing his hands, he was definitely a lighter shade of blue in this fresh air.

Ignoring Aurielle, Blackjack placed the knife point at Crook's chin. The spot of weather where Death appeared was fading fast.

'I don't know what to do! There's no obvious door!'

'Feel for it, use your hands,' implored Aurielle now realising what the aim was.

Crook held out her hands, searching the space in front of her. Defeat splashed across her face; she could find nothing. And the mist disappeared entirely.

Mum was gripping her shirt, Denyse nestled into them both.

Jordi was mumbling through his gag. What was he trying to say?

'You want me to kill him?'

Jordi nodded.

'I'll do it in my own time, won't be told what to do, thanks.'

Jordi groaned, and rolled his eyes, which were also blue.

The sorcerer raised his knife, Crook searched her pockets urgently.

'Wait!' she said.

She turned, took a step, and opened a compact mirror. She stared into it walking backwards, as though reversing in a car. She adjusted the mirror's angle, stuck her hand out, and grabbed at the air. The moment her fingers gripped it, the strange circular shape appeared. It was the size of a netball with fizzing grey matter inside it. Aurielle rushed to Crook's side, gripped the edge of the opening with her bound hands and pulled. The gateway stretched to the size of a yoga ball.

Blackjack gawped in wonder.

'There ... it's done,' Crook said, 'it's hidden to the eye, but a mirror will reveal it, gods forgive us.'

The sorcerer snapped out of his trance and ordered the others through the mystical door.

'No! I'll go first,' said Aurielle.

The sorcerer wiped his brow. 'I say what happens here, girl.' He pointed at Henni, then the others in turn.

The dinosaur climbed in, thinking it would be a "fun adventure". Aurielle's mum and sister followed nervously, then Crook, and finally Jordi-blue.

Aurielle locked Blackjack with her stare. 'So, you've tricked Death to take us all to another world? Gamma Nine is my guess, where there's no magic at all. Dangerous for you though, not being able to use your magic.'

Beardy raised his knife, 'I don't need magic to get what I need. You won't have too much suffering to go through now, but I'll promise you, it'll be me that does it when the time comes.' He sniffed, and suddenly spat whatever was lurking in his throat.

'Hooligan.'

His knife prodded her to climb in.

'Hope you know for certain where this goes?'

The reply came in the form of a boot, which shoved Aurielle into the tunnel. She knew it would lead them to another world.

Not a big deal.

She had travelled abroad many times; it was kind of fun.

Chapter 10. Blaam Rises Again

Prod knew where to find him. A loser with no future, a drifter. He'd been part of a story, a great story but he had chosen the wrong side, made bad decisions. In fact, he hadn't made one good decision since Prod had known him. He was not only the unluckiest god he knew, but the most luckless person too. A fallen god. Undoubtedly the worst of the worst. And yet he did have some positive qualities, for example he was disturbingly ruthless, which was surprising for an ex-god. Or, when Prod really thought about it, perhaps not.

In any case, Blaam's luck was finally going to change. He was going to be useful and do useful things. Just needed the right guidance, that's all.

It was in the third bar Prod searched in the city's darker quarter that he found Blaam. Where the gambling bars and nightclubs gave way to the sleaziest of establishments which sold every human sin in one place, where the boots of policeman never walked unless they were paying, and where people sometimes disappeared entirely.

Prod looked around the room. It crackled with atmosphere fuelled by cheap booze and the croaky laughter of men and giggling women. This drowned the Bon Jovi song playing in the background. Prod circled the tables, taking the longer route to the bar. At the far end, Blaam stood clinking glasses and knocking back shots of liquid gold with a woman dressed in a stage costume, similar to an old-fashioned cabaret dress. Her body language showed she was teasing him. Prod approached.

Leave here, save yourself.

'Shut up!'

The woman shifted nervously at Prod's sudden outburst.

Blaam turned to him. His face pinched into confusion. The woman didn't know what to do.

'Go,' Prod said.

Blaam was an ugly looking ex-god, with his shaven head and generous nose. It said a great deal about a spirit who once had the choice of any human form.

He swallowed what remained in his glass, and leant casually against the bar. 'Hullo, enemy.'

Prod was ready for any trouble, part of him wished for it. 'I've no complaints with you. The past is in the past.'

'Is it, mate?'

'Should be.' Prod leant on the bar, facing the crowing customers, lapping up drinks with banter.

'I should cut that neck of yours right now with me knife.' And to help Prod fully understand, Blaam pulled a face as he pretended to cut through his own throat, ear to ear.

'Maybe you should, but you don't want to miss out on anything. I've got something unique for you.'

The fallen god studied his empty glass, not interested enough to ask anything yet, he needed to be tempted.

'Let me ask you something. What do you see going on here?'

Blaam cast a look around the room. 'Fun.'

'Precisely. Fun. I can provide that in spades and much more besides.'

The ex-god ushered the barman to pour him another drink, even though the labelled bottle was right there.

'Get me a soda water. Pint,' ordered Prod.

Blaam looked at him like he'd gone mad. 'You've gone mad.'

'No, I can get you what you want. It's that easy.'

'Yeah? What is it that I want, Prod Visceral, Servant to the Oglith clan?'

'Like I said, the past is definitely in the past.'

'Yeah, and like I said … you're mad.'

He's right.

Prod twitched to one side. 'I said, shut up!'

Blaam studied him. 'Look mate. I don't know what ya going through, but I don't need any of it. D'you get me? I just want a nice long drink with a pretty lady, and… no offence, you don't interest me, not one bit.'

'Yeah, forget that. Didn't mean it. Look … it's real easy … I can give you Rig Penlip on a plate. Call it fun, call it payback, whatever you want. It's a good option. Definitely fun. I can help you.'

'No, you are mad, mate. I may not be a god no more, but I can still get information.'

Prod appraised the room calmly. There was nothing of concern here, nothing unexpected.

'I know you all, like, went on that trip to that Indochina.'

'Malaysia.'

'Yeah anyway, searching in the jungle for waste pools of magic, fell in it, and poisoned yourself. Careless wacko.'

'And how did you come by that information?'

'Still got connections, mate. Those locals got them water samples to a lab, needed paying, didn't they? They had to sell them to someone. You forgot about all that. Not even bothered to talk to them, have you? Anyway, them samples show poison. And that poison's in you,' he said poking a finger at Prod, 'it's alive, messing with you mate. It's gonna eat you up.' Blaam rubbed Prod's hairless scalp.

Prod snatched Blaam's wrist with an iron grip.

Blaam's eyes brightened, his muscles tensed, ready to act.

'I'm fitter and stronger than ever.' Prod released the arm. 'I will stop Penlip and his magic, and I'm going to have a good time doing it. Now you can help with that, maybe get some well-deserved payback, or you can carry on drinking until your liver splits in two and your human body dies. Up to you, my friend.'

The ex-god grimaced, adjusted his shirt, and returned to his whisky glass.

'I know the future's uncertain for you,' Prod persisted.

Not a flinch, he was waiting for the punchline, new information, anything which might prompt his next step.

Prod continued, 'I'm told you're privileges as a god have largely been taken away, except one of course.'

The unemployed god swallowed his drink in a single gulp.

'Sure, you have connections, you have life, can even move between spirit and your body still, but for how long? How long have you got before they pull your plug? It's all a bit uncertain, isn't it? So, why not get some game-time?'

Blaam turned one-eighty degrees and drank in the scene.

Money was changing hands; deals were being done. Prod could see women taking cash from dumb men looking for company. It was a simple exchange. On the surface it looked harmless, but Prod knew nasty things happened to innocent people who were having hard times. Money talks for some. Others were bound to it, to their futures, but at some point, there were choices to be made. For some, their lives and sanity depended on it.

Behind them, Prod noticed the barmaid fussing busily, wiping the shiny wood surface, refilling Blaam's glass. Working hard and fast, but for what?

'Dunno mate, see I wanna be on the winning side … and I just don't reckon you've got the full picture.'

Prod moved closer. He searched the fallen god's eyes carefully as the rocking music descended to its natural end, 'Why would you think that?'

A smile slipped across Blaam's face, 'You ain't the only player, mate.'

'Whatever gives you that idea?'

'Information.'

'Your information is wrong.'

A Rolling Stones classic song started up and quickly ripped into the atmosphere.

'We'll see, won't we?'

'It ain't wrong. But I dunno know where it'll all lead. Might be fun to find out.'

'I don't know what you've been told, whatever it is … it's irrelevant. I'm the only serious game going, Blaam. If you're serious about getting some fun-time. You'll run with me.'

The fallen god didn't appear entirely convinced, not just yet.

Prod met his gaze. 'One last thing. Remember that Yuki Toro mage you killed on Gamma Nine?'

Blaam's eyes were watery and where he didn't have bursts of red, the remaining eye was a soft grey. He was sick as a dog.

'What of it?'

'Toro said he'd discovered how to generate magic without the presence of magical particles.'

With a scrape of his stool, Blaam immediately straightened to face Prod, eye to eye, god to monster.

'You got my attention, mate. Tell us some more about all that.'

'Find Rig and you'll find out where he's got the mage's book stashed. I reckon it'll be in there.'

'Well, I reckon—'

A shrill bell sounded.

Prod flinched. The same sound his phone made at the apartment. The barmaid who served them answered the phone by the till, she listened intently glancing at Prod and Blaam and shaking her head before ending the call. Smart girl.

Prod addressed the ex-god. 'Anyway, most of the fun will be happening at a small shack of mine on Gamma Nine. Enjoy it while you're there. I have some guests you might like to meet: Aurielle Merlot and family. Think of them as disposable. And if you come across that hopeless Blackjack, feel entirely free to express my dissatisfaction with his service, but whatever you do ... I want Rig Penlip's future significantly reduced. Understand?'

The godless man half-turned, grabbed his glass, and looked at Prod. 'What d'you get out of it, mate?'

'As much fun as you, just from a distance that's all. So, do you want some of that, or not?'

Blaam gave a sickly grin and quaffed his whisky. 'Yeah, I'll go along with it for now, so long as I get to finish him.'

'Is that your only demand?'

'Don't need nothing else. Well, except for this.'

Blaam whipped a large bowie knife from nowhere and rammed its point into the bar.

A glass smashed to the floor.

The hall flushed into an uneasy silence, eyes focused on them and the weapon, its steel blade shone against the spotlights like a beacon for all to see. Blaam means business. Someone could die. Someone *will* die.

Excellent. Prod had found another quality in Blaam.

Cruelty.

It was written all over his stubbly face.

Killing the famous Rig Penlip and bringing an end to all magic was going to be a real hoot, and there was not a single madman about.
Really?

Chapter 11. The Ghost, the Drunk and the Powerless Wizard

The two grizzling ladies abandoned their bench and wobbled away, clutching handbags, and shaking their heads in disapproval. Rig's cheeks warmed. His phone chirped merrily as he considered the drunk and the ghost in front of him. Appreciating the interruption, he answered it.

'Auntie! How are you?'
'Rig? Rig?'
'Yes, it's me.'
'Is that you, Rig?'
'Yes! How are you?' Rig asked while Humphrey gawped at Frank Merlot as though he were a curious new animal at a zoo.
'Oh, hullo darling. I'm okay mostly but my veins keep bothering me, they really do, very itchy, and sore at times as well … the girls…'
'The staff?'
'What?'
'I think you mean the staff when you say, "the girls"?'
'Yes darling, they keep telling me to put my feet up, but I forget, you see.'
'Right, must be uncomfortable, that itching?'

The ghost was pointing to Frank's wine bottle and shaking his head, luckily Frank hadn't got "the sight" so he couldn't see visions, not yet anyway.

'Yes, it is, and also whenever I go to the little room, I find as soon as I start—'
'Yes, alright Auntie, no need to tell me everything. You sleeping okay?'

What was he going to do with these two? That was the real question. Flash's father couldn't do without his plonk, and the ghost wouldn't leave Rig's side, except when needed.

'Sleep? Yes, I'm fine in that department, but what are you up to, darling? Tell me.'

'Nothing much really,' Rig scanned the field opposite the pub and strolled towards the fence, 'just chilling out with some friends in a park.'

'That's nice, darling. You wouldn't be thinking of taking a Slide to another world and rescuing that delightful Aurielle then?'

'What? How do you know that?'

'How do I know? Friends in high places you see, my darling. You're not the only one in contact with the gods.'

Rig rubbed his head, 'I guess not. Which god talked to you?'

Humphrey's gaze switched to Rig.

'Never mind about all that now, you let me know if you need any help.'

'Yeah, but please don't tell Dad, he always worries. There's no point, is there?'

'Worry? That's his job, darling. We all worry. We all want you safe.'

'I know, I'll be alright though, honest,' he said as he watched Frank succeed in the tricky task of standing.

His elderly Great Aunt said goodbye with an embarrassing blast of kisses. Rig ambled to the park bench, a little bird landed on the edge of a litter bin nearby, gave a tweet, shook his beak and dived into the bin. It surfaced speedily and flapped away with a prize.

'I said, what we doing now, Riggy?'

'Don't call me that.'

'Eh?' Frank replied as he crumpled awkwardly onto the seat next to him.

Rig turned, 'Look Frank, see, this might be hard for you, but, um … there is someone here you can't see, and he, sort of … talks to me, and I reply, like normal.'

'Someone? You could at least introduce me properly. Honestly, you really lack manners, Rig Penlip. A "someone" could be offended by what you say, you know.'

Frank's face didn't shift, until finally his forehead moved, and slowly his eyebrows lifted and clashed in a state of gentle bewilderment.

Frank laughed but stopped suddenly. 'I don't know … anything about spirits, but … I can tell you; I know about magic. Can't do it though. Now my daughter, she's …' Frank took a long swig and wiped his mouth with his grubby sleeve '… amazing, specially trained … kills monsters, hold on … what's your name again, lad?'

Humphrey circled Frank, looking him over. 'What a revolting man. I think he's a little under the weather you know. Must be that alcohol.'

Rig nodded and turned his attention to Frank. 'It's Rig Penlip. But what I need to know is what happened to your family. Who took Aurielle, Denyse, and Molly? What happened? Tell me everything.'

'Hey, hold on. Yes!' Frank pointed at Rig. 'You're the boy she saved. Yeah. Protected you, while you searched for a spell, potion … not sure, but you made the gods listen to you. You saved your father from a slow death, something to do with the Oglith clan. Wasn't it?'

Humphrey looked at Rig like he had seen a ghost. 'Well! Goodness … that really is unbelievable.'

'I know, tell me about it.'

'What's that?' asked Frank.

'I was talking to Humphrey, the … um, spirit that's here with us.'

Frank froze, motioned slowly to his left, then right, scanning the space around him suspiciously. 'You sure?'

'Don't worry, it's nothing to get in a bother about.'

'Incredible! Talking about an "it" now?' Humphrey showed Rig his back and lifted off the ground.

Frank shook his head like he was trying to clear his mind. 'It was you, wasn't it? You … defeated that Oglith clan, right? Worked with the gods, in person, they're your friends … aren't they?'

'Wasn't quite like that, it's all in the past. Look, if you want my help to get your family back … I have to know what happened, right now. Do you get me, Mr Merlot?'

The drunk tried sitting up straight, 'Call me Frank. I, er … sorry about … about all your brothers, and your mam.' Another gulp of red wine, 'Really lad, I am.'

Humphrey floated around Frank, looking him up and down. 'I bet he smells. Does he stink at all? I really don't like his sort.'

Rig flashed a glance at Humphrey. 'Stop it!'

'What? Are you talking to me now?' asked Frank.

'Sorry, no I wasn't.'

Frank shut his eyes, rubbed them, and gently shook his head.

Rig looked skywards. Thinking of his family brought physical sensations, not warmth, just a needling pain which always threatened to grow into a fire, unless he refused to think about them, especially *mum*. He couldn't afford to walk down that road. The time never seemed right, maybe it never would.

Frank wriggled to the edge of the bench, as he faced Rig. 'You asked … what happened to my family. I'll tell you, right. Came home … the other night, a tad late, but there you are … we all do that … just a quick drink y'know … with my pals. Where's the harm in that?' Frank studied the bottle, there were some dregs swirling at the bottom. He swallowed the last drop and launched the empty bottle over his shoulder. It clattered against the wire mesh fence.

Humphrey shook his head again. 'Pig. Isn't he?'

Ignoring the spirit, Rig asked, 'What happened when you got home?'

'The house was empty … deserted, like … felt different, something in the air. My, err … instincts maybe … suspected something was wrong.'

'Doubt it,' said the ghost.

'Go on,' Rig urged.

'It was like they'd disappeared, without a fight, without anything happening. They'd just … gone, see?'

Rig moved closer, 'So, there was no sign of a struggle, no clues, anything like that?'

'Nothing lad, not at all.'

Rig leaned away. He did reek of booze. 'Oh.'

'Except ... for the note, gave it to the police.'

Humphrey walked away, hands on hips, shaking his see-through head.

'Oh. Okay, well, what did it say?'

'Something like, "Come get them, come over if you dare", then something about dead meat.'

'Was it signed Blackjack?'

'Wasn't a letter, Rig ... just a note. No, wasn't signed.' Frank gave such a loud burp that heads of neighbours peeked around curtains.

'I'm sure it's him that's taken your family. Why, I don't know, except he wants me. Why he wants me I haven't a clue. Another angry sorcerer. Well, it's me that's angry. How dare he take Aurielle, your family ... and threaten them like this. I'll sort it out, somehow. I will.'

Humphrey was examining the petals of a flower in a particularly well-tended row of pots. Frank had his head in his hands, mumbling. No one was listening.

'Disappeared ... off the face of the earth, not a clue where they are. What I'm supposed to do? What can I do? Coppers are hopeless,' Frank complained.

'Yes, Frank,' Rig nodded. 'They've been taken from this earth ... to another world. Gamma Nine I bet. I'm sure of it. We'll have to go there.'

Humphrey and Frank looked at him as though he had banged his head.

'What?'

'Gamma Nine?' Frank said, nervously. He looked skywards, searching for something he may have missed his whole life. 'Where is it? Why there?'

'It's there somewhere, just can't see it. It's just like here, except there's no magic, doesn't work. So, if we go I can't do none. Can't defend us, not like here. See? That's why they're on Gamma Nine.'

Humps closed his eyes and held his hands in prayer.

Frank's solemn face suddenly brightened. 'But how do we get to this Gamma Nine?' His head turned and twisted, searching for a missing planet that might suddenly appear. Rig didn't want to explain about the existence of other dimensions, mainly because he didn't understand the facts of it himself.

***

It didn't take long to work out that the nearest place they could catch a Slide was on the hill behind them. It was a welcome splash of nature right by the town, not high enough to get anyone dizzy but good for their purposes. So, the ghost, the drunk, and the wizard marched along a curved lane on the edges of the last housing estate out of town. They passed a farmer's shed. More cows. Like he had seen from the bus, larger than Rig remembered them too. Was it because he was in a place where the air was crammed with magic particles, making everything bigger and more dangerous because of the powerful magical potential surrounding them? Or because Rig had not seen a farmyard animal for years? The questions were worth pondering, a good distraction on the way to rescuing his best friend from a nasty sorcerer. Rig kicked a large pebble along the dirt track.

'I hate Slides,' he said.

Humphrey drifted to face him, 'Slides? You haven't even told me what gods you've been talking to! You tell me nothing, do you, Rig Penlip?'

'What's a Slide then, lad? Don't know what you're talking about half the time,' Frank's voice droned from behind him.

Humphrey drifted in reverse, arms crossed, 'What's my life come to when I'm forced to agree with a drunk?'

Rig turned to Frank. 'A Slide? Well, it's like a portal to another world, Earth where I'm from, here, or Gamma Nine, where there's no magic at all. Problem is the Slide feels sort of … well, like it's alive. It squeezes you and mashes you through its tubes. Grim really.'

'Oh, can't wait,' said Frank.

'And the gods, Rig?' Humps leaned back as though he were resting on an invisible armchair.

'Yes, I know Lycka the God of Chance, she's a nice god,' Rig kicked another stone and eyed the woods ahead, dissected by the dirt road climbing through the hill, 'and I've, sort of … met a God of Death, God of Odium, I know there are more, just haven't met them. They've changed anyway. It's not like they're proper friends or anything.'

'Eh?'

Rig glanced behind to see Frank swaying as he walked, swigging from a small silvery object. 'Don't you ever stop drinking?'

'Course I do. But I can still have a little slurp … while we're heading up there.'

'Pig, that man,' said the spirit, 'and I'm awfully sorry, I really can't believe you know all these gods. Anyway, why didn't you tell me? Maybe they could help me. I mean who goes round talking to gods?'

'Plenty talk to a god.'

'Now listen, Rig, don't get all philosophical on me, I just want plain answers, thank you. People don't meet gods and have chats. Who is this God of Odium and God of Death anyway? I mean, really!'

They began walking up an incline, Humphrey strolling alongside Rig for now. The branches of the trees arched over, meeting in the middle, much like Humphrey's eyebrows when he gets confused. The trees formed a natural tunnel with the grey light of day poking through the branches, creating patterns of shadows between slithers of light all the way along the track. It had a heavenly feel, but every now and then the cool brushes of the breeze made him shiver.

'Look, I don't know them okay, I've met them, had to … in the past.' His breathing had gotten heavy, and his heart banged hard as though thumping a message, something about a lack of fitness most likely. 'It's all … in the past.' Rig repeated.

'Eh?' Frank called out, lagging behind.

'Forget it.'

'Forget what?' said Humps.

'Nevermind.'

'Such an enchanting walk through here. Where we going anyway?'

Rig sighed and wiped the dampness from his neck.

'No need to be like that, only asking. You should be grateful for having such good company on your travels, wherever you might be going.'

'Stop,' said Rig.

'No, I won't … I mean you don't seem to realise how lucky you are having me tag along on your … your, er … adventure.'

'Seriously, stop!'

Rig had already halted, the ghost a few steps in front, Frank laboured behind. Near the top of the track was a dull shape. A silhouette. The outline was so big it filled the space between the forest track and the arch of the trees, under which seemed to be … a head.

The earth under Rig's feet trembled, he looked each way into the undergrowth. Frank studied the ground. Earthquake? Rig dragged his gaze to the inevitable cause.

The hooves of a huge monster stamped the ground angrily as it hurtled towards them. Trees shook wildly, leaves rained on them, the ghost disappeared, and Rig's heart sank into his plimsolls as the day grew darker and darker by the second.

Chapter 12. Gamma Nine with None

The brief sense of weightlessness was fun, but when Aurielle spewed from the tubes of the Slide, she knew the landing could go either way.

Her knees smashed into the spine of the sprawled Protector.

'Jeeeeez!' Jordi moaned through his gag.

This could not have gone better.

A big grin escaped Aurielle. There was a surprising degree of entertainment in landing on Jordi-boy, as he yelped like a puppy with his tail caught in the hinge of a door.

The others stood in a semi-circle, with Mum and Denyse hugging nervously. Their eyes sought reassurance from her, so she smiled warmly, or at least attempted to. Laughter was rare and spontaneous, anything else required effort of will. So, smiling wasn't really her thing, she often smiled inside, and just like a poker player she hated to give the game away. It had become a habit to disguise her emotions, and it probably saved her life a few times. Monsters were commonly dangerous, so she always had to be one step ahead, and being hard to read was one part of her armoury. This predicament was similar, except she noticed how Jordi's gangling giraffe limbs faltered as he stood.

She exploded with laughter.

Ignoring Aurielle, Scarlett Crook lifted Jordi's arm in support, but he shrugged her away, moodily. The spirit guide looked startled at the force of it. Aurielle sprang at him, reached up to his neck with bound hands, grabbed his throat and squeezed.

'Listen, Blue … you will never do that again. Understand?'

With watering eyes, chest heaving, trying to breathe, Jordi nodded. He shoved Aurielle off him.

She tripped, just about keeping her balance. She paused; her attention focussed on the boy. Her expression creased.

'I will fix you myself, if I have to,' she said slowly, carefully.

Jordi-blue stared straight back, held his ground and his thoughts to himself.

A spurting plop sounded out. Human waste ejected from the Slide in the solid form of Blackjack. He got to his feet, smelling of … just smelling.

Her senses raced from this dreary fact and focused on their landing site. Gravel underfoot in a rectangular space with a smattering of leafless trees surrounding them. A path wound upwards, north-west under a heavy shroud of grey sky. The link road from the car park snaked to the main road below, running perpendicular to their position. She knew this place. On the tip of her toes, she peeked but couldn't see beyond the mound and bulbous tree guarding the pathway northwards. She wriggled her cuffs. The plastic scraped her skin, shouldn't have been so confident about getting them off.

Blackjack finished dusting himself down and immediately raised his arms, splaying his fingers in strike mode.

'Morietur!' he blared at Henni.

Aurielle reeled on her feet. Henni shrieked, they others stood open mouthed.

The silence had a serrated edge.

But no-one died, nothing occurred.

Blackjack's magic failed, and that could mean only one thing.

Aurielle guffawed, holding her stomach in fear she might bring something long eaten to the surface. But she didn't need to worry, food was a distant memory so she bellowed with laughter.

'Gotta do this again,' she blubbered, 'I've never had so much fun!'

'What's your problem?' asked Blackjack, 'The plan worked.'

Crook, Mum, and Denyse looked confused. Jordi nodded in agreement and Henni, well, she didn't know how to smile, or at least it was hard to tell when she did.

'I can't believe you did it. You idiot!' blurted Aurielle, 'You actually brought us to Gamma Nine.'

'I know! I was testing that fact, my little abrasive captive,' said the sorcerer in his creepy voice.

'Told you, I ain't your *little* nothing. And there'll be no magic at all to stop me once I start cutting you up. You'll be *dead meat*.'

Blackjack flinched at the use of his own words. His gaze jerked to Henni.

'Get them up there. Do I have to do all the thinking?'

Henrietta's bulky shoulders drooped. She nodded her big snout and waved them forward.

'Can't see much thinking going on around here, Blackhead,' teased Aurielle as they trekked single file up the stony pathway.

'Says the girl tied up in a foreign world.'

'Not for much longer Blackhead. Better keep a close eye on me, hadn't you?' She wouldn't choose to fight a man much larger than her while her hands were tied, but she could if needed. It would be a decent test of her skills. Stupid she wasn't, and with her hands free it was a whole different game.

Crook had dropped into a heavy silence, with occasional mutterings to herself, sounded like she was praying. Jordi-Blue mumbled irritably.

'Shut up,' said Aurielle just as Blackhead did the same.

She climbed the track behind her petrified sister. That wasn't quite so funny. He was going to pay for this, she just had to break free first. It was all about the timing, the right time would come. They sauntered along in single file; her mum became increasingly distracted by the fauna.

She pointed to a tree. 'I think they're cedar,' she muttered to Denyse. 'I know where we are. It's incredible.'

'Mum?' Denyse said in a hushed voice. 'Don't.'

They marched along the path, through an attractive glade with azaleas and chrysanthemums nestling between patches of wooded areas. The light was low, and the air lacked warmth. It gave the view ahead a broody mixture of intrigue and doom. The view was of the gardens and moat surrounding the medieval Leeds Castle. They approached the outer building.

'Dino, take a right, up there,' instructed Blackhead from behind.

Henni looked back confused and pointed vaguely at the castle.

'No! I said, go right!'

Throwing her padded paws in the air and giving a strong snort through her leathery nostrils, Henni veered away from the monolith. It took a few minutes trudging up a wooded incline before they found what Blackhead was looking for. An old cottage hidden by the shadows of trees. They neared the long oblong building with its outhouse. There was a cellar, chimney, and a wood-stack under shelter. It would be hard for potential rescuers to find, but good cover for killing sorcerers; casual strollers were unlikely to find them. In normal circumstances, it would be a good hangout.

A shift in the air.

Aurielle spun on her heels, a protective double arm block … swinging arm deflected. She stood in a classic defensive stance, ready to kick some sense into Blackjack's head.

The others turned. Mum gasped. The world seemed to freeze as the two eyed each other coldly.

'Try that again, Jack … go on,' urged Aurielle.

His face was rough, like chipped slate. He glanced at the cellar doors. 'Get down there,' he pointed, 'no-one will hear you or come save you.'

'Thank the gods. I hate being disturbed, especially by amateurs.' She looked him up and down. 'Oh, and by the way. Nice choice of black jacket with black jeans. You're so imaginative.' She glared. 'I'm imaginative too, especially with revenge. It's my specialist subject.'

A childish smirk was all the sorcerer could manage. He sidled up to her. 'Ever wonder what it'd be like to die alone in the darkness?'

Mum and Denyse's faces shrank with fright.

'Sounds like heaven, or it will be compared to what I'm going to do with you, Blackhead.'

Chapter 13. All Powerful Magic

The hulking monster pounded down the slope, arms that looked like they could pull trees from their roots stretched towards Rig. Its face was covered in long brown hair, an overgrown forest-yeti, its whole body a big hairy mess. It was the largest monster Rig had ever seen. The remaining light in the forest retreated as the creature hurtled towards him.

The ground flinched violently as each pounding leg hit the earth.

Rig's knees softened and his stomach twisted. He turned and ran.

Mr Merlot was already tottering as fast as he could back the way they'd come, swerving hopelessly.

If only Rig had taken athletics more seriously at school. His legs wobbled and his thighs strained as he fled. His chest heaved as he lumbered back down the slope, his breathing rapid already. Noise surrounded him. The cacophony made by the disturbed trees grew louder, which had to be bad news. He wasn't going to outrun a monster the size of a detached house. Frank took a sharp left and crashed into the thicket.

Rig stopped and spun on his feet, but lost balance. He stabilised in time to notice the grizzly monster above him about to squash his head. Against his better judgement, Rig dived, slammed to the ground, and rolled between its legs. The ground quaked. A gigantic fist had landed where he had just been. A guff of air broke from the creature's bum putting Rig in a cloud. He choked, then scrambled, shifting backwards. The creature turned clumsily, slowly, like an oil tanker on the ocean. Rig looked to the woods and skywards for inspiration. The monster's enormous furry feet smashed the dirt track, its head brushed the overhanging branches.

He needed a ready-made spell. Had to think. Otherwise he was going to get mashed into a gloopy pulp.

The creature raised its arm to crush Rig.

Particles of magic atoms collided, warming Rig's hands. 'Flecte,' he spat the words out.

The monster halted and stared as the skinny branches of the trees surrounding them recoiled, as if stung. Some crashed together as they raced to the swollen bicep of the forest-yeti. They curled round it like charmed snakes. The yeti whined and turned its moppy head to the leafy canopy above him. It growled. It pulled on the tree's ties, but the shackles held firm.

'Lad! You alright?' yelled Frank from the cover of undergrowth nearby.

'Brilliant,' Rig said, not taking his eyes from the monster. It was gnawing through the bark of the branches, and with one snatch of its head, tore through its binding.

Hell. Rig peddled backwards. He wasn't going to outrun it. The forest had given him its best shot. The yeti crashed to one knee, causing more leaves to rain on them. The fur-ball lowered its faceless head to take a closer look.

'Hullo,' said Rig and grinned meekly.

The thing inched closer.

'Parle vous Englais?'

The shaggy creature snorted, blowing its hair clear to reveal a pair of deep brown eyes, long eyelashes, and a pretty pink nose, facing upwards for some reason.

'Oh, are you a … um, Miss?'

The cute eyes narrowed, and the Yeti's mouth gaped open revealing a double set of razor teeth. The tongue was a curiously dark purple shade with black spots. Maybe it was sick. Deranged for sure.

'Hedera, carpe.'

Her padded palm, the size of a small family car, arrived next to Rig with surprising gentleness while her tongue slithered towards him until it was uncomfortably close. She wiped his cheek with her slippery tongue and sniffed. Her gums pulled back revealing her own steak-knives. She gave a deep, low, grumble which Rig didn't consider a good sign. To the side, Rig watched ivy untangle from nearby trees, creep along the forest floor, winding forward. There were hundreds of the spindly arms.

Rig froze to the spot in horror as the monster's giant fingers clasped him in his middle.

'Can't we … can we … have a chat … about all this?'

'It's a she?' asked Frank from the safety of his hiding place.

The Yeti gently squished him, and tilted her head. Unbelievable. Criticisms from a colossal Yeti about his weight. Nice.

'What's … your name?' Rig urged.

'Killer?' said Frank.

'Not helping!' blurted Rig.

The monster gasped, dropped Rig, and spun to face the ivy wrapping around her legs in knots and gripping her ankles. Rig's call to nature had worked. The creature snatched and fought, tugging and tearing, but the ivy re-doubled its efforts and seized her arms. She was being attacked from all sides. The most savage, relentless opponent … a life-squeezing, relentless, wicked swarm of ivy from the darkest recesses of the forest.

A useful woodland plant as it turned out.

***

A pair of cyclists raced past Rig with petrified faces, legs thrashing, spokes spinning so fast the normal eye would not see them, only a blur. Rig tracked them. When he focussed his concentration on one place, one aspect of what the eye could see, and if he persisted, the object became clearer and larger in view. The world around him on the edges shrunk, became unimportant, and slowed, bringing detail forward, every smallest part of the picture zoomed into full microscopic view. That's how he knew the girl riding had one out of thirty-six spokes in her wheel missing. This was a skill that had always interested him. It was surprising how dull he found most magic. These were skills others would pay dearly for, but for him, inheriting them from his family was not what he wanted –because they were dead. Killed by an assassin from the Oglith clan. It was all in the past, but the anger, the grief was still very much in the present, his own monster lurking in a corner deep in his head. He feared that monster, more than any living creatures with actual claws.

'I said, how did you do that, like? I mean … gods! You're weird. That thing, that monster could have eaten you alive,' said Frank. 'What did you do, lad?'

The complaint, if it was a complaint, shattered Rig's concentration and the world continued, none the wiser.

'I SAID—'

'Heard you!' Rig snapped. 'I do magic. Sometimes … if I have to.'

Rig scanned the area. They were at the crest of the hill surrounded by woodland. Through a gap he could see some of the sprawling town, and betwixt town and treetops he could see the big brown fur-ball of a she-monster's head. Above, the light was changing with the shifting skies. Although swollen clouds followed them there had been no rain. As for Gamma Nine, he had no idea what weather and horrors were waiting there. Where was the Slide? A sign with an arrow would be helpful.

Frank stepped closer. 'So, what you gonna do with it? Can't just leave it there like that, can you? It's not like the monster can, like, help being a monster, can it?'

'You just said it could have eaten me alive! What am I meant to do?'

'Let her go, you bad lad,' Frank's finger jabbed as he spoke.

Incredible. Rig sighed. 'We need to find the Slide to go to Gamma Nine,' Frank looked like he hadn't slept for a week and needed a long hot soak in the bath, 'you could help look for it. A large circular ball of fuzzy light about four feet off the ground.'

Frank looked at him like he was bonkers nuts.

Rig slouched. 'What? Want to save your family, don't you?'

With that, Mr Merlot slumped to the dusty track and slapped the ground in annoyance. 'I'll never find them, what hope have I got? Maybe…'

'Yes?'

'Maybe, if I could just get a drink first, I'll feel better, see, then we can go get them, all of them.'

Out of the corner of Rig's eye a haze grew, and ever so slowly … the outline of a Humphrey appeared.

'Ouch!'

'For the sake of *all* gods, what is it now?' asked Humps.

'How did you do that? Appear out of the corner of my eye?'

'What? Just walked through. I was under the impression you'd want to chat face to face, not through the back of your head. I don't know, Rig Penlip, I don't know why I bother showing up. All you bring me is danger and unjustified continual moaning. Haven't seen you for ages and that's how you welcome me!'

Rig stopped rubbing his eye. 'You disappeared when a large helping of danger started running towards us, but anyway … I am pleased to see you, just a bit surprised how you did it, that's all.'

'Really? I'm pleased to see you too!' Humps waddled nearer clasping his hands. 'What we doing next? Why are we here?'

A new foal climbed carefully to its feet, in the shape of a drunkard which looked just like Frank Merlot, husband, teacher to infants and father to the best teenage, trained killer to have been born on any world.

He belched.

He looked pathetic, had seen such grander days, times where he'd been well-respected as a deputy head teacher and reliable dad, always present, available with a warm heart and wise words for people around him.

'Disgusting filth,' said Humphrey with his head half-turned from Frank.

Rig twisted, his gaze searching behind him and back again. He threw a look at Humps, 'That's mean, that is.'

'What you looking for, Riggy?'

'I hate that name.'

'Is that … um, invisible bloke back again?' asked Frank.

'Not invisible, he's in spirit, ghostly, you know?'

'Actually, he's right, Rig. I feel invisible quite a lot of the time. Sometimes ignored, hated even.' Hump's expression drooped as his words became heavier.

Rig rubbed his eyes. 'Look, do me a favour, I'm trying to find a Slide, so we can get to Gamma Nine and find Flash, her mum, and sister. Remember? Do you see anything odd, out of place?'

'Indeed ... him,' said Humps looking at Frank. 'And that over there.'

Rig swivelled on his feet. 'Why are they always behind me?'

'Yes, I find that, don't know why. But you ... you should look more carefully, Rig Penlip. What is it anyway?'

Frank did his best to speak but failed, muttering something inaudible instead.

Hanging between two pine trees was an impressively large spider's web at head height, below it was a shimmering disc, typical of the Slides that Rig had come to know and detest. Every time he used one, it squeezed him so much Rig thought he would throw up. He never did, but he always felt sick and somehow used, even though he was the one using it to travel. The experience was so bad, he would even take the train if it were an option. Sadly, the national rail company hadn't built tracks to other worlds and parallel dimensions yet, they were still working on getting trains to roll over different types of leaves.

Chapter 14. The Creature Hung Up

Nothing he did worked.

It was like having a scratch you couldn't itch but the problem was the annoying itch was both inside his head and also somewhere on his body. And whenever he thought he had found it and scratched, it moved. An additional and unexpected problem was that his feet were growing, none of his shoes fitted anymore. He didn't mind buying replacements, money was meaningless. He preferred walking about in bare feet anyway.

He patrolled the length of his window, back and forth. How many times had he done that already today? Not important.

A lack of progress was important. Blackjack had wasted time. Blaam would get the job done, but when? He should've done the job himself, there's nothing like the personal touch, the satisfaction of seeing your own job done well. There were doubts in his mind and that was unusual, never happened before. He realised it was since he had found a small section of scales under his arm. He kept checking them, weren't growing, probably nothing.

Except it isn't nothing.

That damn voice again.

The shrill bell of the phone disturbed the air.

Prod searched for it, followed the ring, found it, and pressed answer.

He listened.

So did the caller for a moment. 'Aren't you going to say hi to me Prod?'

It was her. 'What do you want?'

'That's no way to speak to your saviour.'

'Everyone wants to talk about the past.'

'Really? Maybe because the past is important. Because it might influence what we do today.'

'I've moved on.'

'That's not what I've heard.'

'Yes, you released me from that contract, that's it, done.'

'Funny that, not too long ago you said freeing you and generations of your family from the life-long oath of servitude to the Oglith clan was a good thing.'

'Yeah, I'm made up about it but I'm not going to keep bowing to you, kissing your feet, even though you're a god.'

'You've changed.'

'We've all changed.'

'No. Not like you. You're not yourself. You've got a problem my love and it seems you just can't see it, or the scales you're growing.'

She's right.

Shut up!

'What's that, Prod?'

'Not you. Nothing.'

'Hearing voices? Or your own voice, deep, hidden away, nearly gone.'

'What do you want?'

'Down to business then?'

'Anything to stop you calling me wherever I go. Why don't you come here?'

'You know why.'

'I wouldn't hurt you, like you said … you're my saviour.'

'I like the old you, the new version has some unpredictable quirks. The phone works for me.'

'What do you want?'

'Prod, I don't know what you're up to or why you're doing it … but I need you to let them go.'

'You mean Aurielle? I don't have her.'

'Of course not. One of your villainous, mobster friends has her.'

You sort of do.

'I don't have her!'

'Yeah, keep repeating that, still not true.'

'Like you said, why would I want to keep a treacherous, dangerous little imp like that?'

'Hmm … your own words betray you, Prod. What are you after exactly? What do you want? Unlimited power? World domination? What is it megalomaniacs want these days? Recognition? Status? Or just a million followers on your Tik Tok account. Help me out here.'

      With a simple tap of his finger, Lycka the God of Chance was gone. If only his other inconveniences were that simple to overcome. He unclipped the phone from the wall socket and went back to the window. He searched the sky and its thin traces of cloud and pondered. A sole pigeon circled, then drifted to the rooftop of the apartment building and out of sight. His insides gurgled in delight.

Chapter 15. Dimwit in a Cellar

The walls were properly old. They must have been built at the same time as the castle, most likely. An outbuilding for the servants perhaps. But they *were* in the cellar. The cold was beginning to frost Aurielle's skin, and the damp gave off a pungent smell which she thought would bring coughing and bile to most of them in the end. Worse was the humming coming from Crook as she meditated, but worse than all of that, the gag had been taken away from Jordi-boy Blue.

They had released each other from their ties. Crook sat crossed legged with elbows on knees, arms splayed in a strange position as though she were about to catch flies, with her eyes closed. Her bright, red headscarf lay loosely across her right shoulder, the dye matched her lipstick and the large gemstones decorating her chest. She did nothing but hum in a low rhythmic tone, such a gentle, peaceful soul in many ways. And yet, strangling her just for the humming would be an act of kindness. Mum and Denyse huddled in the corner, keeping each other warm while Blue paced the room. Henrietta licked at her leathery skin, apparently in a world of her own. The atmosphere between them all was dark and had been since they had arrived, minutes earlier. The light from the tiny window by the ceiling was dim at best, which was a coincidence, because that was exactly what she thought of her supposed saviour.

Blue was getting tense. 'I'm gonna kill him slow when I get out of here. Can't believe you let him bring us here. I'll kick that door down. That's what I'll do.'

'Hum ... hum.'

Aurielle finished her last press-up and said, 'Go on then ... can't see anyone stopping you, Blue.'

'Hum ... hum.'

Jordi-boy climbed the four steps but found the angle too steep to kick at the door, so he yanked on the cellar doors, hard.

'I usually find that *thinking* helps, probably need to unscrew those hinges.'

Blue ignored her and tugged on the doors, repeatedly.

'Hum ... hum.'

'Oh no, did the bad man lock it? We'll definitely have to use our brains instead. Good luck with that, Blue.'

'Aurielle! Stop it, please!' implored her mum.

'Hum ... hum.'

Another reason why she didn't like taking her family on missions. For that alone Blackjack was going to get a good view of the scratches on her fists. Henni looked up, her tongue wiped her left eye, then her right before she continued to pick muck from under her toenails with what looked like a metal-poker from a fireplace. She seemed disinterested in what was happening around her, but then it was hard to tell with a dinosaur.

'Hum ... hum.'

Jordi leapt from the steps.

He stood over Aurielle, his gaze unwavering, serious. 'Someone needs to shut her up. I'll get us out of this mess, but I don't want a headache to go with it, know what I mean?'

'Hum ... hum.'

A quick analysis of the situation led to the conclusion that crushing the bones in Jordi's feet was the preferred option right now. She held his stare and raised a heel, just a fraction.

'Stop!' said Crook suddenly. All heads swung to her, including the dinosaur's snout.

'What is it, Scarlett? What's wrong?' her Mum asked.

Her eyes were still shut, but it seemed she was searching the space above them. 'I ... I can only tell you what I can see, no more. There's trouble ahead, a lot.'

'Oh my gods, you must be joking me,' said Blue. 'Where'd you get this Seer? There's more information at the bottom of my last teacup.'

'Look at yourself,' countered Aurielle looking him up and down, 'still blue.'

'I can see,' repeated Crook ignoring everyone, 'our fates are entwined, together, a journey awaits us all and a great battle. And there is ... there is ...'

'Death,' blurted Jordi-boy.

The silence in the cellar which followed smelled, or it could have been the damp soil.

Aurielle looked up at Blue questioningly.

He shrugged. 'Death's always around when there's a battle, that's logic, right?'

Aurielle rolled her eyes.

Denyse whimpered, and her mum wrapped her arms round her.

'Be together though, nice to go on a trip too. Not so bad, not so bad,' the dinosaur spoke with a sort of lisp, because her tongue was too fat for her mouth.

Jordi-boy gawped at the large lizard in disbelief. 'That's one you should have done earlier.'

Aurielle thumped Jordi's shoulder.

'Ow!'

'Shut up.'

Crook's fingers moved like long tentacles floating in the sea. 'There is … *suffering*.'

'Names? Addresses? Anything useful?' Jordi began pacing again.

'Shut it, let her finish.'

'I can see … I can see… what they want. Oh. Not us, not us.' Her head began swaying from side to side. 'Oh, no. Not that. They … want it all. They want all of it. They want it … *dead*.'

Her eyes opened wide, staring.

Aurielle rushed to her side, and she clasped Crook's hands in her own. 'What is it? What can you see?'

'I can see … *the death of magic*.'

***

The news sparked a lot of chatter. Jordi continued to think of an escape plan, Aurielle didn't expect any good ideas about that very soon. Denyse had befriended Crook and were getting close, with their yakking getting intense at times. Her sister occasionally glanced at Jordi-boy, curious about him most likely, who he was.

Henrietta the Horrible was living up to her name, had finished picking her toenails, and was now working on the spots on her lower jaw, obliviously content. She just liked to be with people, or at least near them, which was an improvement on things since Aurielle had first known her. A bit cranky when she was a jailer, keen to harm her prisoners, the change was decent and in Aurielle's mind at least had earned a temporary pardon from meeting Red and Midnight.

Her mum's mood was fragile. She spoke under her breath with urgency. 'Why would someone want rid of magic? Doesn't make sense.'

'Don't know, do I? I'll sort it out though, don't worry, Mum.'

'Get me a weapon, anything. I want to protect you both. No-one harms my girls. They'll regret all this, no doubt about that.'

'Mum! It's okay. I'll sort it. Leave it to me. I'm not having you doing any fighting, this is what I do … it's my job. What I'm trained for.'

'Don't be ridiculous, your fourteen-years-old. My baby. No, this isn't your responsibility. But why are they doing it?' She clasped Aurielle to her and squeezed.

'I don't know, Mum.'

Her mum tightened her hug.

Aurielle's ribs were about to splinter. 'Um … Mum?'

'I love you both so much,' she said and squeezed a little more.

Her ribcage threatened to pop open from so much love. 'MUM!'

'What? Oh, sorry darling. Don't want to smother you!'

Aurielle took a breath as she pulled away.

Her mum's expression sank again. 'Your father must be worried sick.'

The sudden mention of her father drilled ice through her veins. They had lost their loving father to the bottle, his drinking, his choice. Her real dad made rare appearances, couldn't be called on, absent too many times. Adorable dad. Wanted so much but constantly disappointing.

Her mum's palms held her temples, their eyes locked together. 'Don't be harsh on him, he loves you. Think of him as … unwell.'

Aurielle wanted to say something reassuring but couldn't find any words that might do it. Her lips failed to find the strength to smile warmly for her mum, those times it seemed, had gone. Both of them noticed Denyse sidle up to Jordi. They started chatting. There were whispers and giggles at times.

As Crook was on her own, resting against the rock-wall, Aurielle decided to try conversation. It wasn't something she was very good at but making an effort seemed the right thing to do.

She sat next to her and nudge her awake. 'Okay? You look knackered.'

Crook opened her eyes. 'Thanks, I'm alright.'

'Seriously, you look rough.'

'Well … okay, thank you for caring,' Crook gave her a weak smile.

She should try nice. 'You did good back there, on Gamma Seven. Blackjack might have killed you.'

'I don't think so, but thanks.'

'What did he say in your ear, he whispered something to you just before you found the Slide.'

'Oh, nothing. Filthy mouth on him, nasty piece of work.'

'Yeah.'

Her jewellery was expensive, lots of rings and colour. Interesting woman.

'But why whisper to you, why not say it out loud?'

'No idea Aurielle … all I can tell you is he's a horrid man.'

'Hmm.'

Jordi was checking out the cellar while Denyse talked to him, a schoolgirl with a crush.

She spoke in a low tone, 'Will we get out of here, Jordi?'

'Yeah, I'll get us all out, whatever it takes.'

Aurielle shook her head, 'What a hero.'

Denyse and Jordi speared her with their disapproving glances. Great, a new double-act.

'Where are you from?' asked her sister.

'Gamma Seven, same as you but I live in the southern quadrant.'

'Oh, I've heard the monsters are really bad down that way.'

'Yeah, pretty horrific, big too, but I give as good as I get. Still alive anyway,' he chuckled.

'Is it your job?'

'Yeah, has been for a while,' he leant against the wall. 'It's something I'm good at, see,' he grinned.

'And, er…' Aurielle knew what she was going to ask. 'How did it happen? Y'know … that,' she asked pointing to his unusual skin tone.

'Trekking in the jungle, on a mission, doing some pretty serious Protecting … got into a fight. Got bitten by this monster, then this happened.'

Denyse took his arm and rubbed it, seeing how ingrained the colouring was. 'Terrible … you must be lucky to be alive!'

'Yeah, I reckon. I'll have to go back there after all this and catch one, figure out how to reverse it.'

'What monster bit you? What will you need to catch?'

There was an unexpected pause, 'Oh, well this really, like big camouflaged, winged demon.'

'Oh my gods!' blurted Denyse.

Aurielle stood up. 'What was this monster then, what type?' she asked. 'You said winged. Winged what?'

'Don't matter. I'm alive, came to save you, didn't I?' He turned away and started tapping the wall, testing its strength. 'That's the main thing,' he added.

'No, seriously what was it?' By now, Henni, her mum, and Crook were standing together staring at him, expectantly.

He faced them. 'Well, actually it was a blood sucking, rabid hoard of butterflies.'

Aurielle stepped closer. 'You got all that from a little butterfly? Ha!' She guffawed, gripped her stomach and laughed like she was going to die right there, right then. The others sniggered and belly-laughed too. Jordi got a right mood on, started yanking on the doors again.

'I'm sorry,' said Denyse meekly, 'to have asked.'

Jordi continued rattling the cellar doors but soon gave up. He sat with his back to them. They gave him a few minutes, then each of them tried to calm him, give some reassurance, but he shrugged them all off. After about twenty minutes, he got busy examining their prison more closely, its walls and the door, striding from one wall to another, testing its strength.

It was time Aurielle took some control of the situation. The problems he brought her she could cope with – tantrums, moods, and all. Not a problem.

She went to him and poked him in the back. 'What's up, Blue?'

He swivelled to face her. 'Don't keep calling me that.' Definitely grumpy. 'Door's locked and too heavy to shift, one window even you couldn't crawl through. All this,' he said looking around, 'solid stone walls and not a pot to—'

'Yeah, thanks for that stunning summary of our situation. I suppose you've found the weakest point of the wall and tested it.'

'It's a solid wall with heavy rocks.'

'That's a "no" then.'

Aurielle scoured the room. An old broom and a large empty bucket, some rotting wood in a corner. All of it useless. She moved to the lowest point in the wall, swiped moss, and dirt away and began pushing and shoving at the stone wall to find a weak spot. She stretched to get at the ones higher up, should be easier to disturb, but couldn't get any force into them. She needed more purchase, more grip to push through them, something to stand on.

She flashed a look at Blue. 'Get me that bucket to stand on, bring it here.'

Jordi blinked at the command, 'Please, would be nice.'

She didn't reply because her attention was with her mother, who was rocking on her knees. Was she praying? But there was something else. Henni. She had started on her left foot, clearing green gunk out her nail with that poker.

Aurielle marched to the dinosaur and snatched the metal-poker, 'Wake up, if you wanna get out alive, Henni!'

Henrietta let out a squeal of confusion, snorted and stood up, hands on hips in defiance. 'What you doing? I didn't know, did I?' What's happening?'

Jordi took the poker from Aurielle, because he was taller than her or at least lanky and skinny. He aimed further up and hammered at a rock. It was stuck, solid, as it was meant to be.

'Not there,' she pointed, 'between them. Where the cement is. Where it's weakest, dimwit.' Aurielle turned her back in frustration, 'How you're still alive I don't know.'

The grouting chipped away with each dig. Jordi worked hard and eventually, with a lot of complaining, as if it was Aurielle's fault, he pulled a large chunk of rock from the wall.

Her mum, Crook, Denyse and even Henni stood behind Aurielle marvelling at his work.

'Well done, Blue, that's really good work,' said Crook. 'Really good,' she said again. Each one of them turned to look at Scarlett Crook, waiting to see what other pointless comment she would make.

'What?' she said perplexed by the sudden attention.

'Don't call me Blue,' said the blue boy with a large fire-poker in his hand. He looked at her with the cold gaze of someone who could chill their own heart if they needed. A Protector who was also a killer and an occasional odd-job man.

He returned to the rock wall and stabbed, repeatedly, and with a surprising amount of venom. Soon he had four fractured bricks at his feet.

'Got anger issues, don't you?' enquired Aurielle.

Jordi pointed to the space. 'There, reckon you could get through now,' he said with sweat glistening his brow.

'Wouldn't want to take the glory from you Blue, off you go.'

'Stop telling me what to do,' he barked.

'Moody, isn't he?' said Denyse.

'Tell me about it!' She'd not heard him like that before, he was full of surprises. Anger issues, for sure.

'I like him,' said Henni, with saliva slipping over her filed razor teeth.

'Give me a leg up,' said the stroppy teen.

Aurielle clasped her hands together. Blue placed his big foot there and pushed. He scrambled his way through the gap, muttering as he went, until finally his size elevens disappeared through the hole. Quite soon, those same size elevens started pounding the door.

'Jordi-boy?'

BANG BANG went the door as it ached from Blue's boots.

'Jordi-boy?' Aurielle raised her voice. She fetched the discarded poker, might be useful.

BANG BANG.

'What?' he bellowed.

'Look for a key, probably hanging high up somewhere.'

The air drifted into silence.

Crook smiled at Denyse, who in turn looked at her mum.

Mum glanced at the dinosaur with questions in her eyes.

Henni, she picked her nostril and flicked a ball of snot against the wall.

'Oh!' said her mum, shocked. She wasn't used to being around monsters.

There was a metallic clunk and rattle as the cellar doors swung open. This brought sighs of relief from behind Aurielle, as the last of the light from the end of the day washed the room.

'Well done finding the key,' said Aurielle climbing out of the prison. Jordi looked flushed; a deeper shade of blue blotched his cheeks.

The woods surrounding them were already dark, and beyond in the clearing was the moated castle, where Blackjack had no doubt decided to stay. It was time she had a chat with that sorcerer.

The others had clambered out and were brushing themselves down, stretching and taking in the thicket surrounding them.

Aurielle addressed them. 'Jordi-blue and I are going to see that bad man, the rest of you should wait in the car park, where we came in.' She pointed in the vague general direction.

'I'll come angel,' her mum said imploring her, 'no-one hurts my family.'

'You're right, Mum. You'll get your chance, just not yet. I'll come for you, I need you to look after sis', well ... everyone I reckon.'

She glanced at Jordi. 'Come on, Blue. Let's go and see if we can find you a new stick.'

Jordi Longstaff had a face full of misery, 'Dunno why I came all the way here to save you, I really don't.'

'Well, thinking is not really your strong point, is it Blue? There must be a stick down there for you. Wouldn't that be nice?' She enjoyed the weight of the heavy poker in her hands, if only she had her twin swords. Blackjack was going to pay for that.

Jordi trudged ahead of her, the sound of his size elevens squelching in a muddy track his only reply.

Chapter 16. Fun for the tourists

The sky was thick with cloud and the day was ending, so very little light was getting through. Despite this, they could never miss the castle with its battlements and enormous moat. It was spectacular in almost every way but there was something else, something hard to put a pointy finger on. It was a feeling. There was a sinister feel to the place. The flowers and fauna near the castle had been left untended, many of them were either drooping or dead.

With the iron fire-poker slung over her shoulder, Aurielle followed on behind Jordi, not because it was the right thing to do but because Jordi-blue had his own battle going on in his head. Marching off like that. If they weren't going to work as a team, she would have to look after herself. She kept her distance, watching Jordi striding with utter confidence onto the drawbridge and up to the enormous, arched castle door. He tried the handle and heaved it open. Yellow light spilled from the fortress as he disappeared inside.

Aurielle hesitated. If all went well, it would be a matter of minutes before Blue had secured Blackjack and was dragging him from his castle keep. Might be fun to watch, if not, it would be fun to see Jordi get a bloody nose. It was a win-win situation. Blackjack was a sorcerer in a land where magical potential didn't exist, he was powerless – except for any other skills he may have learned along the way.

Usually, she didn't like facing an enemy where their strengths and weaknesses were unknown to her. It made the fight dangerous and that wasn't the best way to start. Know your enemy, know what he can and can't do. Reduce the odds of getting yourself killed. In Blackjack's case she knew little about his background. But she was less worried about all that because she had met him, and despite whatever secret skills or martial arts he might possess, Aurielle was satisfied about one piece of crucial information she had gleaned from meeting him.

He was an idiot.

A pathetic shriek sounded out, muffled by the solid oak door to the fort. She would bet money Blue had tried to pocket a goblet or some other treasure and got caught red-handed, if that was possible in his current condition.

There was a lead-lined window to the side, she approached it stealthily, peeked inside and was immediately forced to stifle a giggle. She had laughed a lot since meeting the hapless boy-blue. He was caught, strung up in a medieval roped net like a captured deer, ready for the butcher's knife. But there was no sign of the hunter. Whilst an idiot, Blackjack could be cruel, so she had to be ready. Underestimating an opponent would be unwise at best. But with Blackjack, she couldn't imagine that ever happening. She glanced at the fire-pit poker. It would shatter his skull for sure. She would rather have Red and Midnight in her hands then there would be more artistry and skill in dispatching Blackjack. The weighty black poker would simply finish him. She levered the fragile window ajar, pushed up from the window-frame and climbed nimbly into the castle, slipping noiselessly to the cold stone flags below.

Ahead, sitting below a collection of draped pennants, she spotted her swords resting on a long medieval table. Lining the entrance hall walls were coats of arms, and between these on display were swords, pikes, and other nasty-looking weapons of war. There was a portion of the far wall converted to glass from ceiling to floor. Most likely containing a display of some type. One giant sparkly chandelier hung above them. It was an interesting contrast to the armaments around them. A nice touch that, although it may only be for decoration because a series of candles lit the room. Jordi was waving his arms, trying to draw her attention to something. She ignored the trapped Protector, through force of habit if nothing else. She eyed the knights in armour on each side of the room warily. Each had broad swords, slow and heavy to wield but deadly if you were caught by even one slash. Blackjack would not be stupid enough to lie in wait inside one of those suits of armour. Would he?

In a crouch, Aurielle moved forward, keeping her left side nearest the castle wall, glancing each way she carefully checked each corner of the room. All clear. She lunged for her swords.

'Watch out!' yelled Blue.

She swerved, pulling Midnight from its scabbard as she went.

A metal ball with spikes flew past Aurielle's ear, it hammered into the table. She whirled, Blackjack put up a shield, expecting her to return the blow, but Aurielle held fast. Better to be unpredictable in a fight. He grabbed a short sword from his side, the metal zinged as he released it.

She noticed in an instant the blade was wider than hers. Confused by her delay, he attacked her with a direct stabbing motion.

'Watch out!' Blue repeated helpfully.

'Shut up, I'm working!'

She stepped effortlessly to one side, making herself a smaller target, deflecting the steel blade with Midnight all in one move. She feigned to strike right, then brought an uppercut through his blocking shield. He stepped back surprised, absorbing the blow, he took a high wide arc with his sword to cut her head clean off. She ducked. His shield battered her from the left, she bounced to the floor on her rear. He had anticipated her move well.

'How's work now?' asked Blue.

'Said the boy in the animal trap.'

Blackjack did look the part, straggly black beard, greasy skin, dressed in chainmail with an uncomfortable grimace, although that might have been embarrassment. He did look a prize fool in fancy dress, it was no way to be seen for an ageing man. Blackjack threw his sword and shield to the ground and wrenched a long sword from the wall.

Aurielle couldn't imagine why he would want to make the fight easier for her. She flipped to her feet acrobatically, ready for his attack.

'Come on, Blackhead, give it up. This ain't no way to get yourself killed, is it?' He had the power and weight advantage, whereas she had speed and skill – and the brains. It was awful having to fight when it was so one-sided, no spectacle at all.

'Rooooaaaar!' he roared, sort of, and charged her, broad sword aloft ready to split her in half.

'Watch out!' blurted Jordi.

'Stop saying that!'

He sliced down, she shifted to her right and stuck out a foot. Blackjack launched into the air and splattered face down into the unforgiving stone floor. This was going to be more fun than she thought. He got up gingerly with a mashed nose, blood pouring from it.

'Sorry about that,' she said.

He raised his sword again and raced at her. She admired his spirit.

The steel sword shaved past her shoulders, it clattered into the ground. Sparks flew. And then, somewhat unexpectedly, Aurielle was flying through the air, her legs having been cheekily kicked from under her. Her spine smashed into the cold flags. The sword was a distraction from the point of attack. A decent move from the dunce. Aurielle winced.

Blackjack stood over her with a victorious grin. He held the point of his long sword against her neckline and gave it a little scratch.

'Nooooooo!' screeched Blue.

'You shouldn't have underestimated me, girl,' he grinned nastily.

'Agreed, that would've been awful.'

'Leave her alone!!!' Blue shouted.

Blackjack glanced towards him.

'I bet you haven't...' Aurielle's boot pounded between his legs, '... put a protective box on, the sort those cricketers wear.' Her head angled to find her accomplice, 'Do you know the one's I mean, Blue?'

The knight in dull silvery armour crumpled with a metallic clang. He dropped his steel sword before clutching himself and howling like a child starting primary school.

Aurielle sprang to her feet. 'Ah yes! Nothing like a scrap to lighten the mood, is there, Blue? Oh, well… maybe not for you. Sorry. Didn't mean anything. Forget I said it.'

'Just get us out of here, will you?'

***

Blue did what he was best at while Aurielle did the thinking. He moaned and complained about her dangerous approach to fighting, her lack of skill with the sword and how close Blackjack was to cutting off their heads. He was such a moaner. Aurielle shoved Blackjack into the make-shift prison with the help of the sharp ends of Midnight and Red. She padlocked the exit and wandered back into the grand entrance hall, sheathing her weapons as she went.

Jordi carried on, and on. 'If you had taken notice of me, then I could have finished him off and we'd have been gone ages ago. Instead, I had to hang up there and watch you nearly get yourself killed. I could have done him in a minute.'

Aurielle didn't bother to look up, 'Could've, would've, should've.' She reached over her shoulder for the hilt of her swords, she stroked each handle with the tip of her finger – finally returned to their place across her spine, reassuringly where they ought to be. All was well.

'What's that meant to mean?'

'You couldn't because you were dumb enough to get caught by a simple trap that every hunter has used since time began. You're useless … amateur and completely annoying. Although you do have one good quality.'

Jordi-blue put his hands on his slim hips. 'What's that?'

'You are so funny to watch. Honest Blue, I never have laughed so much.'

'I'm dangerous and serious. I can kill any man,' the Protector hissed as he spoke.

'Yep. You are dangerous to be around. I'll give you that. What do you think of my display though?'

Jordi followed Aurielle's gaze. Behind a sound-proofed glass wall was Blackjack ranting with a great deal of effort, combined with a lot of fist-shaking and shouting. That will be tiring after a while. Behind him was an ancient table and chair with two cloaked figures in medieval costume in a pose. Surrounding them was a variety of tapestries and pennants, with kitchenware from the period on the table.

She had imprisoned Blackjack in a display-case. Splendidly embarrassing.

Jordi chuckled.

Aurielle allowed herself a smirk.

'That'll give the tourists some fun for a few days. He's so generous that Blackjack. Don't you reckon he's a good actor?'

Jordi nodded. 'Sick.'

Aurielle's gaze slid up and down the Protector. 'Thought you looked a bit peaky, Blue.'

'I didn't mean—'

'Don't care,' she said, already on her way to the exit and drawbridge, back to where she belonged with her family. An annoyingly squeaky voice followed her all the way back.

There were hugs and kisses and pronouncements of love on her return, all from her mum thankfully. Denyse even hugged her. Henni seemed happy too, but it was always a crocodile's smile with her, so it wasn't something she could trust completely. Given the chance, the dinosaur would likely enjoy a nibble of one of Aurielle's limbs. She had no qualms about where her next meal came from. With friends like that you could never sleep for very long, and that's why Aurielle worried about taking Henni back with them. Gamma Seven was where Henni belonged but given Aurielle's main occupation was to kill monsters, it was hard to know what to do for the best. As they nattered in the castle's car park, Aurielle noticed the sphere was close to where they'd arrived. Scarlett Crook was obsessed with them and had talked about little else apparently. She dropped to her knees when she saw it, praying like a medieval commoner.

'Line up,' ordered Aurielle, 'let's go home.'

To her surprise, they did just that without a single complaint. One by one they climbed in just like they had done last time. Jordi was the last to go. His face had a miserable look stamped all over it.

'Why so blue?' she asked.

Jordi didn't seem to appreciate her excellent humour. He grunted.

'Missing your stick, aren't you? Don't worry, I'll get you another one from the woods when we get back.'

The Protector gave a snarl, at least that's what it looked like, and then he dived through the sphere to the Slide. She ought to be grateful he showed some interest and at least attempted to rescue her.

But she wasn't.

She didn't do grateful.

Chapter 17. The Decision

The forest was black as pitch. Rig put his hood up, perched on a log and waited. The air was full of fresh pine fragrances, with a small helping of damp bracken and occasional wood-smoke from a nearby fire. Frank fussed with his clothes, straightening them while marvelling at their strange journey. Rig rubbed his pale hands. The night was chilly. Frank went on and on about the Slide.

    'Definitely the best ride I've ever had! Went on a fairground ride once, chucked up my dinner, but this was different, see? Really different. I wanted to throw up but I didn't. It felt alive, like the Slide knew me. I know that sounds strange. But when I started to get a headache, it stopped pushing my head, like, and when I got stomach pains, it switched to my shoulders, sort of like it knew what was happening to me. Why's that? How could it know all that?'

    Rig looked at him blankly. 'Dunno.'

    'You must know.'

    'Must I? I can tell you want I think if you really want … most likely the Slide does know, because they're all connected to the gods. They use them all the time.' Rig took his phone out to get the torch function working. Three notifications pinged onto his screen. 'Oh, that's weird.'

    'What's that?'

    'Nothing, just got messages that's all.'

    'Eh? Are you saying you've got an inter-planetary network provider?'

    'Of course not.'

    Rig tapped the text icon. New messages from Dad and Auntie Ida.

    Hey, you.
    How's James?
    What you doing?
    Have fun up there.
    Am busy sorting garden

& washing car. Dad

Hey, seriously,
how are you both?
Get in contact.

hakkko
Hulllo darling r
ig
U ok/
fron aauntie

 Rig sniggered. Auntie Ida was actually texting him on Gamma Nine. Nice one.
 'Problem?' asked Frank.
 'Nah. No problem. I don't how these reached me though. Must be something to do with the Slide. I'll text them, might send when we go back through here.'
 Rig sent a speedy reply to both that all was well and headed down the slope with his torch swinging in his hand like a lantern, it was all downhill from here anyway. Frank was chatty, even though he was sobering up. Rig hadn't seen him drinking since before the shaggy she-monster attack. Rig used his torch as a searchlight. No sign of Humphrey but he wasn't sure a light would help find a ghost anyway. He wandered down the hill.
 'I can see a castle down there. Can you see it, Frank? Through these trees.' Twigs crunched underfoot as Rig weaved his way through the pines, downwards.
 Frank trailed behind him. 'Yeah, I can see it. Rig, how does this Slide thing know where you are and where you need to go?'
 'I dunno. I end up in the right place, something to do with the gods I suppose.'
 'The gods again, that's your answer to everything, "something to do with them gods".'
 'Yuk! Why do spiders have to make their webs at head height?' He cleared the webs from his face and stopped at the edge

of the forest. Below them was an impressive castle by a lake, and to one side a heavy mist was gathering. 'Well, the gods are behind a lot of stuff. And I know for certain the gods can control those portals. I always have to find somewhere high up to get one, that's what the gods said anyway. It's like, you know, my dad drives a nice car, but he doesn't know how the engine works, see?'

Frank appeared by his side. 'Yeah, well, I bet those gods, your friends lad, I bet they control spiders too.'

Rig looked at him quizzically.

Frank bunched his shoulders. 'You never know.' He stared at the view ahead, 'So, that's where me wife and daughters are, is it?'

'Maybe.'

They descended from the hill, quiet as mice, except for Frank's feet crunching the gravel path to the medieval arched door.

Rig twisted to Frank with a grim look and indicated for him to shush. Frank raised his eyebrows and hands in apology. They continued on tippy toes to the castle wall and hunkered down.

'What now?' whispered Frank.

'I don't know, I'm not used to raiding castles, I missed that lesson at school. I'll take a peek in that window there.'

'That's what I would've done.'

Rig looked at Frank in disbelief. 'Thanks for that, you're a real help.'

'You're welcome.'

Rig shook his head and raised himself just enough to peek through the small lattice window. In the half-light, Rig found the outline of someone familiar.

He gulped and sank to his knees.

'What?' urged Frank.

'I think it's him. Can't believe it's him.'

'Who? What you talking about, Riggy?'

'Don't you start that!'

'But what's wrong?'

'We've got no chance. We've got a killer in there, cold blooded, vicious, a streetfighter.'

Frank's eyes implored Rig to explain more. 'Who is he? Who's got me wife and daughter?'

'A god. Nasty as hell.'

***

Rig's feet slapped the pebbles as he strode to the castle door.

'What you going to do?' whispered Frank urgently.

'Try and talk my way out of this.'

'Oh,' Frank said, utterly surprised.

Rig turned the cold iron handle, heaved on the oak door, and went in, Frank followed.

The room was atmospheric, the light low with just a few candles brightening the walls where they were perched. A massive chandelier hung above a long wooden table which had a large bowl of fruit sitting on it, a few goblets and a large ornamental glass bottle full of what was probably wine. A dangerous god sat lazily, with his feet on the table supping from a very old cup.

'Come here,' commanded Blaam, the fallen god.

Rig approached, his senses scanning for any traps, half-expecting Humps to appear out of his eye, nostril or somewhere entirely unexpected at an inconvenient moment.

'Didn't expect to see you ever again,' Rig muttered.

'Sit down.'

Rig would obey, for now. The heavy wooden chairs scraped the concrete floor, the noise echoing through the chamber and beyond. Frank and Rig sat opposite the god in a man's body. There were old metal weapons on the wall, the type knights used to have. Several were standing around the room on show. He hoped the armour didn't have anyone living in them, or dead for that matter.

The ex-god gulped his wine. 'Ugh! Grapes,' his face twisted in sourness, 'how do they make 'em taste so bad?'

Blaam's eyes fixed on Frank, who in turn was looking longingly at the swan-necked bottle.

'Well, I know what he wants. What about you, Rig? What you want here then, eh?'

'You know what I want. The real question is more like … what do you want, Blaam?'

'Now we've got to it, haven't we? What do I want?' He took another swig. 'We'll get to that in a minute. I want you to meet someone first.'

He looked across Rig's left shoulder, spitting some unwanted wine to the medieval floor, 'Did you a favour, sorted a little problem. Blackjack is now … Deadjack.' An ugly grin appeared. 'See what I did there?'

Rig shifted in his seat. In the corner of the room was a life-sized display case showing a medieval scene by spotlight. This one was a little different because a man with a grim beard and wild hair was stretched across a table with an enormous sword poking out of his mouth. It certainly explained the blood-spurt decorating the window. Frank took a sharp intake of breath.

Rig turned to him. 'Yeah, that's what we're dealing with here, Frank. A mad murderer, a god-killer too. Can't get any lower than that.'

Blaam feigned a hurtful look, 'Ah, look at me so upset by yer words. Not a good way to start, is it Rig Penlip, Master of Magic?' His tone hummed with darkness and shadows, just like the castle. 'Well, guess what, there ain't no magic here lad so you're done for. Just you, your fat stomach, and your boozer friend 'ere against me. Me, who more or less, is still a god with all that goes with it except in name. What do you say to that, boy?'

Unexpectedly, Humphrey appeared from Rig's blind-side and waltzed right through the centre of the table towards Blaam.

'Oh dear, you really are a horrid little man. Anyone with a warm heart could see that, and some that don't too.' He began wagging a finger. 'You,' he continued, 'are old enough to know better. You have done a cruel and wicked thing, and I fear for your parents and what they must've gone through. The big question is …' Humphrey turned briefly to Rig and Frank before going on, '… how on earth, and in the name of all that's good and true, did *you* become a lower god? Answer me that you, filthy man.'

Rig's eyebrows arched. Humps had never been so vexed.

Blaam caught Rig's gaze. 'Is that it? That all you gonna throw at me? Some pathetic spirit … I mean, no offence, what's he gonna do exactly? Why's he even here?'

'Well … I never have …'

Rig sat up. 'Humps has got more soul and goodness in him than you'll ever have.'

Frank sniffed. 'I'm no diplomat, but this ain't getting us anywhere, is it?' he began reaching for the wine bottle. 'You won't mind if I have a wee drop?'

The steely look given by Rig gave a clear answer.

Blaam continued. 'See, the problem 'ere is. I don't need nothing, right. You need to give me something I really want,' he was stabbing a finger to make his point. 'And that's just to stop me from getting proper angry, know what I mean?'

His gaze switched to Blackjack's limp body. He gave a yellow-toothed grin.

'Seems to have a point there, Riggy. What are you going to offer? *What can you offer*?' asked Humps changing his tune somewhat. The light faded just a touch as the flame of a candle behind Blaam snuffed out.

The shadows in the castle inched closer to Rig, while the drunk, ghost, and the fallen god peered at him expectantly.

Chapter 18. Home and Away

They all stood facing her beaming golden smiles and bursting with merriment, except one. Blue kicked blades of grass, as if a football were buried somewhere within the tufts, hands in pockets with a dejected, miserable face. They were on the crest of a hill near town, having been spewed from the pipes of an inter-dimensional Slide and gateway. Wherever Slides actually came from, they worked. They were back home on Gamma Seven.

'Mum!'

Aurielle's mum clenched her like an industrial vice, for the third time. 'I'm so excited we're nearly home,' she said softly by her ear. 'I'll make your favourite meal; spaghetti bolognaise with just a few shavings of cheese on top. Then, we'll have strawberries and ice-cream for dessert. How about that?'

Aurielle pulled away, 'Brilliant. I'd love all that mum.' She gave her a fierce hug, 'Love you', she said. And her mum squeezed her even tighter. Aurielle caught Jordi's sideways glance and shook her head. She would take her mum and sister home, then help Blue. He was useless on his own, and anyway she wanted to see what unearthly, powerful little butterfly defeated him. He needed to get fixed, return to his normal colour whatever that was. She was thinking tangerine.

The walk back through town and onwards towards home was dominated by questions about Blue and Crook. Denyse was interested in the spirit guide and wanted to know all about her.

They walked together under the yellow lamps of the path which decorated their suburb, a route they had often trodden together as a family, from grocery shopping, or doing enforced exercise to the hill and back when younger. Her mum and dad had always insisted on some form of weekly exercise, constantly concerned about health. If only her dad was interested in his own health now. He was lost to the drink. Aurielle didn't know when she would see her real dad again.

She looked up. The artificial light obscured the evening sky. The light from just a few stars were able to find them, along with the chill of the evening in the early night.

'Mum, how do you think Scarlett knows about the death of magic? How can she see all that? What powers has she got?' asked Denyse excitedly.

'I don't know, it's what they do. I expect they're types of people Aurielle comes across in her work.' Her mum turned to her as they ambled home, 'Do you know how they actually know details like that? How they see things, love? How can they see the future like that?'

'No.'

Aurielle could practically hear her sister's disappointment with a change in her breathing. She could never say quite the right thing for her sister. Next, they would argue and that could turn into objects being thrown or worse, and because of Aurielle's skills training in combat she often ended up getting the blame. Speed and agility with some sprinkling of martial arts rarely won-out against full-on weeping in front of a frustrated parent. Another good reason for getting out of the house.

They took the last bend in the road which led to their door. As soon as Denyse glimpsed home, she ran to it, much to Aurielle's surprise.

'Look at that!' said Mum.

'I know. Look at her hands waving in the air, why does she do that?'

'Don't be nasty to your sister, be thankful she's doing some exercise,' she said grinning.

In truth, she envied her sister's curvy shape, when dressed-up she looked beautiful and gorgeously feminine. Aurielle didn't really do feminine. On the rare occasion when Denyse helped her get ready for a party or wedding, Aurielle looked like an awkward boy in a dress, even in the slightest heels she felt like she was about to tumble over and smash her face on the ground. No, glamour was something she would leave for Denyse. Wearing trainers, leggings, and her biker's jacket with Red and Midnight over her shoulder *was* Aurielle. It was her statement to the world. She liked it that way, it felt right and suited her work because killing monsters was her thing.

Mum couldn't resist any longer and bolted to the house too. She opened the door and began checking everything was right. Aurielle traipsed into the hallway.

'Oh, I can't believe we're home, thank you darling, thank you,' her mum's eyes dripped with gratitude.

'It's alright, Mum,' they hugged. 'Let's put the kettle on,' she said watching Denyse hurtle back through the lounge, brush past them and scramble upstairs, breathing heavily as she went.

It took a few minutes for her mum to gather herself, to calm down, and she didn't really do that convincingly until she had checked the whole house. Standing in the kitchen under its central bright light, mum sipped her tea. She finally her hunched shoulders began to lower. She was at last relaxing, with her girls, at home. All was well.

Aurielle kissed her mum and slipped upstairs. In her bedroom she freshened up a bit, got changed and climbed out of her window onto the roof of the dining room extension. She leapt to the garden, took the side gate, careful not to let the wood scrape on the concrete, and jogged back to her meeting point with Blue. She knew her mum would be worried, upset even, but the fact that Aurielle knew her mum and sister were okay meant she could get on with business.

When she arrived, she found Crook and Henni standing with their backs to Blue. He was brooding.

'What's the problem?' she asked, panting.

Henni was the first to reply with her lisp, 'The boy don't want a dinosaur with him, does he? Says I'll slow him down, or something.' Her talon scratched her scaly stomach. 'Won't get better company than me, will he little one?' Her tail started to swing gently from side to side.

She nodded. Henni had no-one now, no keeper, boss, or family. She had even wanted Aurielle dead, but having a family was important, everyone should have a family of some sort. Jordi sat, arms crossed gazing down the road, occasionally giving Aurielle hopeful glances. He was painful to look at sometimes, needed her help but didn't want to ask. He was moody, grumpy, and an awful rescuer but he was a reasonable Protector. Dumb as wood, although wood could be very useful and could burn. One little match could light him up nicely… perhaps not.

She went to Crook whose whole demeanour gleamed.

'It's good to see you. Are you okay? And mum, and your lovely sis?'

'Yeah. All good.'

Crook leaned into her. 'This one,' she indicated behind her, 'he's an angry man.'

'He's always angry, born that way, its stuck with him.'

Scarlett Crook sniggered conspiratorially. 'I think you're right.'

She was a warm woman, the sort that took on the troubles of the world with a cheeky smile. Aurielle hadn't noticed it before. She wore make-up. Some of it was light, some boldly glamorous. It distracted from a few lines etched into her skin which hinted at her age. There was a hard-fought wisdom about her, as though she'd seen trouble in her life but smiled all the way through it. Aurielle could see why some people would hate her; others would give her their lives. She had proven useful so far and was obviously a woman of action.

'I'll go and see what Mr Angry wants to do,' Aurielle whispered.

Jordi Longstaff couldn't hide his long face as she approached.

'What have you said to Henni and Scarlett?'

Blue pursed his lips and avoided her gaze, 'We can't travel with these two, they'll slow us down.'

'You ain't so quick yourself.'

'Gotta long way to go, don't we? I've got to find out how this happened,' he pinched his blue skin frustratingly, 'I've gotta reverse it somehow. These two will be in danger, you don't wanna do that to them. I mean, what'll you tell their families?' He cast a look at Hennrietta the Horrible. 'Well, she must be a rare beast anyways, don't want something rare to get killed, do you? She's done enough, hasn't she?'

'Ha! You'd kill her in a second if you had to, just another monster to you, like all the others. It's what you do.'

'It's what *we* do.' His eyes blared, accusingly. 'It's what you were going to do. I'm right, aren't I?'

'No,' Aurielle said swiftly, catching the dinosaur's attention as she spoke. She loved the way the creature's scales interlinked in that emerald green and her tall ears twitched like a cat's. A claw picked at a scab. Hygiene wasn't great. It was one part of her colourful character though, and Aurielle wouldn't change anything, even if she could.

She continued, 'It's true, we started off badly but that was just the situation.' She watched Henni's eyes blink with affection. 'No, she's my friend now … that's just how it is.'

Henni's tail wagged furiously.

Blue rolled his eyes and shook his head. 'We can't take her. We can't. Whatever it's done for you, or you reckon is important … well, it just isn't, okay? It's dangerous out there … we need to move fast, sometimes go without food, *often* without food, but we fight, we run, we kill. And I don't know what we'll face out there.'

'Pretty butterflies, apparently. Anyway, you don't call Henni an "it".'

Blue threw his hands in the air, 'No, we can't, it won't work, we'll all get killed. No!' He jumped up and down in a great fit and tantrum.

And then he started shouting.

Aurielle studied Blue casually as he leapt up and down on the spot. She was impressed by how high he could go, but this was quickly overtaken by an overwhelming feeling of loathing.

She threw a look charged with electricity. 'Go on your own!' She turned and ushered Henni and Crook together for a three-way hug.

'I will. That's what I'm gonna do. It'll be better that way, no-one to slow me down or test me with their yakking. Peace *and* quiet. And I can tell you …'

Aurielle let him ramble on, and on. She peeked over her shoulder. He was still stamping the ground and switching neatly between a grouchy-child and moaning old man – quite a feat for a teenage Protector. He had obviously had his own way far too much in the past. Bad parenting? Or no parenting? More likely the latter. Still, he would have to get on with it by himself.

She turned to face the stroppy teenager.

He clenched his fists in a rage, swivelled on his feet and marched away complaining bitterly. 'I'll never see you again! I hate you. You've let me down, haven't you? I don't know what to do with you all. I've had it. I'm off. I'm going. Leaving now! Right now!'

'Bye.' Aurielle waved. She couldn't resist the sarcasm, it was peach-sweet.

Henni and Crook waved too.

This didn't seem to help.

'Hey, Blue!'

Jordi turned in a fluster, 'What d'you want now? Told you, I am leaving. For good.'

'If you want the train or bus you need to go that way,' Aurielle pointed behind her in the opposite direction.

Jordi gave a sort of screech in reply. And marched thunderously past them, blushing in a darker blue, or was it a deep ocean blue colour? Hard to know. She was no expert in such things.

The dinosaur, Seer, and Protector watched as Blue marched down the tarmac-path muttering to himself.

'What a temper,' said Crook.

Henni sniffed. 'He's a nice boy really, I mean underneath all of that stuff, I think, deep down,. Don't you?' she said with her big eyes switching between them.

'Course he is, just goes a bit mental sometimes, that's all,' replied Aurielle.

They only had to wait two minutes before he appeared where the road started to curve, just in view. He slouched against a lamppost.

'Come on then!' he yelled and waved them to join him.

They ambled over. Henni's tail swept joyfully.

Blue was calm but still serious. 'Okay, you can all come. But you follow me, I'm the boss, right?'

Aurielle clutched her heart mockingly, 'Oh, you're such a hero, so manly.'

'Shut up.'

Crook laughed. Henni guffawed, and clumps of her snot splattered Blue. She turned away covering her snout with a clawed hand, embarrassed.

The Protector examined his jeans, soaked in phlegm and goo.

Aurielle couldn't help it, she cackled with laughter. 'You can be such fun sometimes, Blue!'

He tried to wipe it from his legs but managed to smear his hands in sticky dinosaur gloop instead.

'That's nice,' he said between gritted teeth.

Chapter 19. Prod Considers

Prod Visceral chomped on his last mouthful of succulent steak, chewy as it was the meat had been a decent cut with a full flavour. He dumped his plate in the washing up bowl and went to the window of his world. The night sky had been brushed carelessly with occasional swathes of thin cloud. Lights from the city shone back as if in admiration of him, because Prod was the master of this place, and eventually, in good time, everything would be his to look down upon. It was as though the lights thought the same and were putting on a display just for him, their Lord and Master.

Nutter.
'Who said that?'
Me
'Who?'
You.
'Who is that?'
Me
'Shut up!'
You're not going to do it.
'What?'
Change. Won't let you.
'The future is set. I'm getting stronger, your voice is fading. I'm improving, in all ways.'
Our smell is definitely stronger.
'You're the last part of the old me. Soon that part of me won't even be a memory. All of the past is melting away while the new me is stronger, more powerful, more successful. You're all but gone. Dead, dead, dead.'
Still here. I do like your green scales by the way.

Prod ignored the voice in the depths of his head and its poisonous comments. Soon it will be gone completely. He walked onto the balcony. The gusts massaged his forehead cooling him, gently, deliberately. He rolled his shoulders and stretched his neck enjoying the bulky feel of his muscles. His large hands gripped the railing, his nails clawed into his skin as he gripped harder.

His mind drifted to that god, Lycka. Something was troubling. His mind kept returning to her. She couldn't be trusted. She didn't understand him, what he needed, what he was becoming. Why was she on his mind?

His body was so warm, but the breeze knew this and caressed his mammoth chest. But still his body burned from the inside like he was cooking. There was one improvement. He was no longer fighting an itch he could never find. That had grown softer then disappeared entirely.

It was something she said. What did she want? That god. Hate them. Gods. All that power, knowledge and they do nothing with it. She wanted him to let the girl go, Aurielle Merlot. Why should he? Her fate was already determined. She was of no value anyway, just bait.

No, it was something else. What did she say? Let her go. No. Let *them* go. Them. Hadn't noticed it at the time. Who was the other person?

Blackjack must be dead. But Blaam? No contact. Either killed or he had betrayed Prod. Unlikely to have been caught and murdered, although technically already dead, his inner self would be trapped for eternity if he had been killed in his current form. No, he wouldn't allow that. Knowing the spirit, he had definitely double-crossed Prod. Maybe done a deal with Penlip. If the girl has escaped, where has she gone? And then there was the matter of the boy. Where is he? There had been no spying on Prod recently, no creaking ceilings, no warnings from his highly tuned senses. The boy had gone. Must have overheard them. What had happened to Jordi when the attack came? Had he been injured in some way in Malaysia? Bitten? If he had been, he would want to go back, get revenge, or find an answer to whatever sickness had taken him. Or would he try and save the girl. Maybe already had.

All roads pointed to one place. Prod would have to visit the Source once more. The pool of negative magic. The place of Prod's rebirth. Something happened to Jordi Longstaff too and eventually that was where he would end up, with or without Aurielle. Prod was betting she was with him, and wherever she was, Rig Penlip, Master of Magic, would follow.

A gust kissed Prod's cheek. He smiled and rubbed the smooth skin of his head, that's when he noticed his hands were stained with streaks of dried blood.

Such an enjoyable beef steak, so much better when the flesh was raw.

Monster.

'This is nothing. Wait and see, if you can.'

Hmm ...

Chapter 20. Godmaker

He slurped his wine like it was cheap beer and apparently didn't care how much spilled. The claret stained the pale skin around Blaam's mouth. He was a vision. A miserable clown gone mad. There was certainly a dangerous, chaotic quality to him as though he hadn't a care in the world and that was probably true, except for one thing. And that was about the only ace Rig had up his sleeve. But Rig wasn't a Seer, he couldn't see ahead to know how it would all work out. He just had to try his best.

The ex-god stared at him, waiting patiently, because he could. Time was irrelevant to a spirit, albeit one in human form. Frank couldn't take his eyes off the pitcher of wine. Humps was examining the stitching of a pennant carried by one of the knights in armour, commenting occasionally on the hideously poor lighting.

Rig turned to Blaam, whose expression was like cold chiselled stone. 'The way I see it, you've fallen further than pretty much anyone in history, except the devil himself. You are a fallen god, an ex-god. A fourteen-year-old and his friends ended your plans for world domination with your puppet sorcerer, Oglith Farweep. You killed your own pal: Erat, God of War, who will spend eternity stuck in rotting flesh and blood, dying in mind and skin, slowly ... while you walk around swigging wine and anything else you want.'

Blaam took another gulp, winced, and said, 'So what?'

'Your time here,' Rig pointed to the castle's flooring for effect,' could be done and finished any minute. You're on borrowed time. The gods *will* take you. Worse than that, you're going to burn for all you've done. You must know that?'

The ex-god carelessly sloshed some wine into his goblet. Frank leant forward, hoping.

Blaam took a satisfying glug. 'You see, Rig, no-one really knows nothing, even that Archiver who thought he knew it all ... you found him out, got him killed, replaced anyways. What I'm saying is it's all up for grabs, no one knows what'll happen, right, not even them higher gods. D'you get it?' His words stabbed at Rig.

'I didn't get him killed! He was a … he was a higher god I heard and spoke to, no more than that. But you … you've done some bad things. Very bad. The end … well, it's going to be very dark and you don't know when it's coming. You need someone to talk to them for you … you need someone to help them find forgiveness. I can help you.'

Humps tottered on his toes holding his hands close to his chest like a hungry squirrel, 'Nice flags on those things there. Can I enquire … were they made here?'

Rig looked at him in disbelief, 'Please Humps, not now.'

'Oh, dear me, I try and bring some warmth into your day, and I get smacked down. I don't know, Rig Penlip … you really are a difficult travelling companion.' He swivelled like a ballet queen to Blaam. 'And you … you wretch, had better take Riggy's help. It's the only way you'll ever find salvation for your soul.'

Rig straightened in surprise.

Blaam raised a foot and wriggled his boot. 'Nothing wrong with this soul,' he said casually. 'And what you gonna do about it? Bore me until I change my mind?'

Humphrey flicked his head, bird-like, in the opposite direction and waltzed back to the cloth pennant.

'No.' Blaam waved a finger. 'I'll tell you what's gonna happen. You're all friendly with that Lycka woman – moves well, easy on the eyes, all of that – you're gonna speak real nice to her and then real serious because your gonna get my old job back. You'll convince her, see.'

Rig gasped.

Frank and Humps looked at Blaam in disbelief.

'Yeah. You'll make me a god again. Convince that woman to get it done.'

Clenched hands. Jelly legs. 'But—'

'If you don't. I'll visit your daddy and that uncle of yours. And that Merlot girl and her boyfriend. They'll all be done for. Know what I mean?'

Rig jumped up, the chair rasped as it shifted backwards and over, all eyes on him.

It wasn't possible.

Not again, death and destruction.

His family.

Friends.

No.

'No, no, no, no!' he screeched.

Blaam sat unmoved. Frank eyed Rig nervously and Humps moved as if a gust had caught his sails.

Rig pounded the table with his fists. 'It's not fair, not right. All that death! My brothers … Kai, Tyson, Zac, Dillon, Bart, and Connor, and my … my…' he spun away, paced to the castle wall, snatched an axe from an armoured knight, and marched back to them with fury in his face, chest heaving, eyes full. He raised the weapon, Frank scuttled backwards, Blaam just supped his grog.

'No, Rig!' begged Humphrey.

He smashed the steel blade into the old oak table, yanked it free, and slammed it in again and again up and down the table in a fury. He went to the nearest knight, practically dragging the heavy axe. He somehow hurled the blade at its legs and arms. The crash and bedlam surrounded them as he swung the medieval killing axe into the empty breastplate.

Frank put a hand on Rig's shoulder.

'Get away from me!' Rig shrugged Frank away, and pulled the weapon back and marched towards Blaam, teary eyes blurring his vision. He lifted the steel battle axe above his head, 'Why? Why? Why?' he shrieked, his eyes fixed on the blank expression of the rubbish god.

Rig smashed the blade into the tabletop, wedging it into the splintered wood. He heaved and heaved on the handle to release it, cheeks flushed, heart bouncing. He heaved again on the handle, it ripped away, soared above him, he smashed it into the table. Splinters flying.

The skin-head god watched impassively.

Rig suddenly stepped clear, as though the battle-axe had given an electric shock, but it was his own reaction which surprised him.

The ghost neared him, 'Dear Rig, I'm so utterly sorry …your family, such a terrible loss you had to go through,' he said, his words wrapped in soft tissue.

Rig's head lolled into his hands. He hid his eyes.

The skinhead looked smug.

'Finished have ya? Ya see, Rig, I didn't kill your family. It was that Oglith Senior. Know that, don't you? I weren't even around.'

Rig took a moment to steady himself.

The fallen god sniffed, 'It don't change nothing, Rig. It is what it is.'

Rig looked up, 'Who says "it is what it is?" That's stupid. Virtually my whole family was murdered, and you get to sit there, drink your body to death, and tell me *it is what it is!*'

Humphrey tried to put his arm around Rig, but his hands passed through Rig's shoulders like they were smoke.

'You'll do it, lad. You will. Talk to that Lycka, make me a god again. I'll leave the rest of your family alone, I swear it. But for them following that Merlot girl, probably all dead anyway with them going back to that jungle.. She's a dangerous sort. Not my fault if a monster bludgeons her to death now, is it? Deserves all she gets that one. Fight by the sword, live by it, get killed by it. Know what I mean?'

'She's a good girl, right, and I love her!' Frank blurted.

Rig leaned forward eagerly. 'Where is she, exactly? Where is she right now?' he said choosing each word carefully.

Blaam wiped his stained mouth. 'Tioman Island, Malaysia.'

'Hell,' uttered Rig pulling away.

'Sure is. Don't bother going you'll be too late.'

'What? Why?'

'All them monsters.'

'But why would she go there?'

'Dunno. Maybe to get some of that poisoned water. Nothing else there except monsters and mad tribesman foaming through their black teeth..'

'Eh? What poisoned water? Why would she do that? Why?' asked Frank.

'Got ponds and streams full of negative magic, don't they? Don't ask me why, mate.'

Blaam switched to Rig. 'Anyways, do what I say … otherwise I might wanna chat with your old man. Feeling very chatty, I am.'

'Don't you do that!'

'Speak to that Lycka,' demanded the ex-god, glaring. 'Make me the god I'm meant to be, Rig Penlip, Master of Magic.'

He held the ex-god's stare, his nerves calming.

Humphrey put his hand up, as if in school. 'Um … there's a dead man back here. Think I know him,' he said gawping into the display case at the end of the hall. 'Or do I?'

'I doubt it, let's go.'

The ghost thumbed through his notebook urgently.

'Come on, Humps,' Rig said, and with a nod to Mr Merlot, Rig strode from the room.

He waited at the castle-keep door, letting his friends go first. The night air was refreshing.

'I'm sure I know that bearded man with a broad sword down his throat,' Humphrey said floating into the darkened castle grounds like an abandoned kite. 'I'm sure I do.'

'Rig?' called the ex-god.

Rig looked to Blaam. His outline just visible in the gloom.

'Don't let us down boy, or you won't like what happens next.'

'Touch any of my friends or family … I'm warning you, I'll come after you.'

Rig paced into the night purposefully, leaving the old fort's misery behind him and the fallen god smirking in the shadows.

Chapter 21. Jeep

It was an interesting scene, not what you would call every-day but then Aurielle's days were often extraordinary. The tropical island was a real paradise. A bleach white sandy shoreline and the sea the colour of crystals, which Aurielle had only seen before in expensive jewellery. The water by the island barely had waves to the extent the sea merely teased the shoreline gently. But the heat was stifling and the atmosphere so close it was intense.

The roar of an engine interrupted the scene. Their rental suddenly appeared from a gap in the forest and sped towards them. It bounced and rattled to an urgent stop. A local, who couldn't be much older than Aurielle, jumped out and approached them. If all was well, he was the brother of the boat owner from the mainland. He neared, rubbing his arms, looking around, checking them and the beach.

The journey across the sea had been fun until they'd all gotten sick with the constant rolling of the boat. Cheap meant small, and this translated into sickness and vomiting. Only Henrietta had escaped that pleasure. They were deliberately light on supplies, which Aurielle secretly worried would be a terrible mistake. They had large bottles of water at their feet and some plastic sunglasses which none of them thought would last the day. Their mission was simple; go in fast, find a negative pool of magic, take some samples, and get out. Just a couple of hours and they could relax by the palm trees while waiting for their pickup. Any monsters would be dispatched if found. A problem free trip in an interesting place with no gods or idiots to worry about, well, maybe one. Aurielle glimpsed the dinosaur hiding behind some bushes while Blue pawed over the jeep they were hiring.

The islander held out an open palm for his fee without a single word. Crook paid up. He shook her hand frantically and dashed away, glancing back as he ran. Earlier, his brother and boat crew had done the same thing – couldn't get away quick enough. Was it because of the large green dinosaur with them, or the fact they were heading inland to monster territory? Whatever.

'Let's get going,' Aurielle said.

'Sure,' she said stuffing some bank notes down her top. 'We've got twenty-four hours until they pick us up, hopefully.'

'Perfect,' Aurielle waved Henni to come over.

Jordi finished checking the large tyres and bodywork. 'It's so rugged … it'll get us over almost anything, have ya seen the tread on them tyres? It don't look a comfy ride but it'll see us through some rough stuff.' He launched his stick onto the back seat. 'It'll get some speed up too,' he patted the bonnet, 'a decent engine in here, water cooled, single carburettor with about sixty horsepower, reliable. Not a racing car, like, but can't wait to give this a go.'

Aurielle shook her head. 'No. Crook will be driving.'

Crook winked at Aurielle. 'Come on my lovelies, climb in.'

'What? No. No way!' Blue stomped round to the driver's side and sat in the seat.

Aurielle approached him coolly, with her unfunny face on. 'Out. Now.'

'Why?'

'I want an adult to drive.' She nodded to Crook. 'All yours.'

Blue launched his frame from the vehicle in one singular annoyed leap. 'Won't be looking for Scarlett when there's monsters that need to die, will you? What good will she be then?'

'None taken,' said Crook tying her blouse round her waist.

'What?'

'No offence taken,' she replied, adjusting her vest.

Aurielle and Blue sat in the back. She turned to him, 'Don't worry I'll protect you from any butterflies we find.'

Blue pulled a face.

Henrietta the Horrible skipped towards the jeep, leant across, and gave Aurielle a big lick with her slobbering lizard tongue.

'Your thank you is accepted,' said Aurielle.

'I'm so excited,' said Henni. 'You know the bushes, over there, see, they are so dense I had quite a snack while I was waiting.'

Aurielle stroked her snout.

'You're the only thing that's dense around here,' grumbled Blue.

Crook started the engine, the chassis juddered like a washing-machine, sounded a bit like one too.

'Ignore the moody teenager who can't play with his toys,' said Aurielle as Henni climbed into the front seat next to Crook. Her squashed tail-end had to hang out the door.

Crook lowered her head, put her hands together and began chuntering.

'She's saying a prayer to the gods again,' said Blue. 'Lunatic.'

'Some people still do that, it's tradition, you should respect people more,' she looked at his blue-tinged skin. 'If you want respect back you should give it to others.'

Blue gave a scornful shake of his head.

Crook gunned the engine.

They lurched forward in unison.

'Sorry!' Crook cried.

'This is gonna be a thrill,' moaned Blue.

'Oh, belt-up,' said Flash looking at his lack of seatbelt.

'Hilarious.'

'Thanks.'

They zipped out of the sunshine drenched bay and raced up a slope towards the hills, the jeep rattled and clanked so much Aurielle figured it wouldn't last long. They were surrounded by bush and fauna which obscured the view. They wouldn't go off track much, not unless they really needed to.

The big eyes of Crook appeared in the rearview mirror. 'All okay?' she asked.

'Outstanding,' said Blue.

Aurielle nodded.

'I wonder what life we'll find. Such a good thing to do exploring, isn't it? So much nicer together. Should've done this before, so much fun, isn't it?' Henni started clapping, she was so excited.

It had been a surprisingly wayward road she had travelled since meeting Blue. She wasn't happy with the lack of control she'd had since then, something to reflect on. Any Protector of any value improved continually: with training, tactics, endurance, applied knowledge, detailed reflection, and good stabbing skills. She snuck a look at Jordi-blue. A thought surfaced.

'You never told me how you found me,' Aurielle said nudging Blue from his coma.

'What?'

'How did you know I was in trouble, and where I was?'

Crook eyed them both in the rear-view mirror.

'I just knew,' he said. 'I have a nose for this kind of thing, told you … I'm good at what I do.'

'Yeah, it's big enough, but how did you *actually* know?'

'I knew someone wanted to get at you, following his mongrel pet was easy enough. It was someone I'd worked for, I guess you did too because he really wanted to corner you. Got some enemies, haven't you? Suppose we all have.'

Aurielle squirmed to face Blue. 'Who? What's he look like?'

'He's changed a lot since coming back from here, gone a bit nuts. He got it worse than me. Prod Visceral. Know him?'

Aurielle's expression shrunk with worry.

'What?' asked Blue.

'He's the one who helped me and Rig; he risked a lot. Sounds like he's turned rotten.'

'Yeah, well, he was a scientist or something, looking at these negative pools of magic, studying them, whatever they do, testing the water, y'know? I think them monsters that bit him sent him crackers. Look at me, I was lucky to get out totally sane, just this colour problem.'

They veered suddenly to the right, Blue almost head-butting Aurielle.

'Get off,' she said.

'Sorry!' blurted Crook. 'Dangerous road this.'

They had climbed high and away from the beach, there was now some serious jungle on either side. The air was a furnace of heat and impossible to evade.

'It was never that Blackjack, the mongrel pet you followed.' Aurielle continued, 'Prod Visceral – he's after me for no good reason. That can mean only one thing.'

'What?'

'It's a setup.'

'Setup for what?'

They lunged forward as the jeep rolled to cope with the bumps in the sandy road.

'He must be after Rig. He was using me as bait, but his plan has backfired. So long as Rig hasn't fallen for it. Hmm. Probably has fallen for it. Does Prod know you got bitten and went blue?'

'Dunno. Maybe. Logical ain't it?'

'Yeah, if Rig knows I'm here he'll come for me, and Prod or his nutters would follow, unless the gods get involved. What an idiot, I hope he doesn't come here.'

'Yeah, idiot,' chuckled Blue.

Aurielle's hand squeezed Blue's windpipe, 'Don't you call him that, saved a lot of people he has.'

'But you—'

Her fingers pinched him harder. 'Doesn't matter what I said.'

Aurielle pulled away, surprised by her own wrath. Blue had the good sense not to react.

The incline levelled out, but there were even more dips, bumps, and rocks. They reduced their speed to navigate the road's potholes, the jeep's suspension bent and twisted to cope with the surface. In the driver's mirror, Crook's expression was full of concentration and determination. They all held on as the wheels toiled.

'Sorry about this people, no choice on this road,' Crook said as they inched down a huge hole on the left side. Aurielle slipped on the seat and squashed Blue.

'Jeez!' he croaked and tried to push her away.

'Do that again and I'll cut that arm off.' She had one hand on Red.

'Oh,' said Crook.

They came to a halt, Crook clambered out.

'Problem?' asked Aurielle.

Blue joined Crook on the dirt track. Aurielle followed suit.

'See what you mean,' she said, echoing Crook.

'What's the problem?' asked Blue.

Henni went to the verge and ripped fauna from it in chunks.

'There's a big storm gathering, fast by the looks of it. Might get lively around here.'

Blue laughed. 'Yeah, we've got some rain coming, we'll get a bit wet for a while. It'll clear away and we'll soon warm up in this heat and dry off. No problem, is it? Tough in the field, I know that. Do as I say and we'll all be fine. Relax. I've done this a thousand times.'

'Not here you haven't, at least not in December,' replied Aurielle.

'How do you know what—'

'Because we're on an island in Malaysia,' Aurielle interrupted. 'In December, it's monsoon season. Monsters like rain, they like to clean their fur if they've got any ... monsoons do that job quite nicely. I would've thought you'd known that having actually been here before.'

'Ah. Well—'

'Yeah. It's going to get busy.'

Crook's expression sagged; her makeup followed.

Henni hustled over and nestled next to Flash chomping merrily, oblivious to the situation.

'Well, I am a Protector. Blue skin and a bit of rain doesn't stop me knocking over monsters,' he said chirpily. 'It's what I'm best at. Good job you're all with me.'

'We're all here *because* of you, Jordi. Remember?' asked Crook with a menace in her tone which Aurielle hadn't heard before.

'Chill out, it'll be okay.'

Aurielle sighed.

The grey horizon gave way to a churning darkness which folded and turned in on itself as it grew. The clouds moved like steamrollers, rushing forward and angrily bludgeoning the remaining light, blanketing the sky in such scale that surely the gods themselves had demanded it.

'Monsters, lots of them. Bring them on,' urged Blue.

Aurielle swept a hand back and stroked the patterned black leather handle of Red and the porcelain of Midnight, their reassuring presence gave her a lift as always. It was only a matter of time before they were active again. All comes to swords that wait.

Chapter 22. Frank Merlot

After the walk back to the Slide on Gamma Nine, they'd squeezed through to Gamma Seven as though it was a perfectly reasonable thing to do. The threat from Blaam at the castle had echoed round his head all the way, and this only stopped when Frank had decided to take charge. This was a new and unexpected experience.

Frank organised the flights to Malaysia and then the ferry from the mainland to Tioman Island. His confidence had grown. Mostly because he had no wine to glug, he was more focused on what they needed to do, and a useful side-effect was the unquestionable improvement in his hygiene, humour, and appetite. The tropical patterned shorts he'd bought them both was something Rig would forgive in time. He looked ridiculous, ready for a beach holiday and the suncream protection stank, but Rig had to admit they were reasonable ideas.

Unfortunately, some bad ideas had come along with these changes. For instance, he insisted they hire a speedboat to circle the island so they could approach from the far side, because Frank knew best … well, he knew Aurielle best and Frank calculated that if she was on the island, she would want to be quick, in and out. Because when faced with a problem she would never do the obvious, go through the front door, the back, yes. If she was seeking poisoned pools of magic, she would find somewhere to land that was remote, give her cover from nasties but also access to what she needed. Looking at the map of the island, that would mean avoiding the port Kampong Tekek and going to the east side of the island. There was a small cove and dense jungle. Frank believed this was the ideal landing point, in his daughter's eyes. Any arguments about this ceased immediately if Rig simply agreed. So, he did.

The problem with all of this was, firstly they didn't know why Flash would want to get any of this poisoned water and secondly they didn't know if Denyse and her mum were travelling with her, or why. Unless they were all prisoners of some mad sorcerer-type, which was the most reasonable explanation, but Rig had another problem … he really ought to be trying to find Lycka, otherwise the skinhead god was going to harm his family. And whilst he was good with magic, he hadn't learnt the art of being in two places at once.

Lycka would have to wait, and so would Blaam.

But would he?

Humphrey appeared and disappeared whenever the journey looked uncomfortable or if there was the slightest tension in the air. When he wasn't complaining, he was scratching notes in his notepad – about what, no-one knew. Although he did spend a lot of time reading a plaque on the first boat: local information giving some background to the island. For tourists most likely. Whatever it was, he was absorbed for some time. What had changed was that Frank could hear Humps, and it wouldn't be too long before he would start seeing the apparition. It always happened if someone spent too much time with Rig. The laws decided by the gods around magic were clear, if a little surprising. For Rig, when his mother and brothers were killed he 'inherited' huge amounts of magical potential from them. And as he used his magic skills sparingly, he literally oozed magic from his pores. That's how those around him benefitted from an upsurge in ability as they absorbed these magical atoms over time. The result being a modest improvement in certain abilities, usually spiritual related, that was his understanding anyway.

Once they had unloaded themselves from the speedboat, Frank's temper seemed to increase at about the same rate as the island's temperature. At least Rig's belly was full for a change, his crab and salad sandwich with chips had been welcome earlier, but twenty-five Ringgits seemed a lot – except when Rig thought about it, he realised, happily, he had no idea what a Ringgit of the local currency was worth. Ignorance translated into happiness where food was concerned, but when it came to wielding his unrivalled ability with magic, he was having a small crisis. In places of astonishing natural beauty, the use of magic with all its quirks and potential to damage just didn't seem right. He wasn't a Seer or psychic in any meaningful way, although he had been lucky at times, but he realised his reluctance to use magic as a first option was going to cause trouble and consternation. Life was rarely dull.

They each carried a rucksack with water and light supplies for their trek, except Humps who even when present was unable or unwilling to be with them on account of being a ghost. Any excuse to get away with not helping. Frank led the way up the beach, as if it were an assault by coalition forces on a beachhead held by the enemy.

'C'mon Rig, let's get up here pronto. There ain't no time to waste, lad.' He marched in a fever towards a pathway in the foliage as though his life depended on it. But it didn't.

'No, well yes … I agree, but we're not going to war, Frank. I'm right behind you.'

'I'm going to find me daughter. I'll give anyone that stops me a good smack and get her home.'

'Err … yeah, okay. Sounds great.' Rig lumbered up a white sandy slope, his feet slipping as he went. His neck already stinging from the rays of the mid-morning sun, Rig couldn't help but wonder where this was all going to end, and when. If Flash was in trouble and held captive in a place like this, they were going to have to be inventive, cunning, and ruthless.

'Ouch!' he blurted.

Frank whirled to check on Rig, 'What's up, lad? What's happening?'

'Nothing.'

Frank approached Rig, turned him round. 'There's nothing here. What's the problem with you?'

Rig pulled his cotton shirt away to show the bite mark on his left arm, 'See? Took a chunk out of me, look. It's okay though, just a bug or something, probably not serious.'

'What?' Frank looked puzzled. He strained to see the injury. 'It's hardly a scratch. Got another arm, haven't you?'

'Didn't say it was bad, Frank. Just don't want to be eaten alive by lots of creatures, that's all.'

Frank blew his cheeks in frustration. 'Can you see all that forest and jungle out there, this side and over there?' he was pointing, as if Rig couldn't see it all. 'Lots of life in a rich habitat, thousands upon thousands of insects, any one of them could land on you, right?' He shook his head and walked on.

'Yeah okay, got it.' Rig said defensively. 'I'm not a botanist or nothing, you know. I'm here for you and Flash, that's all.' It was okay for Frank to get shirty now he was sober and on a mission. If it hadn't been for Rig, he wouldn't be in the middle of the jungle on a forgotten island trying to save his own daughter. Maybe they were both just hot and bothered.

The path widened and they hiked in silence for a while, Frank was operating on instinct, and it was leading him to the centre of the island where, Rig figured, instinct would meet and shake hands with failure, and then they would seek out some locals and ask if Flash had actually been seen by anyone. Doing it this way round was wasteful, dangerous, and not a little bit tiring.

Frank stopped, waited for Rig to catch up.

'See that hill over there? We'll take the left flank, keep high as we can, so we stand a better chance of spotting them. Then we'll head in a downward arc, checking our right flank the other side before having a rest to refuel. Right?'

Rig looked at him quizzically, 'So you wanna go round the mountain, that way?' he indicated.

'Well, yeah that's about it.'

'Fine.' Rig headed off.

Fifteen minutes later, Rig rubbed the sweat from his face with a small towel he had attached to his rucksack. The jungle around him was like nothing he had ever experienced, impossible to see far into it although it thinned just up ahead. He approached. Frank sped past and gave an encouraging gesture. Rig spied into a gulley where a stream snaked between boulders and ferns, the sun's beams skimmed through the leaves and foliage of the jungle leaving dapples of dark and light on the water's surface. Some of the leaves were giant. Two would be large enough to cover most small English courtyard gardens. He peeked at the lush greens covering the hill which led to the curiously inviting waters below. He imagined animals lapping water to quench their thirst, ever aware of predators and the fight for survival.

'Don't fall, Riggy.'

Rig stepped away from the voice, startled. 'Damn, I nearly—'

He lost his footing, swiftly followed by his balance, and tumbled down the hill.

'Aaargh …' His body rolled over as legs and arms struck outwards looking for purchase. His stomach flattened the undergrowth so effectively that a trail grew as he sped into the arms of accident and humiliation. This was familiar and frustrating.

His detour halted when his face plopped into a shallow part of the river, shorts ripped and loose, and a glimpse of his naked powder-white buttocks reflecting the harsh sun for all the island's inhabitants to see.

'Riggy, you have your … erm …'

Rig righted himself with a spluttering cough. He wiped his chin and hitched his colourful shorts up with a sideways glance which launched a thousand daggers towards the ghostly figure before him.

'Oh … oh, dear. You blame me for that, don't you? A nice welcome. I must say, I don't need to be here in this hot hellhole.' He twirled and tip-toed away as if the pebbles underfoot were burning him. Humphrey: the cloudy apparition who could walk on water and disappear in a flash. And that's exactly what he did.

Flash.

That's right. She and her family were the priority.

Frank waved from on high, Rig returned in kind, and realising his arm was itchy, gave it a good rub like a brown bear. After a few minutes of struggling to get back where he started, Frank checked him over.

'Are you okay, boy? Any breaks, cuts, or other injuries? Don't scratch that insect bite, you'll only make it worse, look – you've already got blood all over your sleeve.'

'Yeah alright, you ain't my dad.'

The expression from Frank cooled suddenly.

'Sorry,' said Rig. 'Didn't mean that.'

'Alright. Well, how you feeling in yourself? Only the gods know what's in that stream down there. Didn't drink it did you, eh?'

'I'm fine.' Rig tightened his waistband with the drawstring. 'Let's, y'know … get this done, Frank,' he said striding purposefully toward the mountain.

Chapter 23. Humphrey the Ghostly Traveller

Rig was super-tired. Taking a rest every thirty minutes was not ideal, and Frank considered every pause a risk to Aurielle's status as a living daughter. But Rig's body told him quickly what he already knew, fitness wasn't his thing. Trekking across mountains and terrain better suited to apes was tiring in such heat. He desperately wanted to find Flash and get her home, if she would allow it, but his stomach and general body tone was not built for commando raids in hostile places. Rig was designed for fighting adventurous battles to the death on his game-station, or sitting in a comfy chair with a hot chocolate to hand.

Humphrey had returned previously with his tail between his legs or would have if he owned one. Rig could tell he was in the mood to chat. Frank listened in as he led their search and rescue mission.

The spectre moved effortlessly as Rig forced his feet to comply with each sunburnt command.

'When you think about it,' said Humps, 'there's not much to see really. These big green palm tree leaves are nice, it's just that when you've seen one. I mean really, you've seen them all, haven't you?'

'Yep,' replied Rig.

'The sand is so dazzling too, almost like it's been bleached, Rig. Don't you think? I suppose in a way it has been, with that hot sun sitting on it every day.'

'Yeah, I guess,' the label in Rig's tee-shirt scratched the burnt skin of his neck.

'Must be difficult for you, I mean not long ago you were in a cold castle with Frank chatting to that horrible man-god, now you're in a sort of paradise, Riggy. Aren't you?'

'That's right,' Rig paused, hands on hips, took some deep breaths.

'Not another break, Rig. Let's keep going, eh?' Frank said. He didn't wait for an answer and pushed ahead.

'Y'know, Riggy, I think I might have met that bearded chap before.'

'You said, yeah.'

'Don't know where from, that's all. Wonder if I wrote about him.' Humphrey pulled his notepad from his back pocket and turned to a page in its middle, then turned a few over, and a couple more. 'No, can't see nothing here, Rig.'

'You've got a nice big "HP" on the front there Humps, no way it can be mistaken for anyone else's.'

'Oh, thank you. Yes, I like the style, nice and big, aren't they? I wonder what they stand for?'

'Your name?'

'Oh, could be.'

'What's your surname, Humps?'

'Um … no-one's ever asked me that before, mind you … I don't get asked anything anymore … I really like it when we talk, Riggy.'

Wearily, Rig set after Frank. It wouldn't be too long before they found someone or something of interest, surely. The path they had taken was winding round a mountain covered in jungle, but below they could see a vista of green stretching out to the coastline where the turquoise sea gradually gave way to darker blues.

Humps continued as Rig slogged up the incline, he was searching his book furiously.

'I really can't find anything. Don't know it, Rigs. Don't know my own surname.'

'What did your parents do? Where did they live? Any memories or notes about that?

'Well … err I don't know. Never crossed my mind.'

The light and heat of the day made Humps harder to see but his voice was as clear as the island's tropical streams, especially as he was yakking into Rig's earhole.

'Ah! Here it is. "Dad: very worried, must come home, don't know where he is … etcetera etcetera" that's a strange thing to write, isn't it, Riggy?'

Rig paused, 'When did you write that?'

'What a clever question! You're good at this sort of thing. How are you doing at school? I bet you're heading to the top of the class. I thought you would do well.'

'Thanks, so when did you write it?'

'Write what?'

'The message about Dad worrying?'

'Oh … no idea.'

'Hmm,' Rig took some deep breaths and wiped a sheen of sweat from his face.

'Got your name at the top of the page though. Do you think it's about your dad?'

Rig sighed.

'Sorry, think it might be for you. That's right, I went and had a chat. He's got floppy hair, a very nice slim figure. Um … that might be someone else though. Not sure. Does it sound like him?'

'Probably.'

'He sounds a tad worried. You are okay though, aren't you?

'Of course, I am, I just can't text him because my network provider doesn't extend to Gamma Seven, it's not even that good outside of town.' Rig hustled forward, trying to catch-up with Frank. His friendly ghost followed close by, keen to stay connected and keep talking. He needed the connection and friendship to keep going, but Rig wondered when it might end for him. What happened that Humps didn't go through to the other side?

'Don't suppose I can ask you to tell him and Uncle James I'm okay, and that I'm not on Gamma Seven, just hiking with some friends?'

'What?' said Frank.

'Talking to Humps, sorry.'

Frank grinned.

'Tell who?' asked Humphrey.

Sigh. 'My dad and uncle. If you wrote it down properly there's a chance you'll find what I said.'

'I always remember what we talk about, Riggy. I love talking to you.'

Frank gave Rig a cheeky sideways glance at the comment.

'Sure,' Rig said.

They continued up the incline of the tropical sandy path. It was like walking on a beach but in fact they were climbing up a mountain. Rig's legs were burning, not from the sun but from the effort of hiking, his muscles weren't used to it. And the upside to all this unreasonable work was that he would become half of himself with all the weight he would lose, surely. His t-shirt was dripping like he had jumped in a bath, and his legs glistened with sweat. His chest heaved to suck in more air.

Frank turned to him. 'When we get near the top … we'll take a good break … we'll be able to see a lot of the island … then I can give me head a wobble.' He was a bit breathless but coping well with the march.

'Did … you say … wobble?' asked Rig, also struggling.

'I mean *think*, I can have a re-think what we're doing.'

'Isn't that inventive, Riggy? Interesting what they do with the language, isn't it?'

Rig paused. Frank marched ahead as he often did. Just the thought of a soft bed made Rig want to lie down for a quick kip. Instead, he continued on.

About a dozen minutes later, Rig caught up with Frank at the crest of the hill. Bent double, Rig's lungs were busting for more oxygen, not used to the strain.

Frank put a hand on his back. 'You'll be alright, lad.'

They surveyed the island for a moment like trekkers on holiday, taking in the whole of the landscape. It was full bushy greens like broccoli which peppered the landscape seawards occasionally punctured by enormous outbursts of rock. A strip of white lined the raggedy edge of the island before giving way to the glowing azures of seawater which stretched to a cluster of other islands just about visible in the distance.

'Oh, it's heaven here isn't it, Riggy? Don't you think, Frank?'

Rig looked at Humphrey. 'Yeah, I guess it is.'

'Speaking of that,' started Frank, 'when—'

'Doesn't matter right now, Frank,' said Rig quickly, wanting to avoid any quicksand-conversations about what happened to Humps and where he would end up. Now was not the time for it, but they would talk about it. They had to.

'I love stories. Don't you both?' asked Humps.

'Yeah,' said Rig.

'You can say that again, lad.'

'I won't, there's really no need,' replied Humps somewhat perturbed. 'Anyway,' he continued, 'did you read about the legend on the boat on the way over?'

Rig shook his head.

'No,' replied Frank into the bristling, burning air.

'Well, it said a powerful dragon, Sri Gumom, was travelling to see his sister across the South China Seas but the God Rama refused him permission. The moment the creature touched the sea to hunt for fish, he turned into stone. The dragon was frozen as rock for all time. That rock is this whole island! And now the only power the dragon has is to decide who can leave the island. Interesting local myth, isn't it? I love stories. So don't upset the dragon! Would you like to stay here forever, Riggy?'

Rig and Frank headed off.

'Hey! Wait, wait for me, what did I say?' squealed Humps. 'There's no need to wander off, I mean … really! I was only trying to educate you.'

'We need to get going, I need to find me daughter, don't you see? Her life is in danger, there's no time to chin-wag. C'mon Rig.'

'You ungrateful lout!' Humps shimmied after them, complaining. 'I wish you could see me Frank, you'd know how cross I was. I mean, honestly … you two! You can at least walk and chat, can't you?'

'I suppose so, sorry,' Frank said out loud picking up speed.

'Yeah, I'm sorry too,' Rig offered, trudging behind.

Rig turned in time to see Humphrey disintegrate, arms folded moodily, until his image was washed away entirely by the sun's penetrating rays.

Chapter 24. King of Monsters

It walked the land afraid of nothing.

The atmosphere was sprinkled with the rich scents of creatures and fauna, a few were complex, others basic. But one or two were sharp on the senses. And because of this, the subtleties of some were hard to discern but it knew all of them would become familiar in the end.

There was a feeling of coming home, of reassurance, which was unexpected but pleasant. A flat surface on a moss-covered rock lay ahead. Perching on top gave an elevated view of a natural spring surrounded by palm trees and boulders, with huge ferns overhanging the water. A clearing of hundreds of metres surrounded by forest gave a partial view of an inlet to the ocean. To the side and rear were the beginnings of the gushing rainforest for which it longed to explore, but certain primal instincts wouldn't allow this, not yet.

So, it waited.

A small mousedeer trod hesitantly into the clearing, checking each way as though crossing some great highway, moving forward gradually without snatching at the grass to fill its belly, acting against its nature, its own needs.

The animal was watched by the new predator, coolly.

A group of small macaques arrived with uncharacteristic quietness, as though driven by some unknown force. They gathered with others arriving after them: porcupines, black and red squirrels, large lizards and other small reptiles, and a threesome of pythons. Those that were not already naturally skimming the floor with their chests arched their backs. Stooped, they crept forward in a hypnotic and silent state of respect. A flurry of birds swarmed from the sky in a multi-coloured spectacle, landing to the left side as a hoard, waiting. Other creatures joined the menagerie in spurts of urgency, rushing into the safety of numbers, even if not of their own kind.

It looked on with a mixture of indifference and loathing.

As the island's animal kingdom waited, gazes lowered, and an interesting phenomenon occurred. Behind them came things from the jungle, things which had no name or equal in species. A creature as tall as the largest trees plodded awkwardly from the rainforest as though entirely made of bamboo, its head barely noticeable from its spindly body. It had lengthy poles for arms and legs covered in spikes. Following this, a large muscular monster, bear-like, crashed forward and lumbered to an immediate crouch. The bamboo-like creature kneeled. More came. A grey bat the size of a family car swept to the rear of the group, its orange eyes blinking, fangs dripping – it lowered its head. Others followed, including a large band of pygmy tribesmen who shuffled forward as one, spears and axes at their sides, mouths foaming – all with their heads down.

Unimpressed with the audience, its hand peeled the last of its pink human skin from an arm, examined its texture and licked its surface. It then gnawed on the remnants to get an idea of the flavour. The monster rubbed the scales of its powerful legs, then picked the last clumps of flesh from its hands, discarding some while chewing on the more tender parts, ignoring the sores and lesions it had created. Soon the transformation would be complete and Prod Visceral would be a mere memory, and that memory would be forgotten. Unrecoverable.

Still here.
The monster leapt into the air and shrieked. 'Noooooooo!'
Yep.
It scanned its kingdom of trembling animals below him, all now seeking the comfort of soil and muck wherever they could, getting as low as their bodies would allow. Some managed to bury parts of themselves. They were a sorry bunch of odd creatures, some natural to the island and others borne out of a toxic mixture of poison and negative particles of magic, none of it mattered any more. All of it was his in whatever form. He admired his own seven feet worth of bulging muscle and scales. The new him. Feeling peckish, he launched into the air. The macaque had no chance. He crushed its spine and tore each limb from its screaming body, blood and matter splashing carelessly. His victim's still-warm muscles and tendons twitched in spasms as he chomped on them. He ate hungrily barely aware of the nearest animals dashing for cover.

The others waited, shivering in anticipation of their King's next move.

Chapter 25. Crash

'Watch out!' yelled Aurielle.

The jeep swung aggressively, they all gasped, a second violent jolt to one side, they turned, and in a split second the bonnet smashed against something hard, Aurielle and Blue soared into the forest brush through the open window, shrieks and curses filled the air.

The pair landed with a bump, inches from each other. Their eyes met.

'Ugh!' moaned Aurielle.

'What?'

Aurielle rolled and jumped to her feet, rubbing grass and thorns from her arms. 'Scarlett, Henni ... you okay?'

'Just some bruised ego,' Crook replied.

'Get clear of the jeep! Now!' Blue demanded, already moving away.

They scattered in a rush.

It exploded in a deafening boom. Aurielle shielded her head.

A fire burned from the bonnet of the old jeep, as noxious fumes filled the atmosphere.

The flames grew taller than the nearest palm tree, a dangerous mixture of petrol and oil burning with the flames catching whatever else it could feed on. Aurielle was just pleased they were all in one piece. The injuries could have been horrific, fatal. Henni's tail swished loosely, happy to be anywhere with any company. Scarlett stared into the flames as though a message for her was hidden inside. Blue could care less, enjoyed the change of pace most likely.

'Oh dear ... could have been very bad that,' said the ghost standing to Aurielle's side.

'You!' she said accusingly.

'Me? What about me?' the ghost said tottering backwards.

Scarlett stepped forward, 'It's alright ... it was an accident, no harm done.' Her look switched back and forth between Aurielle and the apparition.

'Who you talking to?' asked Blue.

'Oh my gods!' shrieked the ghost who bunched his shoulders and gathered his hands up as though scolded by the sight before him.

Henni ambled forward with a happy tail swish. 'What is it? What's happening here, miss?'

The ghost froze with a look of horror painted on his face, he slowly dissolved.

Aurielle and Scarlett turned to Henni.

'Problem?' asked Blue.

'What I done, then?' Henni put her claws where her hips might have been, her tongue lashed round her snout with a slobber.

Crook put a palm of reassurance on Henni's ridged back. 'Nothing to worry about, it's all cool. It is.'

'Will someone tell us what's going on?'

'Chill, Blue,' said Aurielle. 'A phantom appeared in front of the car, we crashed, and he decided to go when he saw you.'

'What? Stop kidding me.'

'Serious. Well, look at you.'

It rained.

'Oh.' said Crook, rubbing her hands in the drench.

The fire still raged. The jeep was useless, and the storm wouldn't change that. Henni's lizard-tongue licked at the air and pit-pattering rain. Blue looked at her in disgust.

'We should split up,' said Crook. 'Henni and I could get another jeep, or some help at least. I should be safe with her.'

'Good idea. Any home-grown monsters should leave you alone with Henni at your side. While you're getting help, Blue and me … we'll go find this negative pool and get a water sample, we'll meet you back at the cove, where we came in.'

It looked like Henni was considering what Aurielle had said, it was hard to tell.

'Lovely, lovely, isn't it?' the reptile suddenly burst into a clap in her excitement, 'another new adventure. Be good fun Scarlett, won't it?'

She smiled and gave Henni a hug.

'Hold on you lot. Don't I get a say?' moaned Blue.

The rain turned torrential, sheets of it dropped so they could hardly hear each other.

Aurielle's sopping hair clung to her cheek and neck. 'Go on then,' she hollered over the din.

He glanced into the undergrowth, hesitated, not sure what to add as buckets of water poured over them. His gaze flicked to Aurielle and toughened, 'I agree,' he finally said with pursed lips.

'Well done, Blue,' Aurielle swivelled to Crook and pointed further along the track. 'Keep to the road,' she shouted, 'head east and be quick, try not to get yourself killed.'

Scarlett gave a mock salute to Aurielle, then a big hugging squeeze. Henni copied the salute, but Aurielle put her hand up to stop Henni from going further, the dinosaur slouched a little so Aurielle gripped her scaled shoulders and kissed her crocodile skin cheek. Henni bounded after Crook, who was already on her way, tail swooshing furiously which only served to slow her down.

Blue was already in the bush, 'Let's find this spring-water and get out of this overgrown banana plantation.'

Aurielle dived in after him wondering why a ghost had appeared on a remote tropical island, whatever the reason, she was ready to call on Midnight and Red at any moment.

Chapter 26. Well

They had marched as a legion of two to the next ridge, the one after that and then the next hill. Frank had already started down the other side; Rig reckoned his companion's energy was increasing while Rig's had abandoned him some time ago. He sat at the hill's peak and took in the view. The skyline was darkening fast, and Rig could see a wall of rain approaching the island's coastline. It wouldn't be a problem; Rig was already drenched from his own body-sweat from the sweltering hike. If anything, it would be a welcome shower. He spied Frank rushing back up the hill, thunder in his eyes.

He stood over Rig. 'What you doing? Time's running short, I've got to find her. I want my daughter back and you're sitting there having another break while she's in trouble, probably alone with some terrible people, like, only gods know what might happen to her. Why are you so unfit, lad? We could've been way forward.'

Movement in the distance caught Rig's attention. 'Yeah, we could've been so far forward that we were back at the Cat and Mustard Pot.' Rig bent his neck to get a better view.

Frank lowered to his knees, 'I'm sorry, yeah,' he rubbed his face, 'we wouldn't be here if it weren't for you. I just want to see her.'

'She might be over there.'

'Eh?' Frank did a one-eighty-degree turn. A beacon of oily black smoke puffed into the air in the distance, a plume that could be seen from anywhere on the island. A call for help or a bonfire gone wrong. Either way they should find out.

'Time to go cross-country,' Rig suggested.

'Yes, you're right, laddy.'

Frank embraced Rig, which took him by surprise. But he had to admit was an improvement on a fist in the face, which was a common experience for Rig during his more dangerous excursions. Putting his memories of wicked sorcerers, monsters, and deep underground dungeons aside, Rig followed Frank into the dense undergrowth, heading in the approximate direction of the smoke.

Making progress was awkward and at times just impossible. This was mainly due to a lack of nicely concreted pathways and the reality of an impenetrable jungle, which Rig had the distinct feeling was directing them through areas which it had predetermined somehow. In no sense that was reasonable did Rig feel they were in control. They had no equipment to hack through the forest's wild and enormous foliage, and he suspected they had veered so much from their original course they could even be headed in the opposite direction. To add insult to their helplessness, it was raining. But it wasn't normal rain, not what you'd usually find in England – changeable with light winds.

Instead, it was heavy, noisy, saturating and persistent. And because of that it was persistently annoying.

'Can't you stop this?' yelled Frank up ahead.

Rig climbed over a moss-covered tree laying in his path, and started on the next. It was like an assault course but without any end in sight.

'What?' he shouted above the din.

'You're a powerful wizard, use your magic … do something!'

'I could pull a rabbit from a hat? Not too good at changing weather systems.'

'Eh? Speak up lad.'

'Forget it.'

The gods continued to throw buckets of warm water on top of Rig. The rain battered palm leaves. 'STOP!' shrieked Rig.

They froze.

Rig reached forward and tugged on Frank's shirt. 'Step back slowly, no sudden moves.'

He must have heard him, because Frank stepped backwards in slow motion, carefully, as if broken glass were under them. Ahead and slightly to the right were a set of eyes on the side of an enormous oval-shaped head. Its camouflage meant it was hard to see where its body started and ended. Its eyes flipped back and forth as though monitoring the area with a natural radar warning system.

Climbing over fallen tree branches backwards in the monsoon was challenging. Rig hooked one leg over at a time, in reverse. The downpour must be confusing the animal's senses, it hadn't noticed them, they continued shuffling while the giant bug's eyes scoped the area.

Why did life have to be so difficult? Where was Flash?

The flood halted as fast as it started, so they both slowed but carried on dripping. The air smelled fresh and clean like nowhere else. Droplets pattered to the undergrowth from the canopy above them, dancing from leaves to vines to unwanted tourists.

Rig's shoe hit a log with a dull thwack.

He looked up to see the monster's head peeking forward on the long stem of its neck, eyes twitching frantically.

'Ah,' Frank said.

Two large black pupils locked onto them. It pulled its long spindly legs from behind the tree revealing its full body – an odd shaped animal with stumpy arms and long legs, big head and large flat face.

It launched at them, running like an ostrich.

Frank yelped.

They ran as fast as they could. Rig watched as Frank sprinted past him.

'Hey!' screamed Rig. 'Wait for—'

Rig's left shoe snagged a vine, he crashed into the bushes and then …

… suddenly dropped.

His arms grabbed uselessly at soil in the darkness, legs kicked pathetically but his shoulders splashed into watery mud with great skill, and then hit something solid and unmovable.

'Ow! Hell!'

'Rig!' Frank shouted from somewhere above.

Rig gripped his right wrist as electrified currents of nerve-jangling pain surged through his whole arm. Someone had connected him to the mains and hit a big switch. He gingerly wiped mud from his mouth with his left hand, looked up to see light from the green world he had just been running in. His damaged arm throbbed. He tried to sit up, couldn't use his right arm. He was some thirty or so feet down, caught in a pit, or trap? He looked up. The sides had ridges, not deep enough to stand on, get any purchase.

What would do that? Maybe it was made entirely by nature. Unlikely. Too circular anyway.

    He needed help. 'Frank?' he called out.

    What happened to him and that reptile?

    'Fraaank!' he bellowed.

    No amount of shouting was bringing Frank back, if he was with them at all. Rig checked his elbow, pressed on the bone. Checked further along. He winced. The pain was real, undeniable. Must have broken it.

    Flash's rescue was not going well.

    He closed his eyes and focussed. Must engage his inner magical potential with the charged molecules surrounding him. He sensed their presence; their signature sang in his ears as they collided and started to tingle under his skin. It was so familiar now. His arm reacted positively to the charged particles, didn't hurt so much. How long did a smashed arm take to heal in a wizard? Unusual conditions, lack of rest, jungle trekking to be done. Impossible to know. Rig sat back in the gloom to assess his options. He could feel magic but using it was tricky, maybe impossible. Who can summon magic and discharge it when their arm was damaged? The particles would heal the arm quicker than usual, of that Rig was sure, but left-handed magic? Was it possible?

    Rig leant back. His head missed the wall of the well.

    Behind him was a tunnel, two feet wide. He struggled to his knees, peeked inside. Lightless. Endless? Most likely leads to a secret island plateau of long grass or a thriving banana plantation, or something like that but with happy people and a delightfully peaceful cafe with a surprising range of drinks and cakes for visitors.

    Not a chance.

    Who or what made this? More ridges. Why? He knew it wasn't going to be a helpful, happy farmer. Rig already had a lot of experience with monsters deep underground, he wasn't keen to repeat anything.

    The tunnel appeared to be the only way out available to him.

    Deep sigh.

He reached for his mobile phone, tapped the light on, and clambered into the tunnel trying to stop his head from thinking too much. Turns out the torchlight feature was not so much a feature but an afterthought by the manufacturer, he clasped it in his last working hand, edging forward with a single elbow and shoving his trainers into the earth to push. The light-beam revealed the passageway five feet at a time. The tunnel's contours were smooth, relatively speaking, the route horizontal and straight but also earthy in smell and mind-splittingly claustrophobic. Otherwise, no problem at all.

He heaved himself forward. The pain in his right arm subsided to a severe ache – progress. Except now his left shoulder was beginning to complain after a full ten minutes of limping forward on his belly like a giant disabled mole, just without so much hair, or legs or whiskers. Was the tunnel getting smaller? No. Maybe he should adopt a vegan diet, lose a few kilograms. He hauled his body along the dirt. It would be more difficult to go back than go forward.

What if he needed to?

He wouldn't.

The soil was a bit loose. What if it all came down, sealed him off? It won't. Then again it might. Anyway, he had escaped that giant reptile successfully without needing to resort to magic. He had been very restrained in wielding his magic for a while now. Not something to be frivolous about. It had to be taken seriously, used conservatively and thoughtfully. Unless he was about to be murdered, then anything goes.

But were there any spells for making travelling underground easier? None came to mind. It was definitely getting more difficult. Was he going uphill? Seemed like it. Nothing like an extra challenge to make life more interesting. He paused for a rest. No point in rushing. If it wasn't for the fact that he had no space, or fresh air and no way back … it would be a perfectly safe way to travel, even if extremely tiring. At least he was on his own.

Rig stopped.

The cheap torchlight had found the last idea to be entirely false.

A huge snake, no … worm was lying opposite him. There were no eyes but a large pair of lips, which Rig feared might lead to a large mouth. At least the mystery of the ridged tunnel was solved with creature's segmented body showing how they could have been made. He tried wriggling backwards, it was slower than going forwards, he doubted he could out-wriggle the worm in a race. He might need to try left-handed magic, which meant dropping the phone.

The giant earthworm opened its mouth and lengthened its slimy body, unfortunately this had the effect of moving the creature closer.

Ah. That's how it moved.

It was an interesting answer to a question which might be his last. With few or perhaps no options open to him, Rig screamed.

'Help! Help!'

It moved again.

Rig tried harder. 'Heeeeeelp!'

Chapter 27. Reunion

She hacked at it repeatedly, and the tangled vine finally came away. The going was slow, but they had made good progress, especially since the storm had blown out. The only difficulty was that she had started to imagine she was cutting into the neck and arms of Blue. He was so annoying to travel with, she could easily turn on her feet and lash out. Shouldn't be too much longer, they were moving in a downwards direction, which she hoped was where they would find this spring water that was so dangerous.

'They should come and, sort of like, bulldoze a decent road through this, don't you reckon?'

'That's a dumb idea.'

She ducked under some branches and came to what looked like a more worn pathway, recently used by the looks of it. Now she was a tracker as well as a hired Protector. There was always a lesson to be learnt if the mind was open enough and the senses alert.

'Someone's been this way,' said Blue, as he pointed. 'Look, them leaves have been disturbed, see.'

'That's a real help, thanks.'

'I reckon it'll be near here somewhere, going in the right direction.'

'Yep.' There was a slight incline further ahead. She paused. Thick undergrowth on both sides and hard to see much else, except for a small clearing. Now the pelting rain had stopped the birds were chiming again, and there were occasional screeches of animals in the jungle. Monkeys she guessed. The rainforest was waking up, its sounds and smells singing to them.

'What ya stop for? We need to get on and get out. Wouldn't mind a little R-N-R though myself, know what I mean? But we can rest up there if you really need to.'

Aurielle spun on her heels, short swords raised high. She could easily do it, and the best thing was that no-one would know, and sadly... no one would care either. Blue stepped back startled, his big stick already in a defensive position.

'What? What did I say? Chill out will ya ... we'll do what you want, right?'

She lowered Midnight to the level of his chin, her face pinched with concentration.

'If you—' She twisted her head suddenly. 'What was that?'

'My guts doing a flip?'

'Quiet!' She bent her knees, tilted her head. 'Did you hear that?'

'Hear—'

'Shut up.' She stalked forward, bent like a hunter-dog sniffing out quarry.

'What you—'

'Hush!'

'Heeeeeelp!'

'There!' she said, pointing Midnight to the ground. Blue followed her as she scrambled on all fours, searching along the sodden leaves strewn on the forest floor.

'What is it?'

'Quiet!' She held a hand up, indicating he should stay put.

'Heeeeelp!'

There it was again, she put a hand on the floor, there were vibrations, she followed them with her hand, picked her spot. She raised Midnight high and slammed the sword into the earth. It sank a few inches. But was it deep enough?

'Pleeeeease!'

No, not deep enough. 'Get a rock, now. Bash that in,' she ordered Blue.

Jordi-boy Blue searched frantically, nothing. He launched himself on top of Midnight. It sank another few inches. Aurielle put her palm to the leafy floor. No more trembling. And then a shifting of sediment and soil a few feet to her right. She holstered Red and grabbed Midnight, raised it ready to strike.

'Blue, dig there with your stick.'

He gave her a look, then prodded the loosening soil, breaking it up. He retreated.

Fingers appeared. They seemed to be waving. 'Heeelp!'

Blue dug at the ground, shifting some more of the topsoil.

'Hang on, we'll get you out,' said Blue.

Aurielle sheathed her sword and together they dug at chunks of grass and earth with bare hands …until an arm popped out of the ground, and then after a great deal of heaving, pushing, and cursing the back of a head was born from the jungle floor. Blue and Aurielle staggered backwards … the head twisted to reveal the most powerful wizard ever known.

'Hey Flash! I've come to rescue you … if you could just pull me out of here first,' said Rig Penlip in a tone which indicated he really believed it. 'If you could be quick, I have a flesh-eating worm after me down here. It's surprisingly fast.'

***

'I've mashed up my arm,' said Rig spitting grit from his mouth while nursing his damaged arm.

'Unbelievable,' Flash stood arms crossed, 'now I've got two to look after.'

The older boy was digging at Rig's right side.

'Who are you, then?' asked Rig.

'Jordi. She calls me Blue though. I'm leading an expedition, like, to get some water to study for health reasons, y'know?'

Jordi hauled Rig out. Flash turned her back to them and began cutting and chopping at the nearest tree. She went at it continually and with increasing vigour.

'She gets like that,' Blue said gawping.

'Yeah, I know, seen it many times,' Rig brushed himself down.

Flash ripped at some vines, dragging them away from the tree.

'So … you do some magic, then?'

'Sort of … sometimes, if I really need to.'

'Really? Bet you've seen some action though, right?'

'A bit … y'know,' Rig shrugged his shoulders and immediately regretted it, he held his right arm still.

'Sore?'

'Yeah.'

'Why is your skin like that?'

'Why are your eyes blood red? You sick?'

'What? No. Are they? I feel okay, seriously knackered though, I mean it's been a long trek to find her.'

'Anyways, we should get that broken arm sorted out. What ya think, Flash?'

Rig grinned. 'Ha! Yeah, I call her that.'

Flash marched into Rig's face holding a giant palm leaf, wrapped it under his right arm, 'Hold this, here.'

Rig squeezed the fern together. Flash returned with some stringy plant shoots and routed them round his arm and shoulder. She tied it up.

'Rest your arm,' she said sternly. 'No … higher,' she pushed it upwards.

'Ouch!'

She adjusted the knot. 'There, don't move it around.'

'Thanks! So, what happened? How did you escape Blackjack and end up here?'

But Flash didn't reply, immediately walked into the bush instead, following a gap in the jungle.

'Ain't much of a talker,' said Blue.

'I know,' Rig said and went after her. 'Flash wait,' he said, 'your dad's here. We've got to find him.'

She stopped and faced him. 'What? He's here? You joking around?'

'No.'

Her expression was riddled with worry. 'Why is he here?'

'We thought you were in trouble, he sort of insisted.'

Blue joined them, 'Seems normal for a dad to do, right?'

'Shut up!'

Blue shrank a few inches.

'What's wrong with your face?'

'Eh?'

'Your eyes, they're all red, are you bleeding from the inside-out?'

'No. I feel good, just a bit tired, that's all.'

'You were born tired.'

'Good to see you too.'

Jordi stepped forward. 'Let's go, we can talk and walk, right. We need to get this sample and then—'

'No. We find my dad, then get you some water, if we can.'

She looked at Rig in that way which told him she wasn't going to take any prisoners today, or accept any jokes, even good ones and was very likely to kill something.

'Where's my dad?'

'Um ... I last saw him over there,' Rig motioned with a nod, careful not to make any sudden movements which might bring any violence his way. 'We got separated when I, sort of, fell into a hole in the ground.'

Blue sniggered.

Flash twisted, reached up for Jordi's throat and squeezed. 'Laugh again funny boy and I'll cut your nose off!'

'How far?' she said staring at Jordi.

'What?'

'Not you.'

Rig sidled next to her, 'He didn't mean anything. Let him go.'

She released him. 'How far away is my dad?' she said through her clamped mouth.

Blue gave a short series of coughs, 'I wish ... she'd stop ... doing that.'

She was definitely going to kill someone. 'Just over there, I think. We were being chased by some strange looking thing with long legs and serious teeth. Huge, ran like an emu, y'know? Flat face with bulging eyes.'

'You idiot,' she said unfairly, 'why didn't you tell me?'

'I just did.'

He was going to add some more description which he reckoned could be useful, but she ran into the bush, whipping her swords free as she went. Blue and Rig rushed after her.

'Blue, tell him about Prod,' her voice bounced back through the forest around them.

Rig lumbered behind Jordi, who took easy athletic strides after Flash.

'Prod? Prod Visceral? What … about him?' asked Rig already panting. 'Hey! Wait … for me!'

Chapter 28. The Voices

He could see the narrow shoreline to the south, and the hills and rocky outcrops of the north. His green island. A deserted sanctuary which moved and grew at his command. Every living being answered to him, only him. The god of his own world.

They were gliding in a cloudless blue sky with a glorious view of his new kingdom. Far below, animals raced to open areas, others squawked or barked, and trees were shaken in the thickest parts of the jungle, all effectively bowing to their new leader.

New. Powerful. Unchallenged.

To him they were simple life forms of no consequence, the real prize was elsewhere, and this was a footstep nearer the bigger prize that was always going to be his. This was as good as anywhere to start, it was not important, only the final steps had any real meaning. Next for his attention was the young wizard, the most powerful there was, and the sweet expunging of his magical abilities – take away the toy, dominate the weak. With his kind eliminated there would be little need to control or monitor the growth of magic and all its uncertainty and influence.

He would just kill it.

And that means saying goodbye to Aurielle Merlot and Rig Penlip.

They skimmed the treetops at speed, glimpses of chimpanzees, parrots, and others as they flew. The warmth of the winds caressed him as they rose, once again giving a whole picture of his wild and wonderful new home. They soared with a freedom he had only known in his sleep-filled imagination. It was thrilling, exciting. A strong current of air reduced the creature's speed momentarily; the great wings of the cave dwelling demon stretched out beyond him like those of an enormous kite. He watched peaks of waves pepper the ocean below and noticed how its edges smudged from a deep blue to a lighter jade before finding beaches and cliff edges along the island's boundary. Mountains littered his land, forests swarmed wherever he looked, with a few inlets for visitors if they dared, streams and springs hidden beneath the canopies along the denser parts, and …

… something out of place.

What was it?

A solitary cloud in the distance. He had noticed it once before, when he was last here. Before. At the pool he had dived into to avoid the poisonous mass of deranged butterflies. That's right. A single cloud formation in an otherwise clear sky. Why?

They approached it but then, on instinct, he urged the beast to circle.

He studied the undulating land formation.

A fierce glare far below. Something unnatural caught in the sun's forceful light. It was oblong. Man-made. White. A fenced building. North-east of the isle's centre. The nearest large cove further eastwards. What was it? What was it doing on his island?

They arced to one side then swooped in a long descent back towards his platform. They took several minutes to glide and lower until it approached their starting point; his thoughts tumbled angrily at the realisation there was a stain on his natural paradise. The bat-like creature flapped furiously to slow its decent, the noise annoying. It released him onto the rock gently as it landed, like stepping off an escalator. The winged demon faltered slightly on landing, used its claws to grip the rock edge, the scraping of nail on stone could have been inside his head.

He punched it hard in the neck.

It cawed, distressed, and plummeted twenty feet onto a palm leaf and slid to the forest floor in a heap. He watched it stumble away; no doubt glad to have survived the meeting.

There was no point ruling in your own country unless you controlled every aspect of it. He had to know what that building was doing in his kingdom. There was no democracy here, it was about being on top, ruling everything and moving on and upwards.

You are mad.

'Who's that? Not you again?'

You know who it is. I'm coming back.

'I don't think so. Your time is over.'

You don't think. You react. You're animal now.

'You're desperate, nearly dead.'

He moved to take in the panorama before him. It had misted somewhat.

'Oh, you really are impossibly vulgar close up,' said a new voice and unlikely hallucination standing on the end of his ledge.

'What are you?'

'Gods! You are a devil of the darkest sort, aren't you?'

'Spirit or hallucination, I don't care, you mean nothing to me.'

The apparition put its hand on its hips, 'Now ... hold on. There's a reason I came here. Oh, I know.' He motioned towards the half-man. 'Stop hunting animals, they deserve a life too. Um ... I don't think that's quite right.'

'Your ramblings bore me.'

'Ah, that's right ... I wanted to see what ungodly beast was hunting my Riggy, and now I know!' he grinned, then started wagging a finger at the beast that had been Prod. 'You must be the most gruesome living incarnation of evil I have ever met.'

He kept directing that finger at him. 'Half of you is covered in scales, like a lizard and what's going on with the rest of you? By the looks of it you haven't got any skin.'

'Shut up.'

'You would certainly win a prize for the worst looking creature I've ever seen or even heard of, no ... wait, let me see,' the shape of him was faint in the strong light, and it was far from obvious why he was standing before him. The visitor appeared to be searching through a book. 'I've got some monsters listed in here. Let me see, just a minute,' he shuffled through some pages, read a little, and flicked through some more. 'No, funnily enough the nearest I can find to you is a nasty piece of work with a particularly foul moustache and wicked attitude, killed millions from behind a polished oak desk in the nineteen forties. You've got some way to go ... but honestly, you really are—'

'I said, shut it!'

'No, don't think I will. I think I'll continue until you promise ... um, promise to ... er, now what was it? Oh yes, until you promise to leave Riggy alone.'

'He's as good as dead, soon will be, then you can spend all the time you want together.'

The translucent figure was pacing up and down the platform. He was barely even here, but he was the only being he could do nothing about, the dead ones.

'You won't harm a hair on his head, you will abandon whatever ghastly plans you've hatched and slither back under the rock from which you've come from.'

'I'm going to end his days slowly, bring him great pain because of you, and I'm gonna enjoy every succulent second of it. You can watch for free.'

The visitor recoiled dramatically, as if having smelled something so pungent he had to turn away, 'Honestly, you really are a hideous thing, aren't you? Bad parenting I'd say, and maybe something else, something perhaps that is not of your world mixed in. Whoever you were, you are abominable in a cruel and wicked way now, and I'm going to warn Riggy about you. What do you think about that, demon?'

'You're spoiling my view.'

With more complaining, the visitation waddled away into the sunlight where his form merged with the air more fully, leaving him on his perch to wallow in his thoughts about ending magic.

Rig had arrived. Good. It was time to start the party.

Chapter 29. Left-handed magic

They raced through the bush.

'What?' shouted Rig.

The athletic Jordi paused, waited for Rig to catch up. 'I said, we got attacked here. Prod and me. At one of them ponds he was wanting to get some samples of, y'know.'

Rig's shuffling run became a slow plod as he neared, 'Why? What ... for?'

Jordi straightened as though he were about to give a great lecture to a pantheon of university students. 'We was looking for negative pools of magic, they're like a Source ... because that's where these monsters come from. But then it all went wrong, the water was, like, really bad. Prod lost his head and lost control. I spied on him in his luxury penthouse in London. Saw him change. His skin peeled. Went bald. Even starting growing scales and that. Mad. Now he's this, kind of beast after swimming in it, and them creatures that bit me did this,' he said scratching some blue-tinted skin.

'So ...' Rig used the moment to catch his breath, '... he wanted to collect the water sample, study it, and understand how monsters are born out of it, is that right?' His chest heaved to take in the rich island air.

'Yeah, that's about it,' Jordi's attention was elsewhere, looking for signs of Flash further up the track. 'And like I said, it all went wrong. We have to reverse it all; try and get an answer to all this.'

'Alright, so he's lured me here, to find Flash, all this coz he was wanting me?'

'Maybe, I dunno.' Jordi took off.

'Hold on,' urged Rig. 'Why would he want to get me? What have I done? He could've just called.'

But Jordi had already launched into more undergrowth. Cradling his arm, Rig jogged after him, pushing through gigantic leaves, following their trail. His stomach ached from hunger and his legs wouldn't do what they were told. His brain informed his body there was no choice in the matter and to get on with it.

There was an opening in the forest, he could just about see Flash in the distance, she was waiting and waving them forward. She disappeared into the wood; Jordi soon followed. When Rig arrived at the entrance to the next batch of jungle, he eyed Blue ahead of him. He took a right turn so Rig followed after him wondering how long this could really go on. Blue batted leaves aside as he went, although most had already been cut away by Flash so only a few branches remained as they dashed after her. Rig did his best to keep up and protected his arm. The jungle seemed to be leaning inwards, getting closer and closer as they went. The sky now only visible in patches, daylight struggling to find him. He crooked his back to push through some bushes, snagging his shirt, ripping it as he forced his way through, not really knowing where he was heading, just needing to keep up.

His bonce broke through a thicket of bush and when free of it, he immediately halted. The scene was of a creek decorated with ferns and flowers of all colours and types, with flies and mosquitoes buzzing above the water under the partial shade and gaze of numerous gigantic trees and against one of them was the monster Rig had escaped earlier.

Frank was trapped under its foot. The thing was leaning idly against a tree with its midget arms folded as if waiting. It was difficult to tell if the monster was smirking because its mouth was wide anyway.

Flash and Blue were working as a team. He could see they were standing some way apart to split the monster's attention, making the targets harder to hit.

'So Rig, our powerful mage of magic. How about using some of those skills to kill the beast and release my dad?' Flash said, her eyes fixed on the threat.

'Well, I'm all for negotiating and getting Frank released, obviously. I mean, have you tried talking to it? What does it want? What are its terms for releasing Frank? I'm happy to start the conversation, that's a very reasonable thing to do.' Rig stepped closer.

'Thought so.'

'What do you want, exactly?' asked Rig diplomatically.

It seemed to laugh.

Flash hurled a knife into its throat.

The blade pinned it to the tree. Its arms fell limp and boggling eyes rolled out of view. Dead as a dodo.

Blue laughed. 'Good shot, Flash!'

'Help me then,' Frank moaned as he tried to wriggle free.

The duo jumped across the stream.

'Why did you do that? I'd only just started talking to it.'

'You distracted it. Thanks for that!' She raced to her dad's side.

Blue and Flash prized the dead animal's claws away and Frank crawled clear.

'Unbelievable!' Rig waded into the water and climbed the bank to them.

Flash was welded into her dad's arms. He wouldn't let go.

'Yeah, alright Dad,' Flash forced him away. She hated physical contact unless it was combat.

'Good to see you're alive, lad,' he said.

'Thanks.'

'What in the name of the gods happened to your face?'

'What?'

Flash and Blue laughed sympathetically.

Rig's fingers searched his jaw and cheeks. He gasped.

'Red eyes and a bad beard, but that isn't the worst of it.'

'Eh?'

The three of them were staring at his arm. His shirt sleeve had been torn free, which revealed thick brown fur along his forearm.

'Aaargh!' he screeched. 'What's that?' He rubbed it but it wouldn't come off. 'How did that get there? What's happening?'

'Oh, relax.' Flash said. 'You'll be alright in the end. Worst case … you'll just look like a stuffed teddy bear.'

Blue grinned sneakily. Frank chuckled.

'Must have been something to do with that nip you moaned about, on your arm, remember?' Frank approached him.

A bird swept onto Frank's head. 'Ow! Get it off!'

Flash retrieved her swords and hacked at her dad's scalp, slicing the bird in half.

Its carcass dropped by Rig's foot, blood spitting into the sand. The ground nearby was mottled, he looked up to see hundreds of birds diving towards them.

They zoomed at them like large bullets. Rig hit out as they pecked at his skin, Blue turned his stick like a windmill knocking birds left and right as they bombed. Flash whirled her swords, scything all near her into pieces, their insides splattered them all. Frank was bludgeoning them with a broken branch, like swatting flies.

Rig stumbled to the running water as he flapped helplessly at his head, knocking them clear. The ground was a deadly picture with littered with feathers, blood and entrails covering the jungle floor.

More crazed birds came, but Rig took cover behind a tree nearby. He danced about the trunk as they targeted him, many hitting the tree, dropping dazed to the hot sand underfoot. Rig clutched his head and bobbed and ducked as the winged beasts altered their aim of attack as if by command from an unseen general.

'They're going for our eyes,' Blue shouted.

'Makes no difference!' Flash replied as the blades of her swords swished in a blur as they tried to ram her face.

Frank had had enough of knocking them out, so took cover in the undergrowth.

'Rig!' yelled Flash. 'It's time to do it! C'mon!'

She was right. Rig summoned the particles of matter as he mumbled the words, pictured what he wanted, he could feel the buzz of the magic particles bouncing through his body, fizzing and...

SNAP!

The birds stopped.

Those nearby launched into the air, others ceased attacking entirely.

And then a storm of gunk rained on them.

Blue wiped some from his tinted hand and examined it. His skin looked like an artist's painting palette. The pitter-patter of dirty rain landing on them, and in the river, sounded out. A theme tune to their trip so far – sick and dangerous.

Rig examined the white and black goo decorating the riverbank and his legs.

'What have you done?' screamed Blue.

'Rig!!' called Flash while shielding her face.

It was raining bird mess.

'What did you do, boy?' said Frank as he stepped into view by the forest's edge.

'I meant to knock them out, that's all, stun them a bit. I didn't want to kill any of them.'

'Rig, it's raining bird poo on us. For the gods!' Flash took cover.

Blue followed.

'Sorry!'

'You've given them all dodgy stomachs and they've unloaded on us!'

Flash was cleaning her swords in the palm trees, 'What sort of magic is that?' She slid them home.

'Um … left-handed?'

'What?'

'Left-handed magic … my right arm's broken, remember.'

'Really? You gotta be kidding me.'

'I said sorry,' he said sheepishly. 'I've never had to draw on magic that way, calling on it like that … it's really different.'

'Give me a break.'

Frank wandered towards them, his eyes rooted to one spot. 'Hey, look I think we all need to calm down, right, we've got more problems here.'

Rig found what Frank had been staring at. 'Oh.'

'Hmm,' Flash muttered.

Blue strode forward, spinning his staff acrobatically. 'Excellent!'

The monster was hard to miss, well over six feet of brawn with three horns sticking out of its head, its mouth was in urgent need of dental treatment and had been for some time. Its incisors were protruding outwards which were only matched for oddness by its nose, which seemed to be some kind of weapon, it was so bulbous that Rig thought it could do some real damage close up. It had the expected two arms with the equally predictable long talons growing from its hands, which looked efficient enough to hook out an eye quite easily. It was a regulation monster, not overly surprising but certainly dangerous. It was neither animal nor human in form, more a mash-up of the commonest monsters.

And then its mother arrived.

She appeared from the opposite direction down-river, twice the size, twice as ugly.

'You take the little one,' said Flash.

Jordi watched Flash head the other way towards the big mama, disappointment etched across his blue face.

Frank was pointing at Rig.

'What?' he asked.

A cursory glance to his broken arm revealed fur poking out of his make-shift sling, it was getting worse whenever he used magic. Why? It didn't make sense. He went to the stream and found his reflection.

'Oh, no.' The hair on his face made him look like a mountain hermit, he hadn't started shaving but soon he would need hedge trimmers.

When he looked up, Flash was swirling her blades like a windmill as she approached the giant monster mum. The beast moved slowly but there was obvious power. Flash jumped and rolled as the monster tried to grab her, it whipped a claw through the air. She ducked, stabbing a sword at its knee. It dragged a leg clear just in time – stalemate. Still alive, neither getting the winning blow.

Blue was battling with the younger one. Dodging a hammer fist, striking it with his long staff.

What could Rig do? If he used his magic, he was going to become a jungle monkey himself before long, but he couldn't see his friends suffer.

'Can't you help, Rig?' shouted Frank from the forest opposite. 'Can you see anything we could use?'

'I ... I don't know what to do.'

'Just do something.'

The bushes rustled opposite. Rig looked into the merging greens before him, trying to spot the threat. It was impossible to see anything past the initial line of trees. Rig glanced left and right. The two beasts with semi-circular noses battled with Blue and Flash at either end of the stream. Rig's feet fidgeted. Run or fight? With one arm? Rig turned and ran. He raced towards the river; he'd leap over it easily.

He tripped; legs tackled. He thumped into the riverbed, face buried in the water – not again. He struggled to his side to find a tribesman the size of a child grabbing his shorts, pulling him closer, his mouth foaming, eyes wide with fury or fear and the bone through his nose wriggling.

'Get off!' said Rig batting the pygmy's hands away.

'What?' shrieked Rig, as if the native was going to have a chat.

He wrestled to get on top of Rig, pawing at him, his hands slapping Rig across his cheeks one after the other, then he searched his pockets as the pygmy's mouth dripped bile onto Rig's face.

'Get off!' Rig screeched.

THWACK!

The possessed boy bounced from Rig's midriff. Frank appeared above him with his extremely annoyed teacher-face on, half a tree in his hand. He waved the branch at the native threateningly. The boy scurried off like a demented squirrel.

'Get up Rig, look.' Frank pointed.

A large snakehead the size of a dinner plate appeared, its tongue licked the air as if tasting it before writhing forward, left then right checking each way as it approached, ignoring the carcasses of wildlife in its way.

Rig got to his feet but faltered, he leant on Frank.

The harsh midday sun was not hiding, and the innards of the birds were beginning to swelter and stink. Flies harassed the dead bodies. It was all Rig could do to avoid purging his own guts. Meanwhile, Blue and Flash were still in mortal combat with the over-sized horned beasts, thrashing and shouting.

Frank turned to Rig. 'We need to get out of here.'

The trees shook again, and a gang of pygmys appeared, eyes glaring and mouths gaping as they shook in a mixture of nervous excitement and rage. And this time they were armed.

He noticed Flash glance towards him.

'Run Rig, run! I'll find you!'

The pygmys faced them in a line, six altogether. They fanned out to spread the threat, they inched forward, their eyes on stalks as they peered at the out-of-town visitors. The anaconda slipped forward silently until it was close enough that Rig could see puss streaking from its eyes. They were all half-crazed in some way, had to be. There was a meanness in the pygmys' eyes, they looked hungry, driven – or just mad-bonkers. Either way, Rig didn't like the look of the bones dangling from their necks. He didn't want to be their next takeaway meal.

'Do something, use your magic, quick,' Frank urged.

The tribesman edged closer with raised axes and spears.

There was a loud melodic tinkling sound.

Its electronic tune filled the glade's atmosphere, reaching into the depths of the jungle.

Every monster halted, transfixed. Blue and Flash looked across; their attackers gawping at Rig.

His phone vibrated in his pocket. He took it out. 'Sorry,' he croaked, 'just a minute.'

A raised eyebrow creased Frank's forehead. 'What you doing?'

Rig raised a hand indicating they all wait.

The monsters looked on, puzzled. The snake paused and sniffed the air impatiently looking for a reason for the interruption.

Rig pressed the answer button.

'Rig, is that you, are you there? Rig?' asked his dad urgently.

He grinned. 'Dad! Yes, it's me, I'm fine.' He said realising he wasn't really, arm in a sling and surrounded by nasties.

'Where are you? I'm coming to get you.'

The pygmys took a moment to chatter amongst themselves while mummy-monster was preening her fur, patiently. Junior was sharpening his fingernails, giving Blue angry looks.

'What's going on?' asked Flash.

Blue was shrugging, asking the same.

Rig gave a thumbs up, 'But how can you reach me here? Where are you?'

'Never mind that. Are you okay?'

Rig's gaze swept the clearing, the situation wasn't great he had to admit. He could do with a little help if he was honest. He frowned. The tribesmen were now practising their thumbs-up signs to each other. Weird.

'Rig?' said Frank. 'C'mon.'

'Oh, hurt my arm a bit, but I'm okay, mostly.' The tribe stepped forward. 'Actually … it would be kind of good to see you. Soon.'

As if they understood, the gang of half-naked cannibals rushed at them.

'Hell!' shouted Frank.

'Run!' barked Flash.

Rig dropped his phone, readying his good arm.

'Rig!' He could just about hear his dad's voice as the first pygmy attacked.

Franked knocked one clean off his feet with a hefty whack.

A native lunged at Rig, he stumbled sideways just avoiding the short knife, he must use his magic, had to. The two circled each other. Rig shuffled, keeping out of his way. Frank knocked another to the floor.

'Rig!' shouted Frank.

'Rig, do it!' screeched Blue as he fought.

Three of them launched at Rig from his side.

'Nebula!'

A mist formed at Frank's feet. The tribesman slowed. The fog swirled as if pushed by a coastal wind to Rig's feet.

Too slow.

They jumped at Rig.

He dropped to the ground; the men clattered to a heap. Rig moved, suddenly aware of his knees squelching in the bird droppings and torn flesh, he clenched his teeth. Frank caught another square in the jaw as the mist grew about them, growing heavier. Rig scrambled away from groping hands. His magic had finally worked, been useful. He stood.

His head snapped backwards from a fierce tug. Rig pushed his head back hard, his skull cracked someone behind him, they both dropped. The little man moaned, but as Rig's elbows stabbed him the in the chest, he grunted and sort of squeaked.

Then, in the shroud of the hazy weather Rig had created, he stood and backed off.

'You alright, Rig? Where are you?' Asked Frank.

'I'm fine,' said Rig from inside the fog.

'Let's get out while we can, lad.'

'Sure,' he was disorientated. 'But which—'

His feet were caught, yanked with speed. 'Aaargh!' He hit the ground with a crunch. His legs squeezed tighter, trapped. 'Help!' he shouted.

The mist grew thinner, and Rig realised the anaconda had coiled round his lower half and was slithering up to his chest, wrapping him up. He barely had one hand to defend himself. Frank kicked a pygmy and threw another over his shoulder.

'Rig!' Frank grabbed the snake, pulled on its body. He couldn't move it.

Rig tried to kick out. Stuck. Its eyes glowed. Rig was the prize; it was mesmerising in a non-magical, terrifying way. Its mouth lined with black gums, its teeth small but deadly like tiny knives ready to grip prey, but its gob was huge, and Rig didn't want to end up as lunch. Magic. What to do? He didn't have a spell that would work on a snake. He needed time. Frank started hitting it, wouldn't budge.

'Riggy! Oh dear! What's happening?' said a whining voice.

Rig looked at Humphrey, 'About time, do something!'

Humphrey reached for his notepad, but a garbled message was no good to Rig right now.

Its muscles squeezed Rig's legs tight, a tongue flicked the humid air and a pair of golden eyes gorged on him as it motioned across his chest, slowly, imperiously its head raised until it was fang to eyeball with him.

The anaconda blinked its crazed streaming eyes.

Rig choked on a breath.

Chapter 30. Strange Battle

A gush of blood hosed Rig's face as the snake's head plopped to his side, gagging was its last action.

'So glad you came all this way to save me,' Flash said irritably.

Rig wiped the goo from his eyes with the last remnants of his sleeve. 'Well, I …'

He wasn't sure what he thought of anything right now. Humps and Frank looked bewildered, and it wasn't even them that had been so close to being eaten by a monstrous anaconda. Frank began pulling the snake's carcass off Rig.

Flash went to help Jordi, he appeared to be struggling with the three-horned son, not surprising after the mother had had an altercation with Flash. The ugly mum was nowhere to be seen.

With typical speed, Flash rushed at the monster toying with Jordi, she ducked a swing at her head and stabbed a sword into his foot. It squealed. Jordi poked at him again and again with the nasty end of his wooden stick. If they weren't going to kill him then annoying him was a good ploy. The shaggy creature started to retreat, he turned and lumbered away, smashing through the rainforest, glancing backwards at them angrily like an irritable teenager.

The stream and glade quietened, birds had flown and the pygmys who survived had skittered away noiselessly. The jungle floor looked like a butcher's chopping board after a morning delivery. The harsh sun was burning them all. He wasn't sure Flash had ever seen much of the sun before and hoped she wouldn't suffer for it.

'What happened to you, Riggy?' said Humps putting his useless book away. 'You're all … well, you're growing into one of them. What happened?'

'Now is not the time.'

'For the sake of the gods man! What are you doing in the jungle, in the middle of South Asia?' Frank asked.

Rig turned to Frank, surprised. 'You can see him now?'

Humphrey waddled to a dark green leaf and pretended to study it. 'Well, that's nice. I could ask you the same thing.'

Frank shook his head. 'Whoever heard of ghosts in the jungle, like? I mean it just doesn't happen.'

Rig struggled to stand. Frank assisted but Rig shrugged him away. 'None of us are experts, Frank.'

'Alright, just saying.'

Flash approached, checking the forest's edge warily.

Jordi trod between the clots of blood and guts in the sand and took a water sample from the river. 'That was close,' he said fastening a lid on a tiny container, 'we need to move on.'

'Agreed,' said Flash, alert as ever, scanning the trees high and low. 'We stay together, we run back to the road, go for help, try, and find—'

'Trouble,' said Jordi interrupting. 'Something in the bushes up there,' he indicated with his staff. 'I'll take a look. Sort it, then we move on.'

'I'll come with you,' Flash said inspecting the blades of her swords.

'No. I'll do it, then we go.'

She let him have the final say and he took off, entering the bush nearby to work his way round from the flank.

Rig ripped some leaves free and wiped the worst of the blood and bile from his hands and face. 'I can't believe we're in this situation again,' he said looking at Flash. 'I mean … why is Prod Visceral after me? Why here?'

Flash slipped her swords into their scabbards. 'I don't know why he wants you, but it all changed for him here. That's what Blue said.'

'I've met him,' Humps said.

'You again. You're the one that caused our crash. Why are you here?'

'Crash?' said Rig.

'A weeny misunderstanding, that's all, no need to be casting blame. We're all here to help each other, aren't we?'

'He's with me,' said Rig. 'I'll explain later.'

'Whoever heard of ghosts roaming the jungle,' moaned Frank.

'Stop your whining, Frank.'

'Yeah, Dad,' said Flash scanning the area.

Humps looked surprised.

Flash shifted her feet, becoming anxious about Jordi, probably. 'So, you said you've met Prod.'

Humps looked thoughtful. 'Did I? Well, I might have done. Possibly. Um... Yes, indeed, I have, once met very hard to forget.' He wafted between Rig and Frank. 'I didn't know him before he had the ... the change, but now he's utterly impossible to look at.'

Rig cleaned his hands on his shorts. 'Yeah, but what does he want?'

Flash almost giggled. 'What do any of these nutcases want? Power. You're envied, Rig. That's why you're a target.' She looked him up and down, 'Hard to believe, but that's the truth of it ... but then no one knows you like I do.'

He turned to Frank, 'Was that a compliment?'

'Don't think so.'

Humps put his hands on his hips. 'I would say not if I was forced at gunpoint, to be honest.'

'You're a ghost, no one can force you to do anything.' said Rig.

'Quiet!' blared Flash, her hand indicating them to hush. She was studying the running water and the perimeter of the glade.

He realised what was wrong. It was too quiet. A silent jungle was not a jungle at all. He strained to hear the slightest move of nature or monster.

At the far end of the glade, a partially scaled, skinless creature dropped from the sky and smacked the earth, landing in a crouch with Jordi slumped under his arm. He let him slip from his grasp and tumble to the floor like a bagful of weekend laundry. He lay motionless, asleep, dead, or paralysed. The winged monster which had delivered this new demon flapped away, its form sufficiently large to cast a fleeting shadow on the battleground before them.

Flash had already moved position, circling the thing to her right, swords drawn. She had her fight-face on. The man-monster flexed its muscles, and a deliberate, thin smirk grew on its lips. It looked as though it had recently been caught and skinned, but some parts were well covered by scales which had a smudgy green and blue tint to them, like a new kind of shiny metal.

'Hell, you're an ugly one,' said Rig.

'Look at yourself, Rig Penlip,' came the reply.

'It talks, you can negotiate,' said Humps. 'Oh, hold on. I think I know this one. Or do I?'

'How do you know me?' asked Rig.

'Everyone knows the story of the wizard boy who cheated death and captured a warlock without using any magic. After all, I was there.'

He gasped. 'Prod? Is that you ... Prod?'

Aurielle had settled into her attack stance, moving occasionally, keeping him alert to her as a threat. The creature that had grown from Prod shifted his head, chuntering under his breath.

'Are you okay?' asked Rig. He immediately regretted it. The bleeding sores on his exposed, skinless arms already indicated, quite strongly, that he wasn't.

He peered at Rig. 'You're becoming one of us.'

Flash snuck nearer, ready to spring.

A pull on his arm.

'You should go,' whispered Frank. 'I'll stay and help her.'

The haze which looked like Humps, gathered in front of Rig. 'He's right, you should go, Riggy. It's not safe.'

'Not safe is my middle name these days, if you know what I mean.'

Prod beamed suddenly and dragged Jordi's torso backwards towards the brush. And then the air grew heavy, darker; the forest around them bristled with intent and the hush turned to a rustle and chatter just as the sun withdrew and the world became a kind of grey, dull sight – entirely opposite to how the island would naturally be.

They looked up as one.

The birds were back.

A hoard of pygmys lined the forest's edge and black shapes formed in the higher parts of the trees. Rig looked about him and became aware of thousands of tiny eyes staring at him, willing his end with no logic, no reasoning or sense to any of it.

He wanted to scream.

***

They were surrounded. The battle they thought they'd survived had barely begun – a starter before the main course. Skirting the clearing and facing them were an animal army: monkeys stood shoulder to shoulder, pygmys were shaking with nervous energy, and the birds circling above had created a gigantic swirling vortex over their heads. There was a sense of anticipation, anxiety and most of all, doom. As he stood watching, the sand under his feet moved. Did he do that? It happened again, more obviously this time and accompanied by the battering of branches.

And then the three-horned mother and son turned up.

Rig eyed the Prod-monster at the far end of the sunless glade, one scaly foot resting on the still body of Jordi.

Gradually, step by step, Flash retreated, turning each way, checking, but at the same time threatening them as she went with her beloved swords now held high in imminent attack mode.

'Form a circle,' she said in a hushed voice.

'What good might that be, Riggy? It's not like you want to have a dance right now, is it?'

Rig turned to Humphrey, 'Is there anything useful you could do right now to help us?'

'Um … I've got this book with good ideas and the like, I'll have a read of that and let you know, just give me a minute,' the faint apparition reached for his back pocket and began thumbing through some pages.

Frank approached Rig, 'What are they waiting for?'

'No idea.'

Flash urged them to position themselves, so they were back to back, facing the baying mob of the island's creatures.

'Prod, let's talk about this,' Rig shouted.

The throng of pygmys rushed at them.

'It's time, Rig! Do it!' said Flash.

He glanced at his furry arm.

A young, small man with wide senseless eyes and a foaming mouth leapt at Rig's head, he ducked, his shoulder smashed the midriff of the native and he somersaulted away with a yelp. Flash cut and slashed, arcs of blood careered over Rig. Frank struck a zombie native across the cheekbone, another taken out by a well-aimed smack at the knees. Rig dodged the thrust of a spear to his stomach, managed to grab it and gave the cannibal a swift kick, the man dropped clutching himself as Rig wrenched the spear free, he immediately used it to deflect the onslaught of the next attacker, too many. He had no choice but to use his magic, which would accelerate his change into one of them. With one arm, he had no chance.

He fell backwards, grabbed from behind. The pygmy was kneeling by Rig's head, anger and hate streamed through his eyes, his bone collection clunked as it moved, and Rig was keen not to be part of it. The man rammed the axe downwards to Rig's jugular.

The pygmy's brain exploded.

Shattered skull, brain and blood matter swept across Rig's stunned expression; the pygmy-native had been knocked backwards by the force. Dazed, Rig stood and watched pygmy heads detonate around him like exploding pumpkins. The accompanying fire-cracker noise suddenly made sense. It had to be some type of high-powered rifle. The attack paused; others reluctant to get their brains blown out of their head.

'Can't seem to find much in my book, Riggy. Are you okay? You look a trifle under the weather, if you don't mind me saying?'

Rig wiped the muck from his thin beard and cleaned his eyes. Frank was breathing hard. Flash scanned the clearing, looking for answers. Frank had lain waste to some natives and was clutching a leg wound but Flash was looking peaky, with limbs and bodies strewn around her like lifeless mannequins from an empty shop window. Prod was searching the undergrowth in a frenzied rage for the new intruder. He pointed a finger at the surging mass of feathers holding a whirlwind pattern above and signalled a search of the nearby jungle.

'Hey! Rig, darling!' came the croaky but familiar cry from Great Aunt Ida.

Rig strained to see, then made out a burst of yellow in the wood. Out of place, man-made – and then the hand of an octogenarian waved at him. He couldn't see it but knew his Aunt's liking for rifles and sub-machine guns. She had the strength of an ox and occasionally the stench of an ox too, but Rig didn't like to mention it, especially as she was particularly talented at saving his life. He knew she was camped up there in the trees with a sniper rifle and a big box of ammunition. How did she get here? Where was his dad?

There was a surge in the forest's trees, the sound of a hoard moving from branch to branch in attack. Rig watched as a blur of shapes headed for Aunt Ida. She opened up. The crack of the weapon ripped through the island's atmosphere, ricocheting through the jungle. The monkeys dropped with a vibrating clatter to the forest floor, but one replaced another, they charged from different directions, but Auntie fired repeatedly and the din grew,

Prod threw a steely look at Rig as rifle shells spat into the forest and wild animals crunched to their death below his aunt.

Oversized rats, squirrels, and a group of muscular bears stood amongst the pygmys facing Rig and Frank.

'What to do, Riggy?'

A line of animals shifted forward … they attacked.

Rig summoned his magical potential and mumbled: 'Iter.'

The wave of creatures rushing at them tripped as their legs turned to jelly beneath them. With a glance from Prod a second wave rushed at them. Claws and axes shaking, animals screeching as they ran at them.

'Rig!' shouted Flash.

'Risus.'

The second wave paused; they had unintentionally blocked the advance of all those behind them. They were giggling to themselves in a fit of hysterics, which was a peculiar sight in the midst of a battle, albeit a strange battle. The remaining army of jungle animals ran at them, shoving the others off their feet out of the way, some were merely clubbed to allow others to push through. Flash knocked two down and wheeled her swords through the neck and stomach of another.

Rig turned in time to see a spear fly at his face. As he looked at it, the rod of the spear slowed almost to a stop in mid-air. He could see how carefully the shaft of the weapon had been shaped, and the stone point crafted into a deadly chiselled point. He watched as the blue and grey feathers stroked his cheek as they passed him, drinking the experience like a boy watching an aeroplane for the first time.

And then he was back. A man took Rig's bandaged arm and bit into it, Rig winced and drove an elbow into the native's cheekbone with a whack. He tottered away clutching the side of his face. Another climbed onto Rig's back tearing at his mop of hair, instinctively, Rig buckled and thrust his hips, so the attacker hurled over his back onto a rotting tree branch, a crunch and crack sounded out as the man's spine snapped.

Aunt Ida fired rapidly again and again, downing the animals around her, with only a brief reloading pause. Frank wrestled with two at once and Flash had chopped and maimed several, making it difficult now to move amongst the dead and bleeding.

More came.

'Oh for the gods!' shrieked Rig as a brown bear clomped forward, nearly twice Rig's height, definitely more in weight. What was he to do with one arm and a growing beard and fur problem?

Before he could think, the bear had Rig clamped in a headlock. Its armpit said a lot about its recent habits and behaviour. Rig choked; the bear squeezed harder. He flailed one-handed like a child, growing weaker, his struggles hopeless against a giant of the forest. His long journey and suffering had come to this, a violent, smelly end under the hairy armpit of a fanatical monster. All of this to save his friend, Aurielle Merlot. Pressure in his head. About to lose it. Go under.

ZAP!

The bear trembled and gave a grisly moan which roared through the trees, its grip loosened.

ZAP!

The bear flinched, released Rig, and stumbled; a burning smell stole through Rig. He coughed and retched, gasped for air.

The bear's hair had been fried, blackened. More cracks of gunfire, shouting. Rig turned bleary eyed to see combat and warfare raging in the semi-darkness, with winged demons circling them, watching, waiting.

There was his dad! On the far side of the stream.

He stood tall, wielding his own magic, firing pockets of energy at the most dangerous animals, zipping bolts of energy into the canopy to warn off marauding apes.

'Dad!'

But how did he and auntie get here? Rig motioned towards him. A hit from his side sent him head-first into the back of a crawling pygmy. Rig flattened him. An enormous cat-like beast pinned Rig to the sandy floor, it raised a clawed paw to finish him. A branch resembling a baseball bat struck the arm of the cat and then crushed its nose into its eyes. It gave a high-pitched scream and pounded into the nearest gap in foliage. Frank nodded to Rig and moved to the next threat, seat pouring from him, his expression determined, mean.

Puffs of sand sprayed into the air as magic particles missed their target. They were slowly getting on top, but the animals kept coming.

'Rig?' shouted his dad. 'Is that you?'

There was fear in his dad's eyes, but he hurled magic spells across the running spring-water, disabling, wounding, or confounding the attackers, small or big in nature, but there were so many of them. Realising the situation was in the balance, Flash chucked a sword to Rig. He knew it was like she was giving him her actual arm, that's how important the weapon was to her. He picked it up.

Rig nodded to his dad.

The three-horned creatures smashed their way back into the jungle clearing, and with a swing of their arm brushed some pygmys from their path. It was chaos. Bodies of birds and animals everywhere, on top of which pygmys laid, either dead or crawling for cover, out of the fight. The hairy three-horns pounded towards Rig. Flash stood in their path; Frank close behind.

'Riggy?'

'Not now.'

The monsters approached Flash cautiously, she leapt left and right to keep them focussed on her.

'Run, Rig, run!' she hollered.

He didn't, couldn't abandon her and his dad after all this time.

More pygmys attacked from the side, Frank took three of them with his lump of wood, but he was limping now, slowing. His dad shot a bolt of magic through one. The three-horn mother tried to grab Flash, but she stabbed her hand and danced out of her way in one swift movement. The other tried to snatch Flash's legs, she rolled free and chopped at the thing's ankles. It shrieked.

Rig's dad zapped the second pygmy battling with Frank, and then the three-horns crashed to the sand-ridden floor, their legs disabled by his dad's brilliant magic. It's what Rig should have done. He rubbed his arm, the fur a terrible reminder of what had happened to him, what *was* happening to him.

They were still dangerous, they hauled on their elbows, grasping for Flash. She cheekily jumped between them and struck out with her sword. The smaller of the two screamed in agony, the other swept Flash's legs from under and she smacked the ground on her back. Still floored, the mother gripped Flash's ankles and launched her into the splattered floor like an unwanted doll. She was going to die.

Rig rushed at the prone monster and hacked at its outstretched arm, it retreated, let go, but the smaller monster snatched his ankle, it squeezed.

'Aargh! No!'

He thought his bones would crack. He sliced at the monster's wrist with all his force, cutting straight through. It rolled and screamed. Its mother flailed for Rig's ankle or Flash's, but she was up and already pulling Rig away. His dad was busy stunning smaller rodents, squirrels, and lizards as they dashed forward and back, making them hard to hit. Aunt Ida had fallen silent. He didn't want to think why.

Bloodied, tired, and a little fed up, Flash yanked him to face a growing hoard near Prod.

Rabid monkeys.

Scores of them.

Frank appeared by his side; Humps had already disappeared.

The monkeys rushed forward on all fours with incredible speed, covering the ground from one end of the clearing to its middle in second. Flash was in her attack stance, Frank ready with a heavy looking branch.

A savaged monkey flew at Rig. He cut downwards, maiming its arm as it rolled away. But another launched at Rig, he was about to strike but the sword was clubbed from his hand, falling away uselessly. He collapsed onto his back, the monkey climbed on him and pummelled his head with heavy blows.

Pistol shots rang out.

The monkey's skull tore apart, and its hairy grey torso slumped from Rig's chest.

Monkeys dropped around him, lifeless, to the bloodied ground. He could see Prod's skinless face was furious.

Rig turned to find someone familiar.

She wore a light khaki long-sleeved top, close fitting green trousers, neck-scarf and a matching hat sitting at a fashionable angle. She strode forward firing the last of her bullets at anything moving near them.

It was Lycka. The God of Chance. She must have opened a portal to get dad and auntie through. It was one of the advantages of knowing a god – interstellar travel.

His old friend and saviour reloaded her gun. She ambled towards his dad. Him launching magic dynamite at pygmys as they scuttled to escape the scene, as she cracked bullets from her handgun at the squirrels and snakes still at the forest's edge, all while the birds above turned in their anti-clockwise formation, waiting.

The remaining hoard of hairy apes hesitated next to Prod. He stepped forward, snarling like a true monster, crazy with anger at the turn of events.

'Rig, you okay?' asked his father hurriedly.

Rig nodded, speechless at the signs and smells of death around him.

'Good to see you, Rig,' Lycka said warmly. 'Sorry I'm so late to the party.'

Rig sighed.

'Her again,' said Flash, recovered and scanning the area. She collected the sword Rig dropped, shaking her head – in disapproval most likely.

Prod stormed towards them. Frank readied himself.

Rig glanced at his dad but he had vanished. Lycka fired shots into the undergrowth blindly, then stopped as suddenly as she started. She sent Rig a look of anguish.

And then a tattooed arm locked around Lycka's neck and snatched her gun.

Blaam.

Flash moved forward, swords twirling high above her head.

Prod paused, surprised it seemed.

The ex-god dragged Lycka by the throat to the centre and forced her to the ground by the riverbank. He aimed the pistol at the back of her head. 'Should have made the deal, Rig. Only wanted me old job back. Now she's gonna have to pay, you all gonna pay. Didn't need to be like this, but then I reckon it's more fun this way.' He cocked the hammer of the handgun with a foul grin.

'Run, Rig!' Lycka shouted. 'It's you they want!'

Flash turned to him, 'Go. I'll sort this. Promise.'

He glanced at Frank, who nodded briefly, then switched his attention to Prod.

Rig took his chance.

He spun on his feet and ran upstream. Unable to avoid the bodies of birds and beasts he tripped, got up and ran as fast as he could following the river into the thicket of forest. He wanted to know where his father was. What had he got him mixed up in? And how was he going to get everyone out alive?

Chapter 31. Aurielle Merlot: Angry Killer, And Hero

'Drop them swords or I'll do her,' Blaam urged.

Prod simply stared at Aurielle, muscles rippling in what was undoubtedly the best demon look she'd seen.

'Better do as he says,' urged her dad.

She never had listened to her dad much, she took a step towards Prod and criss-crossed her swords, the clashing steel echoed through the forest.

'Come on,' urged the new and somewhat ugly Prod. 'Keep coming.'

Sweat trickled down her neck, and her palms were damp too, making her grip more challenging than she would have liked. She glanced at Blaam.

'Question is little man, is that little gun a twenty-eight or a forty-two?'

He wrenched Lycka's head backwards and pushed the nozzle into her face. 'I don't know what you're on about, but it don't really matter, does it? You're done here.'

'See, if that pea-shooting gun is a Glock twenty-eight, you haven't got any bullets left because I counted six shots, if it's a forty-two, well … that's a different story, isn't it? So, Blaam …fallen star and god-killer, how many shots did *you* count?'

Lycka's eyes were fixed on Aurielle, hands clenched. She wants to flip him, maybe, can't be sure. Couldn't put her at risk. She would have to deal with him first, dad knew that really.

'Are you ready, dad?'

'Sure.'

Prod was inching forward.

She did the same. She was going to have to risk it.

Holding Prod's gaze, she took a step nearer and started spinning Midnight and Red.

His skin twitched in delight where his mouth should be.

She sprung to her right, swords about to strike at his exposed neck.

A squawk.

She flinched. Midnight ripped from her fist; Red wrenched from her left hand. Stunned, she watched a giant eagle soar away with her precious friend, and a ball of fur in the shape of a monkey bounded to the wood behind Prod with Red.

A heavy fist struck her face, she flew onto her back. The sun-boiled sand stung her fingers and brought her round.

'You're gonna pay for that, Prod.'

As she stood, she was hit from behind, squashed to the floor. It wasn't going too well. She glimpsed an enormous monkey pound her back, two others tied her hands. She could just about see her father dash into the forest, chased by a score of grey and brown monkeys and a plague of rodents.

It was a rubbish day.

***

The hike was short, but the embarrassment and inconvenience huge. They arrived at a rocky inlet not far from the sea after a good walk. The gusts were stronger here and the view out to sea pleasant or would be if Aurielle hadn't also been given the view of a gang of primates surrounding her. It included Prod who had somehow managed to transform himself into a different creature altogether.

They approached a large tree. Rig's Great Aunt Ida was sitting next to a slumped Penlip Senior and unconscious Blue. Auntie's standard issue walking stick stood perpendicular next to the tree. She must be in her nineties; she shouldn't have come here unless she was one of her famous replica selves. Aurielle could never tell the difference between the fake ones and the real version, and she didn't feel right asking. It was a very tidy trick which helped save them all the last time Rig had been in trouble.

'Oh, Aurielle! How lovely to see you, darling. Are you keeping well? I was wondering how you were getting along.'

'Shut up,' blared Blaam.

'Hi Auntie, I'm good. Sorry to see you in this mess. I'll sort it out soon and we can have a proper chat. Are Blue and Mr Penlip okay?'

Aunt Ida nudged the sleeping Protector. 'Oh, yes dear, just not woken up yet. Probably concussion, no obvious wounds.' She shoved Rig's dad, he seemed to stir. 'They'll be right as rain I'm sure, just need a nap. Don't we all!'

'Sure!' Aurielle plonked under the palm tree, which was spectacular: tall, well shaded with gigantic leaves, a fine view with a reasonable wind to cool them. Being a prisoner was never better. A line of monkeys and pygmys hunkered down in the sun opposite them, although who would end up guarding who was still up for grabs as far as Aurielle was concerned.

Hustled by a lumbering ape, Lycka sat next to Auntie. 'At last, we meet!'

'I guessed it was you, darling. So good to meet you properly after all this time.' They kissed and giggled together.

'I said, shut it!' Blaam took a swig of something and shoved the bottle in his jeans pocket.

Auntie took Lycka's hand and stroked it. 'He's a horrid sort, isn't he? I must say the quality of bad guys has really gone downhill since my day. I should have put a couple of rounds in his head,' she chuckled.

Blaam strode back and forth, an unlikely General.

'You're gonna tell us where Penlip is heading, what powers he's got right now, and then we'll give you a good send off. Know what I mean?'

'Right, so if you want an answer you need to indicate who you're talking to,' Aurielle said helpfully, 'then one of us will know you're trying to communicate. Alternatively, you could try using our names. See how communication can work, Blaam, ex-god and General of failure? And yeah, I'm talking to you, no-one else. Know what I mean?'

'Well said,' mumbled Auntie.

'How's Mr Penlip doing?' asked Lycka.

'He's out of it for now, but no serious injuries that I can see.'

Blaam stomped towards Lycka and gave the nearest ape a kick in the ribs. It howled and fumbled to get clear while whimpering. Curiously, it had half of its right ear sawn off, as if by a serrated knife rather than a rival's gnawing teeth.

Lycka recoiled but Blaam lifted her up by her long-preened locks.

'Ow! Get off me you second-rate gangster.'

He glared at her, nostrils flared, spittle running freely and his nose ring starting to weep a little blood.

'Tell us what we need to know, or else … I'll do it.'

'You've done it already, Blaam, chosen the wrong side. Oh dear, and you wanted to be a god again? It's never going to happen is it, honey?'

He slammed his fist into Lycka's stomach, she folded, crumpling to the ground.

'That's brave,' urged Aurielle. 'Punching Lycka when her hands are tied up. Why don't you release me and try the same thing?'

He grabbed her face with his calloused hands, squeezing hard, 'I'll do what I want, when I want, and won't be told nothing else.'

'How about some antiseptic mouthwash? Just a suggestion. Your breath is as bad as your skin, honestly.'

He spat in her face.

She looked away, rubbing her cheek on her vest. 'Hygiene not high on your list then?'

His face screwed up, although it could have been a snarl.

Auntie Ida cackled with laughter, 'Oh, I do love you, Aurielle! Let me have a go at him.' She turned to Blaam. 'Come here skinny head.'

He looked at the pensioner with disdain. 'What d'you want, granny?'

'See that cut on my forehead?' she said.

He rubbed sweat from his eyes. 'No, what of it anyway?'

Aunt Ida wriggled on her rear to get in touching distance to him, 'Have a closer look.'

He stood by her impressive bright blue trainers. He leaned and peered at the minor wound.

A kick.

He yelped, clutching his knee. A second kick swept his legs from under, he crashed to his back, winded and moaning. Auntie hammered her ankle into his throat as he was lying there.

Choking, he rolled from her before Aurielle could slide forward and help. But on the roasting sands he'd left behind a bottle with a bronze liquid inside. Unaware, he limped to a safe distance from them, coughing and spluttering. The Prod-monster leapt from his special rock and ambled across.

As Aurielle snared the bottle between her feet and pulled it closer, it occurred to her that buying time until Penlip Senior woke up and could use his magic was quite a decent idea, and that riling the violent ex-god known for killing was maybe not the best way forward. Fun though. As for her dad, where was he? And what had happened to Rig? No time for that, the poor soul who took a terrible beating from the biggest ugly stick of all approached them. Prod Visceral, one-time servant to the Oglith clan, a champion for scientific research into negative magic, and adventurer. Now he walks alone, a demon without friends or compassion, or skin and apparently any clothes.

Chapter 32. Blue Awakens

There was no doubt about it, they were the ugliest collection of lunatics she had ever met, and it was shameful to be caught by them. The annoyance was triggered by this fact was giving her actual physical discomfort, which in the end would be incomparable to the amount of pain she was going to inflict upon them. Auntie Ida lobbed a small rock to her with a disappointed look stretched across her lined face. With her wrists tied behind her back, she angled the bottle so she could loosen the cap. She poured the liquor into the sand. She had to get to work before the thing calling itself Prod got too close.

The sun blinked from the bald head of Blaam the Ridiculous – the name she had given him. His studded ears and bull-nose ring made him look like a back-street thug from the nineteen eighties. As for his half-formed zombie accomplice, he appeared to be shedding his past identity as well as his skin. Prod had quite clearly developed into a nutter of unequalled madness. All of that on this astonishing island paradise, a place like this where Aurielle had rarely ventured. The strangling heat and the piercing sunrays made the trip demanding on the body and mind. And that was without any dull comments from Blue. He seemed to be coming round.

She perched the lip of the whiskey bottle on the stone and put the force of her weight through it if she could just get it at the right angle.

'Shame,' said Auntie, 'could have done with a little afternoon tipple.'

Lycka sniggered.

There was a scratch and crunch.

In the near distance were some very large boulders which framed the inlet. Giant leaves and wild foliage gaped over the cove as if tempting those rare visitors to stay a while longer. The sand dazzled if looked upon for too long, could blind someone deep in thought and burn skin if touched carelessly for any length of time. The island was beautiful and dangerous. There were undoubtedly some clever metaphors hiding in the undergrowth of these ideas relating to her own brilliance, but she was too modest to look for them, and anyway, she had some ties to concentrate on.

The sea was less than a half mile away, its meandering tendrils had merged with the island's waterways to create a rich mixture of biodiversity – she guessed. Aurielle didn't really care; it was her friends she worried about most and at the top of that impressively small list was Red and Midnight. Rig was on the list somewhere, perhaps over the page at the bottom, crossed out. As for her dad, he was just Dad.

Here comes the monster.'Hi Prod, what's up with you? Or shouldn't I ask? Is it a secret or are you waiting for a fancy-dress party? Halloween is some way off yet, you're a bit early. Or are you just waiting for an all-over skin graft? Don't tell me you've already had it? Any chance of you putting some clothes on. I mean seriously, you are an ugly thing.'

Lycka and Auntie Ida cackled like schoolgirls.

He stood over them, gunk dripping from seeping sores on his face like tiny volcanoes of acne, the heat had dried most of the blood that had oozed from broken and discarded skin, painful cracks appeared in the top layer as he moved. Each limb was partially covered with scales as though he were a reptile shedding one skin, replacing it with another. He didn't seem embarrassed at all.

'What powers has Rig got now?' he asked.

'Good to see you too!' replied Aurielle. 'Why's it always about Rig? Aren't we interesting enough for you?'

'Doesn't matter, the end will be the same regardless.'

His vocal pitch was definitely different, most likely because his teeth had grown somewhat.

'What is it you're looking for?' asked Lycka, 'What do you want?'

'Your questions are pointless; the truth will run its course.'

'Philosophical for a nutjob, isn't he?' said Aunt Ida.

Prod's gaze switched to Aurielle's right. Blue was rousing. Just in time, because Blaam was strolling back to them with a huge knife in his hand. Occasional blinding bursts of sunlight pinged from the blade as he neared.

'Gods I've got a sore head,' he said sitting upright, nodding to them, and studying his bound wrists. Blinking like a toddler under bright lights.

Prod turned to walk away.

'Oi,' blared Blue, not like a toddler at all. 'No, you don't, let us go, Prod. We've done nothing. You owe me anyway, for old times' sake. And I don't appreciate, like, being whacked over the head either. Come on,' he turned and offered his wrists, 'untie me.'

'The past is the past. Nothing from then matters now.'

'This thing is trying to be wise,' Auntie Ida beamed, clearly enjoying a jolly good day out from her care home.

'Just one of life's nutters, isn't he?' said Lycka.

'Would you say he was a megalomaniac darling, or is he simply a maniac?'

'I think you'll find he would only be a megalomaniac if he wanted to take over the world.'

'Oh, yes, that sounds about right, better ask him then, hadn't we?'

Auntie Ida leaned forward, eyes sparkling, 'Could be a dictator if he worked hard, darling. What do you think?'

Aurielle grinned. 'He's a monster, no doubt. I've met loads of them. I mean look at the state of him. Most monsters have some amount of dignity though. He could do with some underpants, or trousers at least.'

'Fair point,' said Lycka, 'No one wants to be faced with all that! But what's in his head? Nutter of the highest order,' said Lycka grinning.

Aurielle beamed; she hadn't had so much fun for ages. She made a note to get together with her girlfriends more often, except she knew she wouldn't.

'What happened in the past got you here and did this to you, idiot,' Blue said glaring at the creature who had been Prod, getting to his feet. 'The reason you're like this isn't your fault.'

Aurielle gazed up at Blue, curious where this was heading.

'What could you possibly know about any of this?' asked Prod through dried blood and split lips.

'More than you think.'

The creature whispered as if chatting to someone next to him.

'The voices are bad, mate. You need to get all that sorted.' Blue looked him up and down with disgust.

'None of you mean anything to me.'

'I'll tell you who did this to you, Prod.' Blue stepped closer. 'Who do you think sent us here in the first place?'

'It's irrelevant.'

'No, it's not, see. You think them scientists sent us here from that Consortium, when we were meant to be collecting them samples?'

'What of it?'

'They don't exist, none of it's real.'

'What do you mean?' Prod's interest piqued.

'Scarlett Crook *is* the Consortium, she sent us here, she knew there was a lot of negative magic going on here, it's her fault you're like that and I went this colour. Seriously, I'm telling you, right. It's the truth.'

'What?' Aurielle glared at him.

He turned to her. 'Crook wants to control all that negative magic, see? She wants to be able to use it for herself, sell it to the highest bidder.'

'You knew her all along? All that time we were held by Blackjack, and all the way here? And when you first found me?'

He looked at her, imploringly. 'I knew what I was doing, I weren't going to let anyone hurt you all. That Crook wanted to be, like, er, anonymous. Yeah that's it, anonymous.'

'You kept her dirty secret?'

'You're a card player aren't you, Blue?' asked Lycka.

'Spy garbage,' said Auntie as though she had dirt in her mouth. And with bound hands she stretched forward carefully, as if she might break a bone, to her walking-aid.

Blaam twirled his large knife, gazing lovingly at the edge of the blade. 'Sit down!' he barked looking at Blue.

Blue ignored him and continued, 'No, I'm not no spy, I was just doing me job.'

Prod turned on what was left of his feet. 'It changes nothing.' He headed to the bush.

'That's it. Mercenary. Got paid, done the job,' sneered Aurielle.

'Aren't we all, Flash?'

'No, we aren't. If I'm paid at all it's by the state. And most of the time, not at all.'

'That's your fault. But it ain't no difference really, we both get paid.'

'Private contractor, killer. You sell yourself to the highest bidder to do anything, sell out against anyone you know.'

Aurielle got to her feet. 'You disgust me, you *are* disgusting!'

'You tell him, dear.'

She watched as the monkeys guarding them rushed into the jungle, keen to escape the situation now their king had gone. The pygmys looked at each other and gabbled ferociously before sprinting away. Blaam didn't seem to care. Lycka looked on, quietly waiting to see how the situation would unfold. Mr Penlip was still asleep to the world.

Blaam moved towards them pointing his huge knife. 'I said, sit down! Both of you!'

It was time.

She released her binding and punched Blue in the throat. He gasped and dropped clutching his neck. She spun to face Blaam.

He stabbed forward, she shifted away from the zinging blade as it grazed past her, she moved into him, thrusting an elbow into his face, and simultaneously grabbing the arm with the knife. Stunned, he tottered as she gripped his wrist yanking it downwards while standing as tall as she could, forcing him to lower, she pressed harder to force the knife to drop. Too slow, his wrist was holding so she reverse kicked into his solar-plexus. He collapsed, gripping his midriff but kept hold of the weapon.

'Watch-out, love!' screeched Auntie. 'This damned thing won't work,' she fiddled with her stick.

Aurielle twisted on her heals in the sand, aimed a hard kick to his face, he deflected with an arm and cut downwards towards her thigh, she edged out of his way, but now was off balance, vulnerable ... the prize shot came. His foot smashed into her knee, and she caved, crunching to the blazing beach floor. He pinned her with all his weight, lifted his knife and displayed a yellow stained smile. He was too heavy. He batted her arms away as she sought to counter him, get a grip, but she knew she was in a weak position.

Lycka gasped. 'Nooo! Don't do it, Blaam!'

'No!' Screeched Blue.

'Nasty, nasty man,' said Auntie weakly.

Blaam twirled his knife, 'Bye, bye little one.'

BANG!

Blaam's shoulder exploded. The force sent him reeling backwards, the steel blade spiralled through the air. Aurielle took her chance, rolled away, and tentatively got to her feet. Blaam ran clutching his shoulder across the inlet to the far side. Auntie Ida was slumped at the base of the tree from the force of the shot, she looked rough with it.

'Tough recoil on it that one,' she said unmoving, lying on her side.

'Auntie! You okay?' Aurielle collected Blaam's hunting knife, which was surprisingly heavy, and hobbled to Auntie. She knelt with her opposite Lycka.

'Where's it hurting?' asked Lycka.

'Just got a little knock on the tree trunk, that's all,' she said. 'The old back is smarting a bit, I'll be okay, takes more than a sunny beach resort and ugly bad guy to knock the stuffing out of me.'

Aurielle picked up the walking-stick and immediately felt the heat from its far end.

'Yes, gives you one shot, darling. So, you have to make sure.'

'He'll be crying about that shoulder for a while. Thank you, Auntie.'

Great Aunt Ida craned to reach Aurielle and gave her a kiss on the cheek. Blue sauntered forward like a dog who'd been told off.

'Turn round,' Aurielle nodded to Lycka as she worked on the knots on Auntie's binds. She quickly worked through them, then released Lycka.

Rising, she looked at Blue sternly, 'Come here,' she ordered, with the knife hanging like a guillotine at her side. He neared her but was careful to stay at a safe distance.

'Listen to me carefully,' she said moving closer, 'if you hurt anyone here, or Rig or Henni … I will hurt you. Understand?'

He nodded. What else could he do?

'Turn.'

Hesitantly, he shuffled to show her his back.

She severed his laced binding. 'Find something to collect some sea water and get back here with it.'

'Okay,' he mumbled in reply, and sprinted towards the beach.

Auntie Ida took Aurielle's arm and stood, her spine and shoulders cracked as she bent upright.

'Oh, that's better my dear.' She rubbed her back and stretched to the sky. 'That Crook sounds a wrong-un. Why didn't you see it, Aurielle? You need to do better than that.'

'I know. She fooled me. There were some signs, there was something that weren't quite right.'

Lycka gave Auntie Ida a rub along her back. She beamed, closed her eyes like a preening cat enjoying a stroke from its owner.

'You must trust your instincts more,' said Lycka.

'Yes Auntie.'

'So darling, what's their past, that Crook and Blue. How do they know each other? What's Blue's past exactly?'

'I dunno actually, never had time to ask. It's been a bit … hectic.'

'What about you, Lycka? With all you're good looks, you're the God of Chance. What do you know about them? Where do the chances lie? And for whom?'

'I … I don't know. I've been busy too, y'know? That's why I haven't been around myself.'

'Hmm.'

Auntie Ida clearly wasn't too impressed with either of them. She looked towards the coastline deep in thought as Lycka gave a soft massage to her shoulders and back. She was hard as steel, dangerous as Blaam's knife, more so. She had seen war, lived it, battled in it, survived it. Under her fluffy exterior was a penetratingly fierce woman. A leader of people. A General.

Aurielle checked on Penlip Senior. Still out cold, had been for a long time, too long. Her gaze scoured the area for Blue. Where was he? She shook Rig's dad. 'Mr Penlip?' she shouted. No good.

'Why's he still out of it? He should've come round by now, surely,' Lycka said.

Shielding her eyes, Aurielle peered towards the trees overhanging the inlet to the sea.

'Can't see him. I'm gonna kill him when I do.'

Auntie put a hand on her arm, 'Cool it tiger, it'll be alright in the end, you'll see.'

'There he is,' said Lycka.

Aurielle strained to see him. Her eyes found something moving.

There … a figure to the left side, sauntering along the water's edge, silhouetted by the blinding sunshine.

'Blue! Get here! Now!' she yelled. He started running. 'I'm going to rip his head off.'

Auntie held her arm lovingly, reassuringly. It wouldn't make a difference to her decision. Probably.

Chapter 33. The Facility

He was deep into the jungle, no proper paths, and no signposts at all. He stopped, hunched over, and chest heaving, sucking in warm air. The scents of the trees were stimulating, refreshing. He looked to the canopy above, wiping his eyes. What now? Keep going, head towards his blind-side, take him from there. Somehow. Pain was much better, he still couldn't move his right arm much though, and the sling was uncomfortable. Running and fighting was definitely harder. He hated both. Worse though, he was no longer sure which direction he should be going in. He trudged upwards and onwards, had been for some time. It was a decent idea, to escape and circle round to catch Prod off guard but it was proving too difficult.

The stream was nearby. He veered to take a look where a gap allowed in the ferns. Clear running water, hurtling downwards to where he had come from. He was dead thirsty, he crouched by it, watched the flow of leaves and silt glide across the stones. The sun's rays strafed the water, illuminating every cranny and nook under cover of trees that all seemed taller than the sky. He cupped his hand and reached forward.

'Wouldn't do that if I were you.'

Rig gasped. 'Eh?'

He twisted on his heels to find Humps standing over him, peering.

'I wish you'd stop doing that!'

'Just trying to help.'

'I could tell that when you disappeared during the fight with Prod's army of animals.'

'Oh, you're so ungrateful, don't know why I bother. Drink it then, see if I care. I mean you look like a character out of *Planet of the Apes* as it is.' He swayed through the undergrowth to a nearby tree, absently inspecting its trunk and branches.

'What?'

'Loved that film, so sad for those apes. They looked good in their fur though.'

Rig arched his back and snuck through the foliage to the track. 'You're a fruitcake, Humps.'

And with immaculate timing, Rig's stomach gurgled.

'Actually, I miss a good chocolate cake. I was always on diets, you see. Worked though, didn't it?' He stepped closer and gave a ballerina's twirl.

'Oh, for the gods!' Rig continued along the trail, swatting wiry branches from his face as he padded forward, ducking under others. Humphrey followed on behind.

His legs were burning, his shirt sodden from the humid atmosphere and constant walking. He had never felt further away from his bed and home – where his family should have been. Only his dad survived. Dad. He had to get help or draw that monstrous beast away from him. He had done nothing, it was Rig who had dragged him into this by his absence, by his intention to track and rescue his best friend. It wasn't going too well.

'Where we going now, then?' Came the droning voice of his adopted companion.

'To … get … help.' Rig said, struggling to catch a clean breath already.

'Oh! Who needs help, Riggy?'

Rig continued up the incline. 'All … of us.'

'That sounds bad.' Humps appeared by Rig's shoulder, sailing up the hill effortlessly as if carried by the gusts from the shore. 'And, er … if you don't mind me saying,' he continued, 'you look ghastly and seem a bit … you know, tired.'

'Thanks.'

The track was barely visible, if it was even worthy of being called a track. The forest covered every space it could, its spread relentless as though chasing away any opportunity for humans to inhabit this beautiful, dangerous paradise. For Rig, it had become a trial. The path was getting steeper, he was pausing more often now, breathing so heavily he wondered if he'd brought on some asthma type of illness. He plodded on. Up ahead was nothing but dense jungle overseen by enormous trees with great green bushy hats on top. Sweat poured like a tap, he longed for a mouthful of cold water as much as he ever wanted anything in his life. Humps chuntered away like he was on an extended vacation without a care in the world. In a way, Rig envied him the luxury of being unaware of the dangers of the journey. It was damn annoying too.

'Isn't it lovely, Rig?'

'What?'

'Didn't you hear me … I said, lovely to spend some time together, talking. It's good to have someone to talk to, share things with, isn't it?'

'Yep.'

'Have we got much further to go, Riggy? Where are we going anyway?'

His feet were starting to sing to him, maybe you're only meant to walk so far in one day. There must be a limit.

'Dunno,' he stopped, stretched his back, gave it a rub, and checked to see if his feet were still attached. Having to repeat answers to questions already asked was starting to nark.

'Is that where we're going? Oh, super!'

Through the green haze of forest sprouted the white walls of a building a few hundred metres away. Against a forceful sun it reflected the light like a beacon, such that no-one could be in any doubt of its presence. And despite its appearance – stark against the backdrop of unending green forest – Rig sensed there was something wrong, or at least out of place about it, and not only because it was a modern building in the middle of a tropical island. It looked both out of place and didn't *feel* right.

'I don't know what that is, or why it's here. Maybe someone there could help. Let's take a look.'

'Oh, goody!'

They slogged nearer, Rig halting after a minute to catch some much-needed oxygen. His chest battled with the heat to funnel life into him.

'Look at the size of those walls, Riggy.'

'It's … like a … sort of fortress. So tall. Probably … to keep them monsters out.'

'Ooh, how exciting … wonder who lives there. What's that on top?'

Shielding his eyes, Rig squinted to see. 'Barbed wire, like I said … looks built to keep nasties out.'

'Or to keep them in.'

Rig looked at Humps.

'Well, you never know, do you?'

'Great.' He continued climbing, as he had done for what seemed like days.

He didn't know how this was going to turn out, hadn't imagined the slog and stress it was going to bring him and his dad. So far, his acclaimed magic had been useless, having to adapt and use left-handed magic was unexpected and had proved difficult to conjure. And yet he knew if he didn't use his magic in some manner, it had the potential to make him sick, which he had known for some time, and still struck him as odd. Use it or else was the message from the universe. One way or another he would have to because that was his destiny, whether he agreed with it or not.

'What's that up there on that wall?' asked Humps as they toiled further up the hill.

Taking the opportunity to slow to a pause, Rig looked again at the monolith before him. There was a large rectangular building inside the walls which stretched into the rich blue atmosphere above to a lip, where there was a railing. And there were four windows that stared out like alien eyes out towards the island's coastline. There was something attached to the side of the building.

'They're letters, a logo,' Rig said pausing, sucking in the air.

'What do you mean, a logo?'

Rig slipped his arm from the sling and flexed it, much better, still a bit sore and not moving too well but better.

'I reckon … it's a symbol. Companies … use them to advertise themselves … y'know?'

'Oh Riggy, you are good at this, aren't you?'

'No, I've … just heard of it … before.'

'Oh look, it says "HP".'

Rig had another look, 'Yeah … it does.' He continued blowing hard.

Maybe they could get help from whoever lived there. What would he say? A monster has my friends held captive. Can you help save them? From what Rig had seen so far, they must know monsters are a problem, hence the high walls. Doesn't mean they would help though.

'But what does it stand for? Why not just put the whole name? I would! Be proud of who you are, let the world know your name and what you're doing ... unless you're a bad person, in which case keeping any information to a minimum is probably a good idea. Isn't it, Riggy?'

'I wish ... you'd stop calling me that.'

'But that's your name!'

'My name ... yes, it is. You're right.' Rig scanned the bright white structure again, his gaze hovering over the letters HP adorning the tower in the centre. 'I've seen that "HP" before, with that exact style of lettering.'

'Eh?'

'Get your notebook out.'

'Oh, okay.' Humphrey rummaged through his back pocket like it was a cavernous supermarket shopping bag, puffing, and huffing and finally produced his little book and pen. He waved it in the air like a trophy, grinning.

'Front cover, look at the front cover, Humps.'

He flipped the book over and considered the attractively etched letters. His attention switched feverishly between the tawny coloured front and the symbol staring at him on the brick building rising in front of them.

'It's the same isn't it, Humps? It's the same sort of letters. You're connected to this building, these people, somehow.'

Humps stood open mouthed, as though he had seen an impossible event, an event he thought could never happen.

He could not utter a single word in reply.

Chapter 34. Jordi Longstaff

It was as though they had attached Mr Penlip's toes to the mains electricity, he woke with start when she splashed him with warm seawater. Unsurprisingly, it took him a few minutes to come round, remember what happened, and what he was doing on a tropical island, miles from civilisation. Aurielle detected a hint of disappointment when he realised, he wasn't on an exotic package holiday. But then that was life, full of work and killing spies. At least that's what Aurielle Merlot found, hunter, killer, and angry teen.

'I'm not a spy!' shouted Jordi yet again.

Aurielle circled him. 'I don't trust you, never will again, and that means you're no use to me. And that ... is bad news for you.' Her eyes followed the sleek curves and edges of the glinting steel.

'Why did you do it?' asked Lycka.

'I did the job I was paid for! Didn't see there was no harm in being, like, an observer, did I?'

Auntie Ida faced up to him, she was less than half his height but had twice his guile and considerably more experience.

'How far does your relationship with Scarlett Crook go back? What was the nature of your relationship with Blackjack?'

He was sweating heavily, but then they all were.

'Crook and Blackjack knew each other from the past. See, I just got paid to go on this expedition thing with Prod, then it went all wrong, but she kept paying me ... to keep an eye on Prod mostly. But then when Blackjack needed someone ... he thought she was, like, a good idea, she could get to know Rig. That's why it was kept a secret. She wanted to get to know him. They agreed it together, it was the best way Rig could help her understand magic. That was the plan.'

Mr Penlip started pacing with that slight limp of his, occasionally gripping his head with a grimace, 'I don't believe you ... why does she want to know my son? Why Rig?'

'She knows he's powerful, she wants to understand how it all works, see him use it … I don't know.'

'No,' Lycka said. 'You told us she wants to use magic, sell it. There's more to this. You're lying.'

'I'm not! I'm not! That's it, she wants to understand it, yes, maybe control it better, but that's it. She probably wants to sell her knowledge on, y'know, become an expert or something. It's all I know, I swear.'

'Sell it?' asked Penlip Senior. 'You're playing a dangerous game, lad. If any harm comes to my son, I'll …'

His sentence tailed off. She could see his fists were clenched like a boxer about to enter the ring, but they soon softened, then his shoulders became heavy with worry.

Aurielle took his arm, 'Mr Penlip, I'll find Rig, protect him, and get us all back home. I promise.'

'It's Melvyn. And thank you, Aurielle. I know you will, you both have history. It'll work out. We need to get going. That monster must be looking for my boy.'

He swivelled to face Blue. 'I want to know everything … and I mean *everything*. Be quick about it. Because I want to find my son and get out of here. Is that clear to everyone?' he looked to each of them and checked the resolve in their eyes.

Auntie Ida's expression brightened like a soldier being given the order to attack, at long last.

Chapter 35. Scarlett Crook

'But ... but how can that "HP" be the same as this one,' the apparition was thudding a finger on his book like an evangelist high on caffeine and rich-tea biscuits.

'Well, we'll find out, won't we? Come on. Not much further.'

Rig forced his aching legs to march again, his capacity for thinking beyond placing one foot in front of another was about zero.

As if blown by a draft from an open door, Humps swept ahead of him effortlessly as though the jungle infested hill was a mere inconvenience.

'Maybe I will find out who I am, where I've been ... or even what the future holds for me. What do you think?' A warm breeze brushed him back to Rig. Humps face dropped an inch, 'Oh gods!'

Rig spun on his heels to see what the fuss was about. But he knew ...

... another island monster.

It shrieked in distress at the sight of him, recoiling in apparent fright. Stick thin, long seeking tendril arms covered in what appeared to be a mixture of nettles and thorns, very creative. It had several gaping wounds in its bark which Rig suspected might act as chomping mouths. It recovered from its shock, stopped trembling and motioned closer with renewed determination and what could have been a snarl.

Sigh.

Rig didn't want to hurt it, be better for all if he didn't have to resort to using spellwork.

A nest of prickles swung at his face from his side, he ducked, a second spindly branch snagged his right foot, he shook it, kicked backwards but the stringy vine gripped tighter. It coiled upwards around his hairy leg, yanking him off balance. He crashed to the grassy pathway and yelped from the thorns biting into his skin like fishhooks, his arm smashed into something hard. He nearly blacked out. Dazed, he sensed it dragging him nearer, his legs had started to soak in his own blood, he worried he might be running out of it. His arm felt like someone was stamping on it, he gripped it as his head smacked a partially raised tube, and glanced to see the pipe was gushing lime-coloured water into the forest.

His focus switched back to his current predicament. There was no sign of any startling eyes to appeal to in the latest monster wanting to end his life. The pits in its craggy bark were munching on air in anticipation of getting a piece of his leg. Its leafy arms were like barbed wire, gripping him. With his right arm properly mashed up, twice in one day, he'd have to try left-handed magic again. He had no choice.

He held out his palm, opened it as flat as he could, allowing the magic particles to tingle his skin.

A thorny vine wrapped round his wrist.

'Aaargh! Somnum!'

Unaffected, the winding branch continued to coil and wrap around his hand, his legs were entirely seized now, soon he wouldn't be able to move his arms either.

'SOMNUM!' he shouted. He wanted to be crystal clear about it.

The hooks under Rig's skin unfurled leaving weeping wounds. Then his fingers and palm were released – scratched and bleeding profusely. The stem of the tree creature withered a little as if suddenly drugged. It shrank into itself, tendrils full of leaves wound inwards.

Rig pulled away, bloodied and harried. He gulped as much oxygen as he could. His legs and arms were no longer hairy, more like fur and matted with stains of his own blood. Every rise in magical particles stirring in him boosted his hair growth, he was becoming one of them, to look at anyway. He held his right arm close. Protected. He got to his feet. The tree-thing had nestled into some kind of slumber, just as Rig had hoped. He turned to continue up the hill, when the long black pipe peeking from under the earth again caught his attention. What did Blue say? They were investigating negative pools of magic, both Prod and Blue had suffered after coming into contact with the island's natural water. He studied the dirty fluid leaking into the trees, down the hill. Maybe the island's natural water was no longer natural? Or had the negative pools infected the whole ecosystem? Either way, something green and gungy was being ejected from this building. But saving his dad and friends were at the top of his priority list. The issue of pollution was not his worry, not really. Wincing from his cuts and scratches, straining from the effort, he stumbled up the slope following the direction of the huge, bleached bricked wall that was acting as a giant reflector for the sun's blasting light. Still, he thought, wouldn't do the suntan any harm.

He skirted the boundary wall and finally reached a bumpy dirt road leading to the front of the building facing him, surrounded by trees, fern and fauna stretching into the road.

A shadow drifted across the gravel, hauntingly.

He looked up.

His gaze followed the menacing flight of a large winged-demon, similar to what he had noticed during the fight with Prod's animal army. Whatever it was its silence was eery and its size formidable. Catching his breath a tad, Rig sauntered to the front of the building – keeping his eye on the wayward beast circling above – where he found a tall bell-tower above an archway, reminding him of photographs of grand villas in Greece. He approached a wooden door. It was ajar. The dimly lit entrance was enticing after such a terribly long and sweltering march, and of course all the violence he had found didn't help his fatigue much. He approached it without thinking, operating on his senses. He must cool down and rest. He entered the lightless porch.

A middle-aged woman with bright coloured jewellery wobbled towards him, grinning eagerly.

'Welcome, come in,' she said, eyebrows raised at the sight of him. 'You look tired, if you don't mind me saying, and thirsty no doubt? Maybe need a shave?'

'Yes, thank you. I—'

'Good, here's some water.' She hurriedly poured a large glug from a jade bottle, losing half of it in the process, and handed it to him.

He swallowed as much as he could, spilling and burping, his gullet struggled to take it all in.

'Steady on,' said the woman.

Rig ignored the spills down him and swallowed more of it.

'Looks like the island has got the better of you,' she said eyeing him up and down. 'Are you lost? And your eyes … what happened?'

He must look a wretched sight, covered in blood matted hair. 'No … I just need some—'

'Yes, well, come in.' She walked ahead of him, ushering him further into the complex.

Rig padded after her, 'I was gonna ask… what are your pipes leaking?'

She twisted on her heels with a strained, puzzled look.

He continued, 'That gunge from here into the ground, through them pipes?'

'No idea, I'll have my men look into it later, but for now there are much more important matters at stake. You see, I'm afraid you've come at a bad time, I've just called the police. We've had a terrible attack on our facility by some very vicious people indeed.'

Rig was just beginning to register in his brain what she had said when they moved into a cavernous atrium where desks with computer equipment were arranged in rows, with pods of desks grouped together at either end, like some sort of factory for computer boffins. Except the boffins had been slaughtered. Row upon row of slumped technicians and blood splattered equipment made the hall look like a scene from a horror film.

'What—'

'Yes, well, I said it was bad. The police are on their way. I just arrived back here after a break when I found all this, my work ruined, vital equipment and information stolen or missing.'

'And twenty dead people, with futures robbed from them.'

'Yes, and that.'

She didn't seem too bothered, or emotional. It was bad alright. Maybe she was bad.

'Well, all except one.'

'Eh?' Rig frowned.

A strong hand grabbed Rig's left wrist, he struggled.

She slapped him.

Stunned, he looked at her as a man splattered in blood clasped Rig's hands together and bound them, wrapping some plastic string round and round before tying a knot. Only then did he notice the fine spray of red decorating her flower-patterned dress.

'Don't want you using that magic of yours do we, Rig Penlip, Master of Magic. It's about time we met.'

Who was she? What was happening now? The man who tied him shuffled obediently to her side like a hungry puppy afraid of getting shouted at, or his throat sliced.

'I can see you're confused. I'm Scarlett Crook. I sent Prod Visceral here where he contracted his illness and went utterly mad. Actually, I did share a slight untruth with you… this isn't my facility … it belongs to a rival of mine actually.'

'And she knows Flash because she tricked them into letting her tag along,' said Humphrey the disappearing and frequently reappearing apparition. 'If memory serves … she was pretending to be a prisoner with them so she could get close to you. Well, I think that's right … hold on, Riggy.' He searched his pockets. 'Now, where is it?'

'Oh,' said Rig.

'Quite,' Crook said barely glancing at Humphrey. 'Needs must,' she said cheerfully. She gave the boffin-servant a nod and the petrified scientist grabbed Rig and yanked him through the room, fear oozing from his eyes and sweat making his cheeks shine.

'But why?' was all Rig could say as he was dragged into a side-room. 'Why me?'

The room was simple and medical, with a line of five leather recliner chairs, like the sort dentists use, and some electronic monitoring equipment on wheels. Otherwise, the room was bland – except for the large green dinosaur lying on the chair at the far end, waving a claw, grinning cheerfully.

The man shoved Rig onto the leather seat and fixed a long leather belt around his middle.

'Hey! What's going on?'

The petrified man didn't answer. He locked the belt somewhere low under the bed, and then he fixed Rig's legs in bindings attached to stirrups, leaving his hands tied, resting on his lap.

'Sorry,' he offered under his breath and darted from the room. As if that made any difference.

'It's nice to have visitors, isn't it? said the dinosaur suddenly.

Rig was about to reply but Crook arrived. Humphrey followed along in her wake.

'Ah, I do believe I've seen that animal somewhere before,' said Humps searching again for his notebook.

'Back pocket,' offered Rig.

Crook took in the scene. 'Zikri!' she bellowed.

'What are you doing?' pleaded Rig. 'You have nothing to gain by doing this, it doesn't make no sense.'

She moved closer to him, 'That's where you're quite wrong my lovely … you're quite different. Unique even. The magical confluence produced between your magical potential and those invisible particles in the air when they collide is powerful, unusual. Some might even say unnatural, deranged perhaps.'

'What?'

'Your spellwork is powerful, it's time it was studied properly and controlled. Makes sense when you think about it. Don't you think?'

Humphrey raced through the pages of his book, urgently looking for something. Meanwhile, Zikri had arrived in a panic and was fussing with some equipment in a drawer near the dinosaur.

The dinosaur spat goo from its mouth as it said: 'Well, I wonder if we should all introduce ourselves? My name is Henrietta. Henni if you really prefer. Do you?'

She didn't seem to understand the situation, not that Rig really understood either. He was used to that feeling. The man came to Rig's bedside and connected a clear tube to a plastic pouch. He reached into a drawer and took out a razor.

'What's he doing with that?' asked Rig.

'We're going to extract some of your blood and examine it. It's a cocktail of wonderful antibodies and magical potential material in there under that fur you've grown,' she prodded his arm.

'You're mad!'

'Quite the reverse, young Rig.'

Zikri dampened the froth of hair in the crease of his elbow and began shaving it off.

'That's it!' blurted Humps, 'Her name is Scarlett Crook, came here with Blue and Aurielle. She's a spiritualist, sort of Seer.'

Rig didn't take his gaze from Zikri, who had now got himself a long needle. 'Great, thanks.'

'Okay.'

'So nice to have friends to talk to. Do you think we'll be out of here soon?' asked Henrietta.

Scarlett turned to Humphrey. 'Yes, it's Humphrey Holliday isn't it?' she asked, ignoring Henni.

'Me? Um ...'

'Yes, definitely,' she said. 'Unfortunately my skills allow me to see and hear you, which in your case is utterly annoying as I could do without you as a distraction ... still, it's good to reflect on one's victories.'

'Holliday? Is my name Humphrey Holliday?'

'Collateral damage I'm afraid ... apparently your parents didn't put up much of a fight. Must be disappointing for you. Is that an understatement?'

'What you on about?' asked Rig as he watched Zikri's hand tremble as he neared with the needle.

'Ouch!'

Crook played with her multi-coloured necklace as she talked, 'I told them if they didn't agree to the merger of our companies, with me as chairman, obviously, then they'd have to be forcibly retired ... killed, dead meat. But they didn't listen, sadly. I think Blackjack was all done in a matter of minutes, you just happened to be in the way,' Crook said with a sideways glance to Humphrey.

'So, this medical facility here,' Humps pointed towards the floor, 'this belonged to my family, they were scientists before you ... before you ...' His voice trailed away, unable to speak of the terrible deed.

'That's about it. I do believe ... yes, their company was put in a legal trust after, so it continued operating. I didn't know they had an office here though, that was a surprise. I mean I knew *something* was here, that's why I sent Prod and Jordi to investigate. It's funny how things work out sometimes.'

Humphrey's ghostly frame began to tremble, but it was difficult to see him now, the glaring light in the sterile room made him more opaque than usual. He was rubbing his hands nervously, then he stepped through the wall, apparently unable to bear it any longer.

'You're cruel, how can you justify murdering Humphrey and his parents in cold blood and ruining lives like that. For what reason?'

'Progress. Your kind need to be studied and understood, and like I said ... controlled.'

'You're barbaric and ... and ... wrong. None of this is right.'

'Well, as in all conflicts ... only the victorious can look back and decide what was right and just. Wouldn't you agree?'

'Murderer.'

'Hypocrite.'

'What?'

'You've killed before, Rig Penlip.'

'Only in defence of myself or others.' His blood seeped into the bag, he felt faint just looking at it, but with the trek and the stress of it all a quick sleep was about all he could think about. It was a great idea except he was worried he would never wake up again.

Scarlett Crook had the look of a compassionate priest about her.

Looks could be deceiving.

And then it came to him. 'Yes,' he said, 'dead meat ... that was the expression used by Blackjack, brought to me by Humphrey ... when Flash went missing, and ...when her family had been taken, there was a note ... the exact saying. "Come get them ... if you dare ... or they'll be dead meat." You and Blackjack were behind this all along.'

'Like I said, needs must. You can't make a juicy sweet pancake without cracking an egg or two.'

'What? I don't know what you're on about.' Rig yawned.

'I do feel a little hungry, don't I?' Henrietta's long tongue lashed her snout on both sides and then she gave a gentle pull on her cuffed arms and legs. 'Any chance of a take-out? Anything like that?'

Rig's mind began to wander, and then he began to wonder … is this it? Is this the end? Here, now?

'Rest Rig, close your eyes, relax,' said Crook. 'Anyway, it won't be long until we make you sleep, then we can take some of that brain of yours. Got to be worth a look, don't you think?'

'What?'

Rig was so tired he wasn't sure he'd heard right. Take some of his brain? She couldn't have said that. He had better get up, if only he could open his eyes first.

'Zikri! Get me the morphine, a couple of boxes should do. I want to make sure.'

Unable to focus or gather his thoughts, Rig sensed her move closer.

'I can see we're going to have a very profitable relationship you and I, Rig Penlip.' He could feel her breath on him. 'With some of you anyway,' she said softly into his ear. 'And you know I'm a Seer, so there must be some truth in that prediction, right?'

There was a feeling of a heavy blanket smothering him in warmth, and all he could hear was the drip, drip of his blood into a cool bag by the bed as Henni clucked away, oblivious to the end which they were all bound to face. But even with his own doom fast approaching, all he could think about was that damn black drainpipe oozing toxic-looking waste into the lush green forest. And his last thought … it was none of his business anyway.

Chapter 36. Mr Melvyn Penlip

They travelled at speed, hacking and cutting bamboo and bark as they went, splinters flying everywhere. Thank the gods for saving her beloved Midnight and Red, found behind the large rock the beast used as his perch. It was him they were seeking. She reckoned Melvyn was furious enough to unleash some harsh spellwork. Auntie Ida was working through the bush in parallel, westwards from their position, covering them with her retrieved high-powered rifle in case any more monsters tried to attack or slow them down, her cushioned running shoes meant she could move swiftly through the worst of what the forest had to offer. Lycka had proved nimble too, athletic at times. Despite her appearance she could really move if needed, and they *really* needed. Rig's life was in danger with Prod on the hunt, and they had to find him fast. The heat was awful, all of them were sopping from the humidity, which never let up. Blue brought up the rear which Aurielle thought entirely right, while Frank and Lycka followed her and Melvyn as best they could.

Aurielle paused, coiled her damp ponytail so it formed a bun and fixed it there. She slipped her hand across the back of her neck, wiping the residue on her cargo trousers. Ahead of her now, she watched Melvyn clamber over a rocky outcrop, quite strong for a willowy man with a bad leg. His anger hadn't subsided, she could tell he wanted someone to pay but most of all to find his son and wrap him up, protect him. Aurielle could understand that she wanted someone to pay too, and the options for who that individual might be were considerable. Her money was on Crook, but if she was deadly honest Blue wasn't far behind her, and Prod, well … he was just another monster that needed putting down. His choice, his end.

Gripping a grey lip of rock she swung her foot up, hauled herself to standing. Their route was full of swathes of greens and browns in a landscape that was hard to see through, the incline was continuous and testing on the legs.

She glanced behind her, her dad continued to do his best, she was amazed he had come this far and had barely complained at all. Below, Lycka followed on with bravery and compassion in each step, she didn't need to be here and yet she was struggling with them, sweltering, sweating, and battling the elements to help them find Rig and get home.

And then there was Blue, yeah … there was him.

'Everybody stop. Quiet!' Melvyn bellowed down to them, his tones seemingly deeper as they bounced around the trees surrounding them.

Aurielle paused, her gaze settled on each of them briefly, checking their response. She watched as Melvyn leant forward, straining to hear any sounds rumble down the hill. They needed clues, they had to find Rig or disable Prod. It was as simple and vital as that.

'Running water. I can hear running water.' Penlip took hold of some rocks and clambered up another moss-ridden mound until he had disappeared beyond.

She followed him, her feet slipping on the gungy, damp moss. Frank and Lycka were just starting to climb after her. Blue was catching up too. Aurielle rose to find Penlip hadn't progressed very far.

Something was wrong.

He stood motionless, staring ahead. Aurielle went to his side and immediately found the problem. Ahead was the creature called Prod showering under a rocky overhang, gulping the spring water, and stretching like he'd just woken up. The clearing would have been idyllic had it not been for the murderous monster having a wash. The stream from the modest waterfall funnelled away to their right side, carving between stones and trees as it cascaded downwards. The brilliant sun baked the space between them and Prod.

Frank and Aurielle appeared next to Melvyn and Aurielle, silently.

The monster took two steps forward, arms outstretched as if he was welcoming them. There was a scratching noise as he moved because his body was almost completely covered in scales.

Not unlike a crocodile, thought Aurielle.

'Good to see you again so soon, forgive my manners. Welcome to my beautiful island.'

His head was only partially covered in protective scales making it easier for him to talk, and fortunately, easier to kill too.

'We came here before you did, lizard-face,' Aurielle replied.

'Where's my son?' demanded Mr Penlip.

Lycka turned to Aurielle. 'Do you think he's totally turned? Or is Prod still in there somewhere?'

'Nah, he's not totally turned him yet. Prod's body and mind is just host to that ugly thing. Well, I think so anyway.'

'Enough of this!' The Prod-monster scanned the trees around him, and sure enough branches juddered, and bushes shook as eyes appeared around them, encircling them. 'Bow down to me, like the animal kingdom here, of which you are now part.'

'Bog off!' bellowed Jordi striding forward with a long stick he'd found from somewhere.

Melvyn grabbed Jordi's shirt, halting him there. 'Let me deal with it. It's my son we're saving.'

'Sure, pops.'

Melvyn shoved him away for that.

'What?' moaned Jordi like the teenager he was.

Melvyn approached what remained of Prod. 'I don't have time for messing around. Tell me where my son is right now, and then maybe, just maybe, I won't burn you to a cinder.'

His tone was mean and full of menace, in fact utterly convincing Aurielle reckoned.

The scaly legs of the old version of Prod took a step backwards. 'I don't think you understand the situation.' He glanced left and right.

Penlip raised a hand. The precursor to his magic-making.

A barrage of stones and wood sticks fired towards them all, each of them ducked and whirled away to avoid the onslaught. There was whooping, cackling and high-pitched laughing all around them as they were peppered with bone-breaking rocks. Aurielle picked some up and launched them back into the trees from where they'd come. Lycka was rolling and dancing to avoid the attack while Blue deflected what he could with his own stick. Melvyn, the biggest danger to the attackers was hammered worst, some striking his side, most missing as he shifted trying to get some space to wield his magic.

Then the forest seemed to explode.

Hairy, black-coated monkeys and pygmys rushed at them, lots of animals. Shots were fired. Ripping the air in two. Auntie Ida must be close! A monkey dropped, rolled around with arms flapping wildly. Two pygmys dropped their axes and ran back to the protection of the trees. A third was felled by another piercing crack from auntie, blood and brain tissue bursting as his head jolted backwards. But the others were through. Each of them battled with a pygmy while small wolves snatched at their ankles. The apes shrieked as they tried to get some purchase on their limbs.

Aurielle arched her back to avoid the swipe of a monkey with a heavy tree branch, but another swung at the back of her legs. She jumped and swirled, punched one in the face, and chopped the stick of another in half. That was sufficient to send them running. But they were all attacking in pairs, as if instructed to do so in a deliberate battle strategy. A pygmy thrust a spear at her face, she deflected it with Red, chopped it in two with Midnight just as an axe launched at her expose neck. A reverse stab of her sword blocked the initial slice, she swivelled and kicked the man in the ribcage. Another rushed at her. Her balance was good, so she cut the spear down and kicked him in the face, then twisted and redirected another spear attack without thinking – she was good at this. She was working on instinct and relying on her training. She weighed up the scene, made a swift judgement about where the next attack would come from, and a stone hit her in the side of the head. She dropped. A glance found Prod who was being hauled into the air by a huge, winged beast, up and away and out of the fight.

Cheat, she thought.

Aurielle leant on her elbows, a little dazed, head beginning to clear as she watched the bewitched animals of the tropical island scamper back into the shadows of the jungle, pygmys following. Lycka and Frank helped her up, fussing nicely and begging her to tell them she was okay. Like Melvyn, she was more focussed on the direction of travel of the island's animal king who was now hard to see. Where was he headed? To do what?

She noticed there were some scratches on her dad's face, but this wasn't affecting his chattering. Some bruises were already rising on Lycka, which Aurielle knew would be a foundation make-up issue had they not been trapped on an island with a nutjob like Prod Visceral. Auntie Ida appeared, sniper rifle across the back of her mauve cardigan, walking stick prodding the ground where it was less firm. Her little pearl necklace hung neatly between two long bullet belts criss-crossing her slim torso. She could have been the action-hero Rambo's elderly grandmother. And yet she still moved with speed when she needed. She was an odd, wonderful sight.

'Bugger,' she said. 'Where has that nasty animal gone now?' she asked looking into the cloud-free sky above them.

'Dunno,' said Melvyn. 'Looks like he's heading to the west of the island though, and where he goes, we go.'

'I need to take a pee first,' said Blue checking his damaged long-staff.

They all turned to him with a pinch of disbelief and ton of disinterest.

'What?' he asked with a whimper.

***

The trek had continued, uphill. This was of particular worry for one of their hunting party, not ninety-year-old Great Auntie Ida riddled with arthritis and balance problems – replica or not – but Blue, who wouldn't shut up about it. In fact, it was a small miracle that they reached the summit of their particular hill with Blue in one piece. To be truthful, the view at the top was spectacular and this dissolved almost all temptation and thoughts of abruptly ending his trip. Surrounding them was a splendour of natural hues below a scorching sun, with tropical cawing and wild shrieks occasionally sounding out from its wild inhabitants. The island stretched lazily to its edges like a resting lizard on white sand. But Aurielle didn't care about that, she just wanted, no, needed, to cut Prod in half and be done with it. The urge was becoming breathtakingly strong in her.

'What's that?' Frank asked indicating in the direction of a white walled building dead ahead of them.

Penlip turned to them, determination in every move, every decision. Aurielle liked him.

'Blue and Aurielle? Go and find out what's going on there. See if there's any sign of Rig. Or talk to anyone you find. It doesn't look like a villa from here so something else is occurring. Find out what, and meet us over there,' he said pointing, 'on the west side where that large inlet suggests a beach.' His look was intense, but not unfriendly. 'Got it?'

Aurielle motioned towards Auntie Ida and said, 'Sure.' She gave auntie a hug, who beamed.

'The rest of us will head that way now, westwards. That's where the creature is heading.'

Blue approached Melvyn. 'But *we'd* be better hunting Prod. Anyways, that's what we're trained for.' He turned to Aurielle looking for her agreement.

'My son, my decision. Get on with it. Go! And then head west, meet us on the beach.'

Blue's shoulders slumped as he trudged forward, dragging his new stick in the general direction of the strange house in the middle of the jungle. Aurielle followed. She pondered what kind of terrible accident might befall the young Protector. Practically anything could happen in a place like this. The possibilities and dangers were endless.

They headed down, deep into the thicket of the bush, occasionally hacking their way through but moving quickly with the energy of two Protectors finally unleashed to show what they can do. And then Blue tripped on a vine and flew headlong into a rather attractive looking bush. It had lush fragrances, sweet and subtle, possibly jasmine, like you'd find selling in a natural cosmetics shop.

'Bloody hell! I hate this place,' said Blue, standing.

'Yes. It hates you too,' she said, brushing past him.

Chapter 37. Henrietta the Horrible

Rig woke with a gasp and splutter. A crocodile face was peering into his, its big eyes blinked at him, the eyelashes long, feminine. But the teeth in its snout were savage, nothing would escape once snared. It spoke.

'Hey there, you! You're alright now, aren't you? Only I had no-one to talk to, see? I thought you were gonna have a big sleep. Maybe you were even in some troubles, how would I know? Not a doctor or anything, am I? So now you're awake we can have a good chat, yes?'

Rig tried to inch away, but he was tied up like a goose at a food festival. Henni saw him struggle, her crocodile tail swept the floor.

'Oh, I can help with that, I can.' She placed her claw under the leather belt and started to saw through it, slowly but effectively.

'What happened to the crazy Crook woman?' Rig asked.

As if in reply, there was shouting and crashing of equipment next door. Also, quite a lot of grunting, yelling, and yelping. It sounded like two small armies battling and went on for several violent minutes.

'Thought she was a bit mean, that woman. Dunno why, I just did, didn't I? I said she has to leave, didn't like that at all, did she? Had to do my best snarl, I did. Wanna see it?'

'It's okay, I believe you.'

A moment of quiet interrupted them. Henni finished cutting the leather belt, and in a jiffy sliced the ties around his wrists. Free at last but still woozy, coming round.

The double doors suddenly flew open via a black boot.

Blue shoved Crook into the laboratory, arms secured behind her.

A moment later, Flash walked in, nonchalantly. 'Here you are. Still alive then? At least your dad will be pleased.'

A hint of a smirk was enough to suggest Flash was pleased to see him. He understood now that her insults were only a sign of affection – that's what he believed anyway – giving actual affection would be wrong and awkward, and out of character. This was the best next thing.

'This is no way to treat your employer,' said Crook, glaring at Blue. His shirt was ripped, and a swell was starting under his left eye.

'They know about you and my past, so don't try tricking no one, okay?'

'There are always more details I can give, you fool.'

Blue turned to Flash. 'Can we gag her? I want to gag her.'

Rig got off the medical bed, pushing off with his left hand. He faltered, sat back down. 'That's not nice, gagging someone,' he said, cradling his right arm.

'Not nice? She just tried to kill me! And look what she did out there,' he said indicating back through the swing doors.

'True,' Rig agreed. 'How did you get in and capture her anyway?'

Flash rolled her eyes. 'Yeah, Blue used his brains and turned the door knob and pushed. He's excellent at doing that.'

'Whatever,' he said maturely. 'Put up a fight though, she did. Got her in the end.'

Crook tittered, 'I knocked you down three times.'

'Like I said, I got you in the end, that's what matters.'

There was a sigh. 'I so wanted to cut her, just a knick from Red.' Flash examined the sword lovingly, and sheathed it. 'It was so hard to control myself, resist. Y'know?'

'Gods!' moaned Rig. 'I'd almost forgotten how addicted you are to violence.'

'Let's call it necessary persuasion.'

'Right.'

Henni shuffled to Crook and raised a single, hooked talon. 'You need to be quiet now, see? Sometimes life can be dangerous, and knowing when to stop them words is real sensible. You get what I mean?'

'You are *so* dull. So, who's in charge around here anyway?' she asked her gaze skirting across each of them. 'Does any one of you have a single, working brain cell?'

Aurielle put her in a headlock.

Rig stood again, protecting his mashed arm as he rose. Success – finally on his feet. He motioned for Flash to calm. 'It's okay, we'll tie her up here, or something, until we can decide what to do with her. We won't do nothing bad to her, even with all she's done, just wouldn't be right.' Rig couldn't help it; he stifled a yawn.

Flash released her. 'Give me any excuse Crook and I'll finish you.'

Crook rolled her eyes. 'Gods, you are a hopeless lot. No wonder you're in this mess.'

Aurielle was about to strangle her again when Blue grabbed Crook by the throat.

'When we were held by that Blackjack, and you and me was under cover, like, you did that Seer thing. You saw the death of magic, you said. Well now, I see *your* death you old hag!'

Crook grinned.

Blue slapped her.

'That's enough!' bellowed Rig. 'Tie her up, Blue, and for now, we'll leave her in here.'

'Sure will.' He released Crook and noticed the syringe and morphine phials in the metal tray. 'You been shooting up some good stuff, Rig? I'll give this one a bit of gear to relax her a bit, yeah?'

'No! Leave it. Bind her to this chair. Let's get out. I need to find my dad.'

When they were in the computer hall with bodies, shattered glass, and debris all about them, Rig had to lean on his new friend, Henrietta. The effects of the morphine, the whole expedition in fact, were making it difficult to concentrate and stand upright for long.

'Need some fresh air, don't you?' Henni looked concerned or would be if only her scaly armour would urge her brow into a frown.

'You look rough as hell,' Flash said, politely. 'Red eyes, legs and arms are almost furry, and your face ain't much better, just like a yeti. Not only that but you seem to have trashed that arm! You're useless, Rig. Dunno how you're alive without me.'

'Thanks for that. I need air.'

They sauntered to the balcony, the nearest place to get the clean, fresh jungle air, albeit terribly humid. The lab over-looked a garden, much of the raised vegetable patch was under cover from the baking sun. A path skirted the walls all the way round. Next to the path were a hotch-potch of fauna native to the island sprinkled along the base of the wall. Some of the bushes grew the largest flower-heads Rig had ever seen. They surrounded the garden, all except the far corner where two umbrellas gave shade to a set of tables and few chairs. Rig leant against the balustrade and described his journey. To give Flash credit, she rarely interrupted. That her dad had come after her was the biggest surprise to her. He'd stayed sober long enough to take part. That didn't make him a saint, she had admitted. But Rig could tell it meant a lot. For just a moment she became child-like, humbled, even embarrassed. But this was soon forgotten, and she began her own story. They only travelled to the island to get some water samples to send for analysis. Then she revealed how Blue had tricked them all. He did this in tandem with Crook, under her direction, in her employment. It was hard to accept. Rig straightened at this news. Blue apologised, he'd try to make up for it. In the end they actually shook hands. Henni nodded in agreement, whereas Flash had her hand gripped on one of her swords. The white of her knuckles told Rig all he needed to know.

Flash went on to describe the route they needed to take to reach the western most bay, to link up with the others.

'A track will take us part of the way, then I think we need to veer off, go through the bush.'

'Roughly how far?' asked Rig.

'About six kilometres.'

Henni dug into her ear with a claw and scraped out some yellowy goo. 'How long will it take? I know we need to rush, don't we? Don't want to hold you back, I don't.'

There was a barely perceptible whoosh of wind.

'Aaaargh!' Rig screeched as he was lifted into the air, massive talons pinching his shoulders so hard they were millimetres from stabbing him.

He was flying.

Aurielle and Henni shouted uselessly as the winged monster took him further and further into the island's cloudless sky. The view was tremendous. So was the searing ache in his shoulders. The wind buffeted him making it hard to breathe and think. He glanced up. A nasty curved beak was above him. Powerful claws would never let him go.

If he could just raise his left arm … magic was needed. But to achieve what?

They were gliding now. Its wingspan was as glorious as it was scary.

He raised his left hand. Magic while flying. That's a new one.

The prehistoric bird's amber eyes flicked to him.

It let go.

'Oooooh!' he dropped.

Thoughts of how he might die queued in his mind.

He flailed wildly.

He also plummeted. The air rushed at him.

Left arm snagged.

'Ouch!'

Wooooah! Rig's world tumbled and turned, his senses were slow to catch up, giving him a generous sick feeling from head to stomach.

The demon squeezed Rig's bicep so hard it went numb.

They levelled off and flew like this for a few minutes. Rig waited for his senses to adjust and for some good ideas to gather. They were reluctant to surface, but the view of the tropical paradise was wondrous and disabling at the same time.

They were about to pass the shoreline a long way below. Instinctively, Rig thought this a curving line in the white sand he shouldn't cross.

And then they did.

Definitely not a good thing.

Rig felt their height lower. The crystal blues of the seawater became darker in swathes below them like an artist's lazy strokes had painted around the island haphazardly and in a rush. The creature tilted and they banked as they soared, flying lower and lower. They were spiralling downwards towards the sea.

No, towards … a ship?

No. A yacht. They were heading for a boat below. Why?

Someone was in the boat.

It wasn't a yacht.

They approached from the side, skimming the waves.

It wasn't even a boat. There were numbers and letters in black on its side.

A dinghy? It was a dinghy.

In it was Prod Visceral, friend and scientist turned into an astonishingly ugly, murderous monster.

Hell.

The creature hovered over the dinghy and let its passenger go.

Rig plopped into the craft opposite Prod. 'Urgh!'

He landed. Could have been worse.

He sat upright on a board.

The monster appeared to be smiling. It was hard to tell. Its mouth was split to each ear, and the gash was sore looking with puss and blood oozing from its wound. Nice.

Chapter 38. Meeting Dad Again

They arrived on the white sands of Tioman Island with Jordi Longstaff in a huff. Henni was not far behind. They'd tried not to travel too fast for her. But it had been arduous, not because she was tired and hungry and the track hilly in places. No. Jordi Longstaff was about to get clubbed with his own stick if he didn't stop complaining. The odds of a beating were exceptionally high as, generally speaking, complaining was a natural part of his personality. She just had to accept he was like that, and so would he, and the very bruising consequences that accompanied his habit.

    Penlip, Lycka, Flash's dad and Auntie Ida surrounded them on their arrival. Mr Penlip was keen to know details of their encounter with Crook, and precisely what happened to Rig. She gave it all, with Blue adding some extra information when he could be bothered. Crook came out of it quite badly, but it was the truth as she saw it. Rig's dad cursed and became flustered at the news, not knowing which way to turn. He stormed to the shoreline and began to pace up and down. Lycka went to chat to him. Ida would look for her binoculars, somewhere in her handbag, do something useful to occupy her mind, she'd said. Blue sat in the shade of a palm tree and began performing some unusual and painful looking stretching exercises.

    She watched on. It was understandable that Melvyn was anxious, but hobbling back and forth along the beach would not achieve anything except add to his reddening skin. Then Henni plodded onto the hot sands with some banana skins hanging from her lower jaw and a smashed coconut under an arm.

    Aurielle summoned some energy from the bottom of her boots and approached her father. He was lying down, arms over his eyes.

    'Are you okay, Dad?'

    He got to his feet, eyes glistening. He tried to cuddle Aurielle. 'I had to find you. Just had to. We were so worried about you.'

'That's a first. Why now? You've never been bothered before.'

His gaze was worried and intense. 'That's not fair . . .' he paused. His tone softened. 'I suppose ... maybe I've not been a great dad recently. But it wasn't my fault. If they had supported me better at work, I wouldn't have started drinking. It would've been different, all of it.'

Silence. A warm wind washed over them. She stared at him in disbelief.

He looked at her.

'What?'

His expression implored her to say yes, he was right. She understood him.

'No. You're fooling yourself. Take responsibility for your own actions. That's what you've always said. Actually, that's exactly what you did tell me when I had to go to court that time. I lost my temper, and those girls caught their faces on my fists. YOU told me, "Take responsibility for your actions and your behaviour." So, no. That's rubbish! You're a drunk and full of excuses as usual.'

'No, no ... I'm not. It's them. Honestly!'

She spun on her heels. Blue looked down, not wanting to get involved. Wise. She climbed the boulders behind them to see what was going on with Auntie Ida. She had apparently found her binoculars. Leaning on her walking-stick, rifle across her back, she scoured the coastline, inland and out to sea.

'Please!' her dad urged as they neared the base of the rocks.

She ignored him. She felt guilty about it. Still ignored him though.

Auntie Ida kissed her cheek. She always did the right thing. Aurielle thought she might love her, in a great, great, granddaughter way.

'I can't see anything, darling,' she admitted. 'Nothing. Only that out there. Don't know what it is? Can you see?'

She handed the binoculars over. They were small and heavy – in fact petite, vintage brass, and ceramic viewing glasses. The kind you'd find very old people using at the theatre or opera. She looked at them quizzically and gave Ida a sharp glance.'

'What is it, darling?'

Aurielle studied the small blip that was some way out in the bright turquoise sea. It looked like a boat. Must be it. The only possibility.

'Hey!' she hollered to Mr Penlip and the god, Lycka. She indicated beyond the shore. 'Something there. Worth a look,' she bellowed.

Humphrey appeared with a stifling hot breeze, surprising her momentarily.

'Oh yes, didn't I say? He's out there. Why, I don't know. I mean why go on a boat trip right now? What for?'

'Yeah, alright. Thanks anyway.' And then she shouted again, but Melvyn was already
trying to run through the clear waters. He took a leap suddenly, dived in, swimming like an Olympian.

Henni looked up at Aurielle. 'Can't swim, can I? Would help otherwise,' she said. 'I just sink you see.' She waved her arms. 'Can't get any purchase with these. It's not my weight.'

Blue and Lycka were in the sea up to their waists, watching, waiting, like her. The ruthless sun continued to burn them with the limited shade giving only the smallest relief.

Chapter 39. The Death of Magic

'What happened to you?' asked Rig.

'I could wonder the same of you,' was the monster's reply.

The thick hair on Rig's legs and arms was not reducing. And he really needed a proper shave now. His face was uncomfortable. Are you still Prod Visceral?' Rig persisted.

'He departed a long time ago.'

'Where is he?'

'Search me,' it shrugged.

'What do you want from me?'

'Oh, that's simple. I want you to die, Rig Penlip.'

Rig gripped the thin wooden bench under him. 'Why?'

'Your kind are dangerous. Magic needs controlling at least, or better ... eradicated.'

'Eradicated?'

'Killed off, powerful sorcerers and mages will, in the end, be extinct. The practice of magic is abnormal and favours certain untrustworthy people.'

'But that doesn't make sense. All the violence in the world to do with magic, is *against* mages, not started by them! They ... we, have been, um, hunted, blamed for all the world's worst events. Your anger is based on a lie. A misunderstanding of the facts!'

'Now you're calling me stupid. Is that clever? Because this is your last conversation, after all.'

The dinghy rolled as Rig shifted forward in his seat. 'No, I'm not saying you're stupid, not at all. Look, this is a mistake. Give us all a chance to tackle some of the world's worst problems and you'll see, I promise. I mean, take this island. There's dirty green waste water being allowed to drain into the forest. Why? What affect is it having on plant life, animals ... and the water basin. We need to find out and magic can help work it out. It can be used for good things!'

'Not interested, and I'm sorry. I think by allowing us to talk, *you* have misunderstood. This is not a negotiation of any sort.'

As the creature rose, some flesh tore from his stomach and slapped into the hull of the little boat, like a stranded fish might. He was still changing, slowly, relentlessly.

The monster produced a piece of white bone. A homemade weapon. He gazed at it as he turned it in his blistered hand.

'This little monkey was delicious,' it said, bile dripping from its mouth. 'Can you imagine being cut by the jaw of a primate from my wonderful island?' He moved forward and the sea wobbled the boat. 'Well, you won't need to wonder.'

The creature with more scales than skin lunged at Rig. Only, as he shifted, in that exact moment, he slowed like a film winding down. If there was such a thing as automatic magic, this was it. Rig didn't feel like he controlled it, or even summoned it. It must be an unconscious action – or someone else was doing it. He was sure that gods didn't employ magic though. As he looked, the picture in front of him altered frame by frame. It did so in such a way that Rig could move nearer and examine the bone structure he would have been murdered with. The edge had definitely been sharpened to allow some proper damage, except the monster's muscular forearms could have dispatched Rig efficiently enough without it. The blisteringly red sores which were not covered by blue and green scales looked incredibly painful. Even Prod's face seemed to have changed shape his skull had morphed into something else.

What happened to the real Prod? Where is he? Is he lurking deep down in this monster's consciousness somewhere waiting to be freed? Rig inched nearer, peering at the metamorphosis that had taken Prod. A very curious thing.

He tripped on the creature's huge feet.

The dinghy rocked as if in a tropical storm. Rig waved in a panic searching for some balance. He swung to his left and right, the wooden boat following. The rocking and rolling got worse. One last gamble. He shifted his left foot to stabilise his weight and calm the craft.

Prod tipped over, splashed into the sea, and sank.

Rig followed, and as he entered the sea, he recalled a terrible fact.

He couldn't swim.

Never had.

He swallowed seawater, head bobbed up and down as he scrambled for the boat. Fingernails scratched the dinghy, looking for grip, some safety. He floundered and fought but couldn't rescue himself. An image of sunbathing on a beach came into his head. No chance. His arms and legs fought and grasped. Useless. He went down and down into the deep azure, body sinking.

His weight took him down faster, he was sure of it.

He *so* regretted those chocolates.

Does magic work underwater? Right arm useless.

Not much breath left.

He struggled and battled and wished for a response.

No magic particles. Not one.

Magic was going to fail him again, like last time.

When he most needed it.

Family gone, now him.

Magic … a curse. *Hated it.*

Last chance. Rig coughed, choked, arms and legs pushed and strained – desperation, death.

A scaly hand.

The beast.

The world went black.

Chapter 40. Other

Prod Visceral woke up as he sank deeper into the azure.
Life was full of surprises.
He was at least alive and had some breath left.
He took a moment to take in the underwater heaven surrounding him.
The soft blue tones of the sea grew darker in the distance while the seabed was crammed with mounds of green, rusty orange and yellow coral. A turtle swam past him in the gentle currents below – heading somewhere, searching for its dinner. A school of goldfish moved as one across banks of rock and open sands.
He could move his body, seemed to be in control again.
He was back. The original, real Prod. Why? Why now?
The monster was silent, like he'd been gagged, drowned, or extracted from Prod's body in some way that Prod couldn't understand. What a shocking mess his body had become. And then he noticed how delicious the salt water tasted. Odd. But then nothing, or very little, could be described normal.
No one wants to drown in their favourite drink, unless a drunkard, so he waited another second. He would enjoy this brief moment before facing the harsh world above him.
Rig Penlip drifted limply past him into the depths. Prod grabbed his arm and headed to the surface. He gasped as he burst through the surface, tasting the air as if for the first time. His tongue found salt in his mouth, on his teeth and in between. Why was it so satisfying? He drank as he swam, cautious but also somehow knowing it's what his body needed. He pulled Rig along as he headed to the shore.
He didn't know if this was the start of a new beginning, or if his body would ever be the same again. One step at a time, or one swimming stroke. It was more than frustrating to have been prisoner in his own body, hosting some kind of evil entity in his body and brain, and to witness what he had done to his form, and his wickedness to others. He hoped not to be blamed. The fierce sunrays were drying what remained of his exposed skin on his scalp. Blisters were starting to sting, a curious mixture of pain and

pleasure as he lapped the saltwater as they went. He could see in the distance people on the sandy shoreline. A welcoming party of sorts.

Nearer, floating, was the body of a man. Weak, mumbling.

He appeared to be missing a leg but there was no blood or obvious injury.

Prod moved closer.

It was Rig's dad.

He had both Penlip's with him. Both about to drown if he didn't intervene.

Prod paused, considered the situation. How do you rescue two people at sea?

He could pull one in with a make-shift rope. It was then that Prod realised he had no clothes on. That was two good reasons for taking Rig's shirt from him. It was a bit awkward, even in calm tropical waters, to the point Rig might have taken some water in as Prod undressed him, while at the same time trying to keep him above water. He ripped the t-shirt a little as it peeled off. Tied it round Penlip Senior's chest and pulled. All Mr Penlip could do was to keep above the surface as Prod heaved through the water with both of them. His body part scales and part open wounds, but he had also become muscular. His strength allowed him to drag them as he lurched through the water on his side. As they neared the island, a multitude of possibilities for the future ran through Prod's head, but his full recovery from whatever this was had to be his main goal.

The seawater became lighter in colour and soon Prod was able to touch the sandy sea floor, taking some of the strain from his torso to his legs. With relief, they were at last at chest height.

But with far less relief he found the girl Aurielle Merlot standing in the water in front of him, swords drawn and ready to lop off his head. Her gang watched on from behind.

She clashed her swords together.

The metallic zinging a message which needed no spoken words.

She looked pretty angry with it.

Chapter 41. Dangerous Interview

'Put some clothes on,' she ordered, 'before I start slicing parts off you.'

The man that was Prod halted with a Penlip under each arm. To be fair, the monster had done a great job in rescuing both of them, except Aurielle didn't entertain the idea of fair – never had. It was the sort of notion she stamped on and kicked down the road into the path of busy traffic. That's just the kind of cool kid she was, she supposed.

Wading through the crystal waters Blue and Frank approached the trio of survivors.

'His leg!' Blue shouted. 'It's gone! Must have been bitten off by a shark!'

'Hell!' said Frank.

'Can you see blood?' asked Aurielle nonchalantly.

Blue leant in for a closer look. 'Err ... no. That's kinda weird.'

Aurielle rolled her eyes. 'Looked at yourself recently have you, Blue?'

Blue's face pinched as he took Melvyn from the creature.

'Ah. I remember,' Frank grabbed Rig under the arms and dragged him ashore. 'You said he'd been hexed with a flesh-eating spell when the rest of Rig's family were murdered.'

'Oh yeah. That's right. A while ago now. Just get him to shore and let him rest. He can barely stay awake.'

Frank called back. 'Yes, boss.'

The lesser god took a break from sunbathing and approached Frank. 'Let me see them Frank. How's Rig? And Melvyn? Melvyn's not right. Rig is out cold.'

'Funny, coz it's proper hot ain't it?' said Blue.

Lycka shot Blue a look that could tame a fire.

'Jus trying to lighten the mood, is all.'

The young god shook her head as she tended to Rig, made him comfortable.

Aurielle glanced at the creature from the sea and grimaced. She stopped Blue as he hauled Penlip Senior, grabbed the t-shirt from Penlip Senior's chest and threw it at the the monster to cover up. Relief. 'That'll do,' she said. 'Now, odd-monster, let's be honest, no mucking about. I appreciate you bringing these two back, I really do. But unless you surrender, I'm gonna do what I intended,' she twirled Red and Midnight threateningly. 'So, what's it to be? Give up or carve up?'

Prod shoved his wrists forward for tying. 'Yes, I understand. But I can assure you I'm back to my old self. That other one has gone. The thing, the virus, it's disappeared,' he said, drooling.

Not quite.

'What?' Prod turned round but couldn't see anyone else.

'Yeah, right.' Aurielle said using some spare vine to fix his wrists tightly together. She pushed him towards the shoreline. The urge to pierce his lizard skin with Midnight was overwhelming, but she forced herself to sheath her beauties. In any case, stabbing someone in the back was rude, unless in a proper battle of course and then it was just, well … fun.

With Melvyn recovering, Blue approached her. 'Need any help with it?' he said gawping at the monster.

'No. Sit down over there where we can keep an eye on you.'

Blue raised his arms in frustration like a moody teenager. 'But I ain't done nothing, I swear! Jus' trying to help.'

Aurielle indicated with a pointy finger: 'Sit. Over there. Keep out the way. Actually, no. Build some shade for us out here.'

He gave a harrumph and started up the sandy slope.

'Hey!' called Aurielle.

Blue paused and turned to face her.

'Leave your stick here.'

Shaking his head, Blue wandered off into the forest with a job to do.

Lycka followed. 'I'll give him a hand,' she said, hips swaying as she tracked after Blue.

Aurielle and the prisoner reached a small rise in the sand, so she shoved the creature. 'Sit there,' she ordered.

'Well done, darling.' Auntie Ida shuffled her feet in the baking sand, using her rifle as a walking stick, butt down. She handed Aurielle a jumbled knot of twine.

'Thanks.' Aurielle said, pulling a length of thread free. She secured its ankles.

'It needs to answer a few questions, I reckon,' Ida said rolling her shoulders as if getting ready for a fight.

'Yeah, I'll try *really* hard not to kill him. It's SO tempting, Auntie.'

'No, darling. I'll do it. We don't want him dead yet,' she turned the muzzle towards the monster.

Frank sauntered towards Aurielle, protecting his eyes from the sun. 'I'll talk to it. No problem.'

Auntie Ida swivelled to him. 'I said I'll do it! Are you deaf?' she shouted, wafting the rifle in his general direction.

'Okay, okay!' Frank held his hands aloft in surrender and backed up.

Auntie looked at Aurielle, 'Sorry darling. When I say something, I mean it.'

'I know. It's all good.'

Then their own monster waddled forward holding a tree stump in his claws.

'One minute,' he said his tongue whipping at the occasional fly resting on his snout. He dumped the wood by the nasty monster. 'Wanted to give you this so you could sit on it, see? So, you could be near to it when asking them questions.' Henni said, giving the sea-thing a quick look.

Auntie stared at Henrietta in disbelief.

'It's okay, Auntie. Henni is so thoughtful. She wants you to be comfortable.'

Auntie beamed.

'You got me so right,' said Henni. 'And I thought if it's no good you can always club it on the head with the edge. Very useful lump of wood, I thought.'

'Thank you so much,' replied Auntie. 'It's a fabulous piece of tree.'

Aurielle gave Henni a kiss on the snout. The crocodile tail swished sending a wave of fine sand over them all, but Aurielle didn't have it in her to complain in that moment, and Auntie simply waved it from her eyes and perched her bottom on the tree stump.

She pointed the tip of the gun at the monster's left eye. 'You will answer my questions, or I will take my time injuring you. Understand?'

'I can assure you—'

Auntie Ida poked the muzzle in the monster's gaping mouth. 'Did I ask you for a chat? No. Just answer my questions.'

Aurielle crossed her arms, watching intently. This was going to be a positive learning moment. She could sense it. She was good at noticing opportunities for personal growth. She glanced at Rig and his dad. Rig was unconscious, and Melvyn had a brief chat with Frank before falling asleep. He was suffering exhaustion, not surprising really. Intense heat, no water and no food gets to you.

'Why have you come to this island?'

'I ... I'm not sure. I think the other one wanted some sanctuary somewhere.'

'Liar!' Auntie put the end of the rifle's barrel against the monster's left knee.

'Again, why have you come here?'

'I really don't know. Violence isn't going to help, you know. It was the other one controlling me, doing all sorts.'

BANG!

The gun recoiled over Auntie's head; the bullet embedded nicely into the mound of sand to the side of its knee.

'Liar!' shouted Auntie. 'Lie again and *I will* take your knee.'

A metallic ratchet noise sounded out as she loaded another bullet into the rifle's chamber.

'Last time. Why have you come to this island?' She balanced the gun on its knee again.

'I told you, I've no idea. It was him! The other one. I think he wanted to capture Rig, kill him, most likely get rid of all magic in the end. I think. That's what I think he wanted. But shooting my—'

'BANG!

The monster recoiled in agony, clutching where its knee used to be, where now there was only shattered bone. Blood and muck poured from the wound.

It groaned and moaned loudly. 'But I told you ... I told you everything!'

Auntie Ida winked at Aurielle. 'That's for being a particularly nasty, and ugly monster.' She shifted on her seat a little and rested the rifle's end on the creature's ankle. 'If that's true then why did you save his life in the sea, just there. You're contradicting yourself. You've said one thing but in fact the opposite occurred. Are you lying again?'

'No, no! I ... I think it's because in the water I started to feel like the real me again. The other one started to go. I don't know where he is.'

Quite close.

Prod yelped and called out in agony.

Auntie Ida slotted another bullet in the rifle and rammed the bolt handle home. 'You can stop all that crying because I can easily put another one of these in your other knee, then you really would have something to complain about.'

A kind of animalistic whining slipped through a terrible grimace and clenched teeth.

'Oh dear, you'll have to stop that too I'm afraid. Can't be having that.'

The monster quietened.

Auntie continued, 'So, let's carry on. Are you saying you're now back to being Prod Visceral? And you're not the monster you were in there?' she glanced at the forest's edge.

'Yes. That's what happened . . . after I went into the sea. I came back ... somehow.'

Auntie Ida's expression narrowed. 'Don't believe you. You're a wicked, dangerous, liar. Are you not?'

'Excuse me, please?' Someone nearby called out.

Auntie Ida's gaze searched for the source of the voice. 'Can't see anyone, darling.' she said turning to Aurielle.

She squinted. 'It's the ghost. He's back.'

Frank stood next to the visitor who at times was entirely invisible due to the sunlight's strength. 'This is Humphrey. He came with me and Rig to find you Aurielle. He's a good lad, honestly.'

'Thank you for that, Frank.' Humphrey moved closer to Aurielle. 'Yes, there wasn't time to say earlier ... I'm terribly sorry your car crashed today, a little misunderstanding I think. Or was there?'

Auntie Ida got up and stretched, leaving the rifle aimed at Prod's other knee. 'You look a nice chap, although I can barely see you in this light,' she shielded her eyes to get a better look.

Aurielle smiled. 'No hard feelings, Humprey. Can you help us at all?'

'Well now...' he said chirpily as he neared her. 'Oh my gods!' he shrieked when he noticed the Prod-monster and his injuries. 'He's even worse! And what happened to his leg?'

'We had one of those misunderstandings you talked about,' said Auntie cheerfully. 'I blew his kneecap off with this beauty,' she said looking at her sniper rifle.

'It's okay, Humphrey. We just had to get some answers out of it.'

'But ... but you tortured him? That's wrong.'

Aurielle sighed, 'You're right, except this is a monster, and he would have killed all of us and worse.'

'Yes, but ...' Humphrey's voice trailed off.

'Look young man,' said Auntie straightening up, 'we're going to need a new car—'

'Jeep,' interrupted Aurielle.

'That's right, darling, a jeep thing. Do you think you could help with that?'

'Oh,' Humphrey brightened, 'of course I can. Now, where's my notebook? I'll just write that down. It's so good to see Riggy too. Is he okay? It is him, isn't it? I mean he looks, sort of, changed. Quite manly with all that hair, I must say. Is it him?'

'Riggy?' A wicked smile grew very wide on Aurielle. 'He's okay. Will be anyway.'

'Oh, that's nice,' Humphrey said, easily satisfied. He began searching his pockets looking for his notebook, muttering, complaining to himself. He quickly developed a terrible fluster as he searched each pocket repeatedly for his notebook.

Henni was busy eating a large dark green leaf from the edge of the jungle, inspecting each part of it before chomping merrily. She was oblivious to what was going on, but wonderful with it, thought Aurielle. Frank sat and watched them all, keeping an eye on Prod, Rig, and Mr Penlip. But Aurielle knew they were all getting a bit too cooked by the blaring sunshine. They needed cover, protection. They could simply move into the bushes, but Aurielle's instincts told her to wait.

She didn't need to wait long.

It was a new sensation, being pleased to see Blue. She heard him and Lycka before she saw them. Blue burst through to the beach with a make-shift shelter on his shoulders. It was tied up with a variety of ferns and leaves, bamboo, and twine. Lycka strode after him, her glamour a constant in their day, barely a hair ruffled after their battles, but she had lost her sunhat during the jungle fight. She checked on the Penlips' and halted when she noticed the destroyed knee of the monster. She looked with suspicion at Aurielle, disappointment perhaps, but said nothing and went to sit by Henni.

'Put it there,' ordered Aurielle, 'dig it into the sand so it holds.'

Blue gave her an evil glance but did as he was asked.

'Found it!' announced Humphrey.

'Good lad,' said Auntie looking him up and down.

'What?' asked Blue.

Auntie replied, 'Don't worry kid, that ghost has turned up again.'

He looked up, his blue tones quite appealing in the light. 'Gotcha,' he said digging in more of the shelter's stakes into the sand.

It was usefully going to protect all three of them. Two Penlips and a scaly sea-monster lying half dead on the beach. They'd need help getting everyone out.

'You wanted pizza?' asked Humphrey.

Auntie Ida giggled; Frank nodded fiercely.

'That would be great,' said Aurielle, "but I want you to go find a jeep, maybe up at the laboratory or far side of the island, get someone to bring it here. Yes?'

Humphrey started writing. 'You want a what?'

'Jeep.'

'What's a jeet?'

Blue gave a quizzical look as he took off to the jungle's edge. He plonked himself by Henrietta and Lycka.

'No. Jeep. Je- eep,' she said, careful with her pronunciation. 'Car that will go on dirt roads, and through some types of jungle, I dunno. Okay?'

'Yes, miss,' he replied and started to fold away like a cheap road map. He suddenly stopped and peered at Rig and the monster. 'Did he try and leave the island?'

'He tried,' grinned Auntie.

'The island didn't allow it, then?' said Humphrey, his eyes widening.

Aurielle shrugged. 'If you want to see it like that.'

'No, you see it's the legend of the island. I read it on the boat on the way over. The God Rama turned a powerful dragon into stone when she touched the sea,' there was an unnecessary display of Humphrey's arms gesticulating to enhance the story, 'the rock became the island … and now only the dragon decides who leaves the island.'

'What rubbish!' said Aurielle.

'Don't be like that darling, we must treasure local myths, otherwise they disappear forever.'

'She's right,' said Frank.

The mirage of the ghostly man looked away, apparently offended. And then he folded inwards, left, right, up, and down, repeatedly … until there wasn't a single pixel left of the picture that was Humphrey Holliday.

Chapter 42. Remember me?

Rig coughed so hard he was convinced his insides would jump out. Saltwater bubbled in his gums. Gentle hands moved him onto his side. He blinked furiously. The light was impossibly bright. He spat grit from his mouth and wondered if someone was standing on his head. It seemed unlikely. He noticed the shapes of Flash and Lycka tending to him, and then hands hooked under his arms and raised him to sitting. He trembled for what seemed like an age. They stood around him gawping with a mixture of wonder and worry.

'I'm okay,' he said weakly.

Aurielle Merlot squatted in front of him. 'You've been out of it for ages. You're a nightmare. Always in a mess, somehow.'

'Thanks. What … what happened?'

'Not now, rest,' she replied with surprising warmth. 'I mean it, but just so you know your dad is not conscious yet. He swam out to find you, got into trouble somehow, and lost his false leg. Turns out the monster saved his life, and yours. And to think I was looking forward to killing it.'

'Eh?'

Rig twisted to see his father lying unconscious or sleeping, but at least he was breathing. Next to him was the remains of Prod with his hands and feet fastened.

'Saved us? Prod saved me and Dad?' Rig asked.

Lycka switched places with Flash. 'It's true, Rig. And we're just happy you and your dad made it. We'll deal with him later,' she said glancing at the prisoner, 'but yes, he did save both of you. We can't understand it.'

Blue's skinny legs appeared. 'I'd still kill him. Just saying that's all.'

'Get out of the way, you,' Flash ordered, so Blue retreated to sit with the others.

Rig turned to his dad, checked him out. Seems okay, just not with it yet. Thanks, the gods for Dad.

A few minutes later Rig was up and marching along the beach, getting himself together. He enjoyed the sensation of hot sand sinking between his toes and the sun's heat on his hairy back.

Yep, still hairy. Looking at his arms though it didn't seem quite as thick, but his broken arm still ached, albeit not as much as before his first attempt at swimming.

The coastline stretched for some way before it curved into an inlet and disappeared, but apart from the yak and screech from a wild bird or two, it was all quiet. The sun had begun its climb down. It would be dark soon, but before the light crept over the horizon completely, a dramatic sunset looked likely. Pastel colours were growing in the distance. Worried about losing the light completely, Rig decided to check on his dad.

He could hear Aunti Ida giving a short talk on the history of monster-hunting, and some of her more questionable decisions when younger. Frank and Flash were listening intently. Lycka and Henni sat next to them, all perched on a rotten log by the forest's edge. All were keen to hear what she'd been up to, although choosing her next leaf to grind was just as important for Henni. Rig turned to see Blue collect some seawater in a broken coconut shell and take it to the scaly creature wearing Rig's t-shirt round his waist.

Rig wandered over. If the thing was speaking the truth, then the saltwater was somehow keeping the other creature inside him silent. They didn't know how it had used Prod's mind and body as its host, that was for later. For now, Blue was the water carrier. The only job he could be trusted with, according to Flash. Prod was gulping in the fluid as Blue poured. He wore a grimace, as though he were emptying watery filth into a drain. He noticed Rig, nodded, and took off for more. His dad was still asleep. His top-half was protected by Blue's portable bamboo shelter – quite a decent construction. Rig watched his dad's chest move with each breath and held his hand.

His dad's eyes opened with a flutter.

'Son?'

'Dad? It's okay. You're safe, we're all safe. We'll all make it out.'

'Thank the gods,' he whispered, as that was about all he could do.

'Lycka is here, you can thank her later if you like,' Rig grinned.

His dad shook his head, 'I'll get up in a minute, feeling a bit *legless* though! And I haven't even had a beer!'

'Enough of the jokes, Dad!' But his incredible dad had fallen asleep again.

'Sorry about him,' the Prod-monster suddenly spoke up. 'Your dad, I mean.'

Rig fired a look at him, unable to decide if he was grateful for their lives being saved, or if he should squeeze his neck until he was no longer breathing. After all, he'd caused all this, along with Scarlett Crook – businesswoman, Seer, and murderous criminal.

'I don't know who you are, and I don't know what you are.'

'It's Prod.' He sat up, though trussed like a turkey on Christmas morning. 'Prod Visceral.'

Rig plonked onto his rear. 'We've been through a lot together, and I know you were … well, sick in some way. But you've caused all this; you and that Crook woman.'

'I know. I underestimated the dangers. I didn't know, couldn't know. That's why we came, to investigate what's happening here. These pools of negative magic breed monsters, look at me and Jordi. It's not what we thought we'd find, such strong poison, this warped magic. But we did. And I'm sorry about what's happened to you. But I'm better, much better.'

Not really. I will kill the boy as soon as I feel sufficiently well enough. Promise.

Prod twitched as if stabbed with a sharp stick.

Rig noted the mess Prod's body was in. 'You're right, you underestimated everything, but you're not well yet. You can't be trusted. We'll talk again when you're better.'

The creature laid back down, shivered and gave an odd stare, as though he was concentrating really hard on something Rig couldn't see. Blue arrived with more seawater and tipped it into Prod's open mouth carelessly, some spilling over the creature's chest.

Rig joined the others and sat on the end of the log.

'Good, you're here, Riggy,' Auntie Ida said. 'I've only just started this story.'

Flash laughed.

'How did you—'

'Never mind now, darling,' interrupted Auntie.

Just as she said this a large shadow swept across the beach, and circled. They looked up to see another monstrous flying creature spying on them from above. Auntie looked for her rifle, but it was a few feet away, out of reach.

'I can knock that thing out of the sky easy,' she said, 'pass my little death-bringer, Rigs.'

'It's okay, Auntie. It's quite high up there, won't be a problem. If it looks like it's getting too low, you can have a go at it.'

'Alright love, if you're sure. I'd be happy to bring it down you know.'

'I know you are,' he replied.

Flash prepared her short swords. 'It's okay. We'll get it this time.'

'Why are you all so violent?' asked Frank.

'Lucky for you,' said Flash. 'None of us would've made it otherwise.'

'Yeah, but it's constant.'

Adjusting her ponytail, Lycka said: 'If you've noticed, Frank, the monsters and nasties are pretty constant!'

'Anyway…' Auntie butted in, 'as I was saying …'

Auntie continued in full theatre mode. She explained how she was once attacked by a foreign assassin whilst on a search and rescue mission in the desert. She knew he was coming and predicted his strategy. She outwitted him and during the inevitable knife fight she destroyed his elbow before forcing him to surrender. But after his defeat, instead of killing him during her usual interrogation, they had productive chat while enjoying afternoon tea with English jam and scones. All while under some shade in the baking sun. She admitted a bruise under the eye and her broken foot was awkward, but she overcame the situation to make a pleasant day of it.

Her audience were giggling and in awe of her all at the same time.

She continued with a mean snarl. 'And you know what, of all the assassins and monsters I've met, not one of them were as ugly as that.' She stabbed her walking stick in Rig's direction.

Rig frowned. They all turned to look at him.

A sharp blade scratched his throat and his head yanked backwards. 'Ouch!'

'Remember me?' said the ex-god Blaam with a heartless grin.

Chapter 43. Half an Ear

'Bunch of losers, look at the state of all of ya. Crook stuck in the lab, tied up. That Prod-monster were just a fake in the end, weren't he? And the most powerful mage of them all can barely raise a spark for a fire. Can you, Rig? Useless, the lot of you,' Blaam said mockingly.

Auntie Ida struggled to stand after sitting for so long, so she leant on Blue's special stick for balance. She caught Rig's gaze. 'Can I kill him this time? Doesn't deserve any mercy this one. Desperately ugly too. Don't you think, Lycka darling?' she said facing the young god.

'No doubt at all!'

Blaam's expression scrunched in disapproval. 'Sit down grandma!'

Frank stood at once, 'Don't speak to Auntie like that!'

Above them, Rig noticed the flying dinosaur was swooping lower, neither helping nor hindering but it's shadow a reminder of what the animals of the island were capable of.

'Or what?' teased Blaam, 'cause, to be honest, like. I'm gonna just head off down that beach with this lad, 'he pulled on Rig's hair again, 'and I'm gonna finish it at long last, and no one … not anyone, is gonna get in my way this time.'

'Told you he wasn't nice, didn't I?' Henni said while chewing over her olive-green supper. 'I did say, I did.'

Blaam urged Rig to stand and started backing away down the beach towards the next inlet. His killing knife scratching against Rig's throat as they went.

Lycka followed, Flash not far behind her. Both keeping near the ex-god and Rig. He obviously didn't think of Lycka as a threat.

'You're making a terrible mistake Blaam, again,' she said.

The circling monster in the sky gave out a series of piercing shrieks that could literally wake the dead. They all looked up in surprise, but it was merely gliding on the island's breezes, watching, waiting. Or so it seemed. Auntie Ida was now targeting her gun at the creature. She shifted her aim between it and Blaam.

'Go back home, girl', urged Blaam, practically spitting the words at Lycka, 'you ain't no use here, or anywhere for all that.'

The blade pressed against Rig's lower neck; he could feel a trickle of blood down his chest. If they moved suddenly for any reason Rig was probably done for, the edge too sharp, too close.

'Hey!' bellowed Mr Penlip Senior, 'that's my boy!' The Prod-monster appeared at his side.

'What's going on?' Blue ran forward, dropping the coconut shell. 'Damn it! I miss all the good stuff.'

'It'll be okay, Dad, don't worry.' Rig hollered back.

Blaam tightened his grip. 'Kinda won't be, y'know.'

Lycka walked closer, her eyes widening.

They moved back and back, keeping them all in view. Blaam's stubble itched Rig's ear as they went. If only Rig could raise his left arm. He was so tired he couldn't tell if the tingling in his hand was from magic particles fizzing, or blood loss.

Then, he suddenly tipped backwards.

Him and Blaam landing in a heap.

There was shouting.

Hands dragged Rig away. Rig saw a black-haired monkey with half an ear pummelling Blaam with its enormous fists. Blaam fought it off but was quickly swamped by a stampede of monkeys, some red-haired and other smaller white-furry types.

Up on his feet, Rig backed off as Blaam was swallowed by the hoard of forest creatures hitting and biting him. His calls for help were ignored, and Rig was unsure how he would help at all anyway. And as he was thinking about this, the larger two of the apes dragged Blaam kicking and screaming into the depths of the tropical forest where the light was already fading.

'Good,' said Flash. 'That's the end of him, then,' she said cheerfully. 'He's been a proper pain, liked to have got hold of him though, bit annoyed about that,' she said turning back to Auntie Ida. That's when the hum of a jeep sounded out as it thrashed down a slope, bouncing and rocking, then onto the beach skidding to a halt.

Their ticket home had arrived at last.

Excellent.

Chapter 44. Lab Chat

The sun had dropped over the horizon. The sounds and smells of the night had surrounded them quickly, and three police helicopters had made a terrible racket. Searchlights and guns sprouted from the choppers which landed at the front of the laboratory. It was like an action scene from a Hollywood movie as dozens of gun-wielding officers dressed in black with motorbike helmets ordered them to "kiss the dirt". At least that was the translation the jeep driver had offered – him being the only scientist to survive Scarlett Crook's blood-letting fury.

  They were herded into one of the smaller clinic rooms while the police scoured the building for evidence, and any useful drugs they could steal, apparently. The Malaysian language was a tad less pleasant when it was screamed at you, especially when a pistol barrel was placed between your eyes. And the broken English was unkind at best in the rare moments it was spoken, but then to be reasonable about it there were a lot of butchered bodies lying about the lab for no obvious reason. The killer was an expert with a knife. And to overcome so many she had to be an expert in martial arts too. Flash and Blue had shown their own skill and bravery in capturing her. She had fooled them all. Who would have predicted a middle-aged, round lady with a multi-coloured dress and jewellery would be such a ruthless assassin? A Seer, Rig supposed, which she also claimed to be.

  They all sat in silence for a moment because they were beyond exhausted and drained of energy – and because Scarlett Crook had been gagged. There was a row of chairs against a white wall in a white room with nothing but a dentist's chair, and one large single cupboard, also white. It could easily have been a dentist's room. Perhaps it was.

  Rig rubbed his bearded jaw, he didn't need any teeth fixing, but some food in his stomach and a decent sleep. He glanced at the rest of them. They certainly looked how he was feeling. Nearly drowning and almost getting your throat cut was tiring. He snuck a look at Auntie Ida, she was looking remarkably alert. She gave Rig the gift of a warm smile. Was she one of her army of replicas? Or was she travelling as her true self? Frank was having a nap and Henni was biting her claws, cleaning, and sharpening them, she'd said. The lab scientist, Zikri, was staring into space, in shock or fed up, either way he was not quite in the room. Rig's dad had tried to talk to him, but he'd closed down, shock, anger, fear – it could be anything. So, his dad set about texting Uncle James, only to realise he was in a different world. This didn't improve his mood whatsoever.

For Lycka, the day was done. It was only a matter of going home. She could disappear right there, but she didn't want to abandon her human body just to escape. She was rather pleased with it and had become attached to it. It surprised Rig that there were limitations for a god, albeit a Lesser God. He thought she could produce another human body just like it, but then he didn't know how it all worked.

Humps had come and gone like a wet wind. Most likely he would return before the night's end with his usual swagger and cheer, whilst being relentlessly forgetful and fabulous. Prod was strapped to the dentist's chair being fed from a bag of liquid on a stand. It was a simple mixture of seawater and rock-pool samples – presumably laced with negative magic. Despite the look of him, he did appear brighter, although he was quiet with it.

'How long will he need that for, Auntie?' Rig asked.

'We don't know, darling. No one does.'

Dad leant forward, 'He'll have to stay here and get the treatment he needs; they'll work it out eventually.'

'What about me? No one seems bothered about this?' Blue said, rubbing his skin.

'That's 'cause no one is bothered. You're right for once,' said Flash.

'Nice. You're just annoyed 'cause they took them swords away, right?'

'It's temporary. I'll have 'em back soon, one way or another. Don't worry about that.'

Blue examined the skin under his arms. 'Has it gone lighter? I think it's fading, 'cause I did try drinking some of that saltwater.'

With the soft moves of a ballerina, Lycka went to Blue, kneeled and said, 'Listen, when Aurielle said no one is bothered by your skin colour, she was right. It's not the tone of your skin but who you are and what you do that's most important, see?'

He suddenly had the look of a much younger boy about him, as if his mother was being so nice it was uncomfortable.

Lycka laid a hand on his knee. 'It's you who is important, and what you do. Okay?'

'Yeah, I can tell you what he did. He's a spy and a rat!' Auntie blurted.

Flash looked mean. 'Yes, he is!' she massaged her hands. 'But …' her voice relaxed, 'we should give him another chance, I suppose.'

'He's okay really,' added Henni, her tongue lashing her chin.

'Thanks. Just can't wait to get home,' he said.

Rig's dad poked a finger at Blue, 'You'll stay here. We don't know what else has happened with your brain. You'll stay in the clinic until your sorted out.'

Blue stared at the floor. He wouldn't argue with Mr Penlip. He at least respected him.

'You'll all be okay,' said Lycka. 'I'm sure of it.'

'Yeah. I suppose I'll have to stay as well,' complained Rig.

'Most likely son, but where ever you go, I'll be going. I'm not leaving you for a minute.' His dad put his arm round him and squeezed.

Rig rubbed the thick hair on his arm. 'This tropical paradise has poisoned me, and Blue and Prod. Its animals have tried to kill, eat or starve me to death. These negative pools of magic, whatever they are, we don't know why they're like that. And there's some muck being pumped into the jungle from this building. The island's just sick. We're sick. And I just don't know if I'm ever going to look normal again.'

Flash fought to stifle a chuckle. 'Normal?'

Mr Penlip spoke up, 'You might laugh, but Rig came to this place to look for you, remember? Thought you were in trouble. He did this for you.'

Aurielle shrank a little.

Rig's dad turned to him and continued, 'You improved when you swallowed that seawater, and Prod says the monster in his head has gone or is going. The salt seems to be the key to this, but we have to give the scientists a chance to work their own kind of magic, on this and the water system here. But you *will* get better. I'll take you to a shaman, witch, warlock, or sorcerer, whatever and whoever you need—'

'Or a head doctor,' Flash said.

'Never heard of one of them,' commented Henni. 'What is it?'

Blue stood and stretched. 'You mean, "what are they?"'

'A psychologist,' said Frank waking from his slumber.

Blue, hands on hips, replied, 'No, psychotherapist.'

'Psycho is about right,' Flash said cheekily.

Scarlett Crook mumbled an opinion through a tightly bound gag. 'Hmmblipmphblah wah.'

'Psychiatrist,' Prod said bluntly.

'Eh?' this was alarming for Rig. 'I don't know what any of those are.'

There was a crack of bone on bone. Great Auntie Ida raised up painfully and went to check on Crook's bindings. She gave them a good tug. 'You won't need any of those do-gooders, darling.'

Rig was sure that Henni was none the wiser, he certainly wasn't.

Noticing his confusion, Flash beamed from ear to ear. Then she joined Auntie Ida and checked over Crook's ties. She suddenly gripped the woman's neck. 'You're a proper psycho aren't you, Crook? Well, I defeated you out there, don't forget it. And if you think Blue helped me much, you're wrong. If anything, he got in my way. Remember that for the future although I'm not sure yet if I'm gonna let you have a future.'

'Let her go,' ordered Mr Penlip.

Frank jumped up. 'Aurielle!'

'Leave it, Flash!' said Rig.

She continued, 'You've caused a lot of pain and suffering. To think you put my sister and Mum in danger. That is unforgiveable. And we believed you when you said you could see *the death of magic*. I'll tell you what I can see …'

Crook gurgled, her face pink and straining.

Auntie Ida put a hand on Flash's shoulder. 'Not now, darling. Let her face justice.'

And then a policeman burst through the door.

His mop of thick black hair swishing about. He brushed it from his eyes and glanced at Prod, who still looked like a cross between a lizard and Frankenstein's monster. The man raised his handgun and began ranting. He had a deep, growly voice which sounded on the harsh side of brutal. Zikri translated.

He said, 'I am detective in charge. You do as I say with no arguments or chat, chat. I'm going to find what happened. You answer questions or suffer. Okay? You do as I say!' He searched his pocket and read from a crumpled piece of paper. 'First, who Riggy Penlips?'

Rig put his hand up as if he were in his geography class.

The man barked at Zikri.

'He want me and you to follow,' he said.

The detective wafted his gun at Rig and the exit.

Rig held the detective's gaze.

'Um … just wondering,' he asked, 'have you ever seen a ghost?'

Chapter 45. Detective Love

The narrow room had no windows. The junk outside the door told Rig the space had been hastily cleared. Zikri sat on his haunches at the end, behind Rig. He and the detective sat on office chairs, with Rig's seat partially splattered with human remains. And this is where the detective began.

He nodded grimly to Zikri and spoke. The language was heavy and guttural with angles and chimes to it. To him, it was harsh and abrasive and he couldn't imagine how the sounds were formed. In contrast, Zikri's meek, gentle voice relayed the first accusation aimed at Rig.

'He say, "You responsible for this death in the main corridor. You will hang."'

'Eh? What? No, it had nothing to do with me! I was just trying to find my friend!'

Zikri began to explain.

The officer interrupted, shouting.

'He say, "You liar. You have blood on hands. If not you, who? Who did this?"'

'The woman did it, she killed them all.'

'He don't believe.'

The detective pointed to the next room where his dad, Crook and the others were still being held. The man laughed, then barked something incomprehensible at Rig.

'What?' he turned to Zikri. 'Please tell him! You must have been there?'

'He don't believe you, and me, that she, the fat woman, could murder so many computer operator and scientist on her own.'

A high-pitched scraping sounded out as he shifted his chair uncomfortably close. His knees so near they dovetailed with Rig's. Inches from his face, Rig's interrogator spoke again. This time his tone was calmer but he locked onto Rig's eyes as if looking for signs of guilt or secrets that might flicker behind them.

'He say, he knows what you are. Hairy arms, face ... they know it come from the jungle. They know you poisoned, and you do tricks of the dark. Not natural, he say. The green monster with you, and him with scales. You should all be, err, deleted.'

'Eh? He must understand, these murders, they're nothing to do with us,' he implored.

The wafts of scent coming form the detective were bold and unforgiving. Rig sniffed and gave a little cough. Zikri and the detective swapped a series of impossible exchanges. Although this time it sounded like the conversation was a little more reasonable.

Zikri moved. He crouched by Rig and in a whisper said: 'He testing you. He understand it all, but hard to believe. He know you innocent.'

'Oh.'

The detective grinned into Rig's face, apparently enjoying the interview.

'But you hang unless you give something.'

Th man nodded earnestly, as if he could speak English himself.

'What? What does he want? Money? I don't have any.'

Zikri whispered into Rig's ear, like someone might overhear them.'You give gift of love to him.'

'What you talking about?' Rig twisted to face Zikri, to meet his gaze.

'He knows you magic. Give him gift of love or you hang to death.'

The detective giggled like a child.

'What does he mean, "the gift of love"'.

'He like this woman but she no respond. Make him, err, irresistable. Give him gift.'

'But that's not right. I don't do party-tricks. Look at my arm,' he grabbed a fistful of hair, 'this is what happens when I use magic here. If I use it again I'll be completedly covered. Look at me,' he ran his fingers through the tufts sprouting from his cheeks.

The detective pulled a pretend, anguished face, as though being hanged. And sniggered.

Chapter 46. DNA

Sometime later, in the newly named Tioman Research Centre, Rig sat in a clinc room with his dad opposite Zikri and his assistant. He wanted to go home. Desperately. But even though the police had apparently dropped all charges against him, he was to be isolated until he had improved sufficiently.

Zikri glanced at the young assistant and expressed something unknowable. The girl, suddenly flustered, flicked through a handful of papers, scanning them and picking out pages at random before placing one by Zikri.

He glanced at the form quickly, as if reminding himself. 'So, treatment working well, we know that. The symptom improve.' He pointed to Rig's arm, which had been malting hair since his treatment had begun. 'And you feel better.'

'Yeah, thanks,' Rig said.

'We did not know why, now blood result back we have idea.'

'Great,' dad said shuffling in his seat.

'You result not normal. You deoxyribonucleic acid, D-N-A … have this, err, *quadruple helix*. Always double, not triple or quad. Never. Understand? Two helix human. Normal. Okay? I think third helix, um … may be magic ability. Fourth not right. It in tangle like a dead snake,' he twisted his hands in the air in demonstration, 'and this, err, disease affect other cells. Understand? All this wrong DNA give the problem.'

Rig shifted to face his dad. 'What?'

'You've got unusual molecules in your body, the poisoned part is giving you all the hair problems, probably the same for Blue and Prod.'

'Yes, yes,' nodded Zikri enthusiastically.

'So the poisoned part was from the negative pools of magic here. We thought that. But why has the treatment worked?'

Zikri waved a hand.'Yes, yes, I come to this. Salt in water, it, err, dissolve in body but electric signal in body increase and this affect the DNA. Okay?'

'Eh?' he turned to his dad again.

'The salt water is helping the cleansing of your body, and getting rid of this fourth helix.'

'Hmm …'

'It's why you like the taste of it, whereas usually you'd spit it out.'

'But it's just salted water. How can something so simple, like, get me better?'

'Not sure,' said his dad, and put a hand on his arm, 'it might be boosted by the magic abilities you've got, we don't know.'

'Weird.'

Zikri grinned at Rig. 'Any question?'

Rig closed his eyes for a moment. 'When can I go home?'

Chapter 47. Garden

The walled garden remained intact, untouched by the violent events of the previous days. A stroll around the various tropical plants, flowers and greenery could be relaxing, but today his best friend was with him. She brought an edge and ferocity to almost every conversation, as though she hated the world, and Rig's existence was only tolerable on a good day. She was interesting. Rig loved all things interesting. With her, there was rarely a dull moment.

It was mid-morning and the air was hot and humid already. He would kill for an ice cream, instead he just dripped with sweat. They sauntered along the paved edge of the garden, stopping occasionally.

'So when do you head home?' asked Rig.

'Tommorow.'

'Okay,' he said, his tone low, 'Where you been staying these last few days anyway?'

'At the beach.'

'Oh, nice. Yeah. Some swimming, and chilling, right?'

'Not exactly. Been on a few treks to get fitter. Bit of tracking practice in the bush. And as there ain't no-one about I've done some sword drills on the beach, y'know, stuff like that.'

'Right.'

They sat on a bench in the shade under a giant plant with leaves shaped like elephant ears. Rig wiped some sweat from his brow.

'It's good you're dripping,' she said, 'you could lose some fat.'

'Don't go on at me. Let's talk nice. Um, what happened with Crook?'

'Dunno, police took her away, suppose she'll be in prison, go to court and all that.'

'She so deserves it. And your dad. He okay?'

'Yep. Lycka took him home.'

'Oh, right. And where is Henni now? I hope she's gonna be okay.'

'Nothing wrong with her, apart from being a dinosaur and jobless. Promised I'd watch out for her. Lycka will settle her down near where I found her.'

'Oh, that's nice.'

Flash gave him a strange look.

'What?'

'Nothing. Seen anything of that Humphrey?' Her right hand touched the hilt of each sword. Still there. Security. Power. She glanced at him.

'He's around somewhere. I'm sure he'll be back. Coming to terms with what we found out, his parents business, their murder, y'know, and his own murder as well. All hard to take in, right?'

'Suppose.'

Rig blew his cheeks out. 'Phew! I'm getting hot. Want a cup of tea? Hot chocolate?'

'Don't be stupid. A pint. Iced water.'

'Oh. Right.'

Rig fetched the drinks. He sat with her while a group of bees fizzed and buzzed amongst some bright purple and pink flowers. The sunlight strafed the courtyard highlighting the different shades of green foliage, and the light picked out the flush of red, yellows and orange petals surrounding them. He sat and handed Flash her glass.

'So colourful them flowers aren't they. No wonder the bees like them so much.'

Flash looked at him as though he were speaking a different language.

'What?'

She took a sip. 'How long they gonna keep you here anyway? Your hair is better, it's all dropping off.'

'I know. It's going well. I guess once it's all gone I can go, probably need to take the serum for a while after I leave. They said the same to Blue. He's in there,' Rig pointed towards the building, 'he's much better. You seen him?'

'No. Don't want to.'

'Right. Well that Prod is still strapped in and taking his medication too, getting there but he's got a long way to go.'

Gently, she placed her drink on the paving stone. 'I came to this island with Blue to help him. You thought I was in trouble, came to find me. I ... appreciate it. I do. I'm ... sorry you're stuck here.'

She stood, kissed him on the forehead and walked off.

Stunned to silence, Rig watched as she marched into the research centre without another word.

Gods.

That's a first, he thought.

Chapter 48. Message

It was the dead of night, and the air was black as pitch and cool with it. It was one of those nights where Rig seemed more awake than asleep. He wriggled and jiggled to get comfortable. But it wasn't the physical comfort that was the problem. Visions teased him, the nightmares pained him every night and his hopeful dreams were just that. He couldn't rid himself of the images of battles with pygmys, monster worms, and Prod himself – whatever he had become back then. He wanted to forget it all and move on. His dad had tried everything to keep Rig calm and happy and safe, but neither of them could deny the truth of what occurred. It may have come from Prod's accident but there were selfish, misguided, and deathly actions that came from it, to say the least. For Rig, he simply couldn't get it all out of his mind. He needed a positive distraction of some kind.

He turned over in his bed, his body seeking a colder patch. Sleep would come. It would. A breeze from his open window tickled Rig's exposed neck. There was some comfort in the cool breeze.

Except the window wasn't open.

There was no breeze.

There was a cough. 'Ahem!'

Standing at the foot of his bed was Humphrey Holliday. 'Is this an awkward time? Only I thought ... I must go and see Riggy. Seems like ages since we had a good chat. I mean where are we without good friends? And I said to myself, he won't mind. He's so good at talking too. He likes me. Now if I'd left it a bit longer, you'd have thought I'd have deserted you, or something silly like that. And then—'

'Humps?'

He was rubbing his hands excitedly. 'Oh ... yes?' he paused.

'It's the middle of the night.'

'Is it?'

'That's why I'm in bed.'

'So, you are! Why don't you get up?'

'Because I sleep at this hour, try to. And by the way … we had this very same conversation last night.'

'We did?'

Rig sat up. 'Yep.'

'Don't remember that.'

'Didn't think you had.'

Humps explored the room. 'It's a bit too dark in here for my liking. That's just my opinion.'

'Yes, I guess it is.'

'You could open those curtains for a start. Oh! Why are you're clothes on the floor?'

'They belong there, some of them.'

'Really?'

'Yeah. Anyway, must be getting back to sleep.'

'Ah, that's what I was going to ask … have you heard from Flash? Nice girl. A bit violent though.'

'She's good. Fighting monsters somewhere I expect.'

'And Blue and Prod?'

'Like I said yesterday, Blue is mostly better, and Prod is well on the way. The scientists are doing a great job. Prod should be well enough to give his account in Crook's court case.'

'Oh, that's nice,' replied Humps ignoring Rig.

Rig followed Humps gaze. The ghost found a small book of notes on his study-desk. After a few moments he was able to turn a page.

'I've got a notebook too! What a coincidence!'

'Yeah, really incredible, isn't it?'

'Now, that reminds me … where is my notebook?'

He searched his pockets urgently. 'Can't seem to find it.'

'It's pretty much always in your back pocket. I keep reminding you of that.'

Humps continued searching. 'It's here somewhere, I'm sure of it. Hmm … Ah! It's okay, it was in my back pocket all along.'

'So, do you have a message for me?'

'Message? Oh, alright, no need to be pushy y'know! Hold on … I'll have a look.' Humphrey flicked through his notebook.

Several aching moments limped by. 'Nope. Can't seem to find it. Where could it be?'

Rig rubbed his eyes. 'It's fine, really, keep looking. I've got all night.'